MW01169612

BROKEN
SOUL

KEVIN WALLACE

Copyright ©2013 by Kevin J. Wallace

Print ISBN number 978-1-7323214-0-3
Ebook ISBN number 978-1-7323214-1-0

This book is dedicated to the men and women of America's armed forces. Their bravery and dedication to our freedoms will forever be engrained in our hearts.

Thank you for the protection of our way of life, and for your willingness to pay the ultimate sacrifice to defend this great nation.

ACKNOWLEDGMENTS

To all the readers who have enjoyed Jake Bedford's dark journey, THANK YOU! It has been a wonderful, and very humbling experience talking with fans of the book.

To my beautiful wife, Vanessa, thanks for your patience on the many nights and weekends I toiled over my laptop. I love you so much, and couldn't have done this without your support.

To my Mom and Dad, thanks for your unwavering belief in my ability to follow through with this bucket list project.

To my brothers, Mike and Matt, thanks for the laughs (and a few bourbons), when I needed them most.

To my wonderful sister, Amanda, your input and creativity were critical in helping make this novel complete.

To all my friends and family, who provided support, feedback and insight. I thank you from the bottom of my heart. I appreciate you sharing this moment with me.

Lastly, a big thank you to all the men and women who serve, and have served, in the armed forces. Not a day goes by that I don't think of the sacrifices that you've given to provide freedom to our great nation. You are truly America's heros.

CHAPTER 1
HOMECOMING

THE ENGINES OF the C-130 Hercules roared. It was the most welcoming sound I could have imagined. The constant humming of the four turboprops symbolized closure and security. After ten months, with the grace of *God* and good fortune, I'd made it through the most hellacious combat deployment in my military career. I shifted uncomfortably in the tightly packed quarters, looking at pictures of Michelle on my phone and yearning to hold her in my arms again.

As the hours passed, I found myself drifting back to the nights I had spent with my brothers of the 22nd Marine Expeditionary Unit. Our minds tired, soaked with anxiety as the mortar blasts filled the dark, silted sky. All we could dream about was coming home to some sense of peace. I closed my eyes and eventually the hum of the engines allowed my weary mind to drift to sleep.

BOOM!

My ears rang and the passage of time slowed to a crawl. My eyes struggled to focus and I looked at my hands to make sure I was OK. No blood. I was alive…but what had happened? Dust and sand swirled around the pitch darkness of the desert night. The Humvee driver slammed on the brakes as we exited and crouched in combat positions behind the door panels.

Crouching down, I yelled to the men, "Hold position, twelve and six."

There was yelling coming from every direction and I could see a blur of red tracer shots firing from the Humvee behind us. Our convoy was attached to an army infantry battalion and we were heading back from a mission outside of Kabul.

Blinking rapidly, I tried to regain focus and quell the ringing in my ears. I lowered and quickly adjusted my night optics, and the world went green as I peered through the lenses of my PVS-7 system.

The right side of the Humvee in front of us had been hit with an IED. Smoke plumed from the car. Radio operators were on coms ordering a medevac chopper, and a team assembled to provide immediate medical treatment.

I fought the pounding in my head as the men looked at me.

"Xavier, Jason, take positions immediately! Juan, Mason, over there and provide cover!"

"Yes, Sergeant!" they yelled as they began firing to move any enemies away from our detail. I moved with Chris to provide cover fire while our men got safely into position.

The mission was fucked. We had a Buffalo MRAP vehicle leading the team, but the IED must have been trigger-detonated by some shithead watching our platoon.

We unleashed hell for the next five minutes…defending our position and hoping for a clearing to allow a medevac chopper to assist the wounded. Through all the gunfire, I could hear the screams of the soldier from the Humvee. Our team worked to create a safe perimeter and I tried to keep my unit busy to focus on our task as the medics gave treatment. But we all heard it…the piercing screams emanating from the flames and smoke.

"Help me…my fucking leg! Oh God…please help me, help me…"

Through the haze of gunfire and yelling, I crouched back behind the Humvee within shouting distance of the carnage. I could see through my optics the blood congealed on the desert sand.

"Stay strong, marine, help is on the way. We've got you secure…medevac is coming."

Counting my men, I looked to ensure everyone was in position and we had incurred no further casualties. We returned fire repeatedly, praying that we could conserve enough ammo to get out of this alive. Dust swirled through the air as the soldier screamed while the medic applied pressure to the tourniquet. This was what Hell looked like…the screams, the dust, the…

"JAKE! JAKE!"

I awoke, startled, a hand grabbing my chest. Sweat beaded down my face…I was drenched.

"JAKE, it was a nightmare.… You are OK. You're here, man, you're with us."

I scanned my surroundings, eyes wide and darting around the C-130. Some of the other soldiers were looking over. DeShawn Davis was quietly talking to me and holding my chest down through my uniform. I breathed deeply and wiped the sweat pouring from my forehead. Thrusting my hand into my pocket, I pulled out my pocket watch and held it tightly to my chest, feeling the cold metal against my sweaty palm. Trying to gain my composure, I started fighting back tears.

"Sorry, man."

DeShawn loosened his grip on my uniform and gently held my shoulder. "It's all right, happens to me too sometimes…. Take a deep breath."

"Thanks…I don't know what happened."

"You're fine, brother. We're heading home…. It's going to be OK. You are safe, crammed in this plane with a bunch of other knuckleheads."

I sighed in relief and took a minute to compose myself. "I hate that shit. Wish I could just wash all these memories away."

DeShawn looked at me with an inquisitive stare. "No you don't. It's those memories that make us who we are. It's those memories that make us realize we are human. When you come to the realization that life is so fragile, it makes you appreciate who you are and how much time with your family really means."

"I'm ready to get home, man. I've seen enough…just want to hold my wife."

"Me too. You got kids?"

"Not yet. We're hoping to start trying real soon though."

DeShawn took out his cell phone and handed it to me. It was a picture of his wife and two little girls. "My little angels," he said, smiling as I held the phone. "They grow up so quick. It's the only thing that keeps me grounded out here…knowing I can come home to them.

"They're beautiful, man. Lucky they got Mom's good looks," I joked

DeShawn laughed and we spent the next few hours talking about our past deployments and what we were going to do with our time back in the States. He was getting ready to go back to Georgia and wanted to start a career as a firearms instructor. As we talked, the hours passed until the voice on the intercom told us we were almost home. We both enjoyed some silence, mentally preparing for our transition to civilian life.

I stared at the metal rivets on the floor of the C-130, slowly tracing the brass case of my pocket watch and thinking of Michelle. Months after we were married, we'd saved enough money to travel to the Marshall Islands for our honeymoon. A family friend had retired there and let us use their house for a couple weeks so we could afford to take the trip.

While perusing a local marketplace, Michelle had found a small brass pocket watch with the Marshall Islands flag on it. It never kept time and was perpetually stuck at 5:00.… She thought it was the perfect gift for me. For one, "It's Five O'Clock Somewhere" was one of my favorite songs. And the fact that I was always so punctual drove her crazy, so the idea of a "broken" watch made us both laugh.

The worn brass watch had scratches that surely told an interesting tale. On the top side was the flag of the Marshall Islands, royal blue, signifying the ocean, with orange and white stripes radiating from the lower-left side. There was a large white star on the flag that signified the Northern Hemisphere archipelago. On the bottom she had engraved, "To the love of my life, take time to enjoy each moment. Love always and forever, Michelle."

For most people, carrying a broken pocket watch makes no sense. But from the time she had given me the watch, not a day had gone by that I hadn't carried it with me. As my fingers traced the engravings, I thought about the ten months since I'd seen Michelle.

I was nervous about "the change." Had I changed? Was I about to enter the tragic storyline about a returning vet grasping to regain touch with reality? I could only hope my beautiful wife would accept and love me as she had when she'd kissed me goodbye at the airport. The desert had ways of messing with your head as you adapt to the fact that you or your soldiers may die at any moment. As the mind becomes so entrenched on staying alive, the life you came from, the life you miss more than anything, becomes foreign.

The landing gear emerged and we prepared to set down in South Florida. I was grateful to have escaped a world of unknown fear and heat.

My mind raced as I carried my rucksack through the tunnel into the terminal. My feet felt heavy. I stared at the diamond pattern on the walkway, trying to picture what Michelle would be wearing…trying to think of what to say. I'll never forget the smile on Michelle's face, seeing her beautiful brown eyes well up with tears as she ran toward me. I dropped my bag as she embraced me and whispered, "Kiss me."

As I held her in my arms, I smelled the lavender in her hair and felt the softness of her neck. I closed my eyes, sighing in relief. For the first time in nearly a year, I was at peace. Michelle kissed me and then looked me over, as if to make sure I was actually home.

"Jacob, I missed you so much."

"I missed you, baby. I don't ever want to leave you again."

I kissed her and we held hands on our way to the parking garage. Coming home was always a surreal experience. It was wonderful to hear the civilians clapping in the airport, but for some reason I could never get used to it. There was a part of me that felt guilty for being able to come home. Many of my brothers never got that opportunity. I was one of the lucky ones.

CHAPTER 2
SETTLING IN

We began the journey home and Michelle told me about everything I'd missed during my deployment. It was just wonderful to hear her voice again and to know I'd sleep next to her all night.

I stared out the window, watching the sun fade behind the Florida palms…just listening. I was finally home, with the woman I loved. I breathed freely without fear for the first time in months.

Michelle smiled at me. "What do you want to do for your first dinner back?"

"Definitely pizza! Let's get some pizza, a bottle of wine, and just chill tonight."

"Well, it just so happens that there is a killer coal-fire pizza place that opened up not too far from the house."

"Perfect," I said, holding her hand as we drove.

We pulled into the driveway and parked. I pulled my rucksack out of the trunk while Michelle headed inside. I stared at the house, our little castle of solitude. Michelle looked back through the door. "Come on in and get settled. I'm going to go ahead and call it in." I nodded and smiled.

I walked through the door to the house, closed my eyes, and

breathed deeply. The cool, clean air was at once refreshing and foreign. While Michelle placed the order, I dropped my bag upstairs, took a shower, and headed downstairs to pick out a bottle of wine. I opened a bottle of merlot and so began my journey back to the normalcy we call life.

As I poured our glasses, Michelle set the pizza on the counter and looked at me. I stared at her, getting lost in her beautiful eyes. "Come over here."

I leaned down to kiss Michelle, she jumped up and coiled her legs around me as I lifted her onto the kitchen island. I kissed her deeply, working my way down her neck as she let out a sigh.

The duress of recent months melted away and I removed her top and began unbuttoning her jeans. As our clothes piled on the kitchen floor, I could feel the warmth of her breasts against my chest. Sweat beaded off my forehead and slid down her thigh. We spoke a language without words as I pinned her against the granite and she bit my ear gently, her breath against my neck.

Our naked bodies embraced across the cool countertop and I stared at the mason-jar light fixture above us. Michelle's arms and legs draped over me. We struggled for breath. Looking at each other, we began laughing. In every sense of the word, the moment was perfect. Everything in my world seemed so wonderfully simple. The passionate escape of our intertwined bodies dancing in the kitchen was a reminder that no matter how horrific the outside world could be, we always had each other. That was all I would ever need.

We got dressed and then toasted to being together. Michelle prepared a salad as I put some pizza on our plates and sat down at the table. Devouring the first slice, I reached for another. "This is great! When did this place open?"

"A few months ago. We should go eat there sometime with the family. They have a cool bar area and local bands on weekends. It's always jamming."

"I'd love to. Maybe we'll go again this week."

Michelle rubbed her hand along my cheek, feeling my stubbly beard. "I'm so glad you're back. It just doesn't feel right when you're not here…the empty bed and quiet house." Her hand gently slid down my forearm and she held my hand.

"I prayed every night for you and your men. Trying to picture where you were, what you were doing. I tried to concentrate and picture you in my head. With your scruffy five-o'clock shadow and sunglasses…looking so handsome in your camo."

I intertwined my fingers with Michelle's.

"Not a day went by that I didn't look at your picture and think the same. Well, maybe without the five-o'clock shadow."

We laughed.

"How was the deployment? All your guys all right?"

I hated talking war with Michelle—it seemed to cloud the perfection we'd created together.

"Happy to say all my guys are alive and well. Xavier and Juan got a little banged up but they're gonna be fine. Other than that, still dealing with a little back pain.… Nothing I can't handle."

In all honesty, the deployment had been tough. Most Americans didn't think we were at war, but our platoons were constantly battling splinter cells of radicals that devoted their existences to killing us. My unit was always being tested, and I'd seen firsthand the horrific toll that this never-ending war took on our men. I would never complain, though. Plato once said, "Only the dead have seen the end of war."

I raised my glass and looked down at the ground. "May they rest in peace, those brothers who have fallen in the name of our country. May their families find peace and may the Lord bless them with prosperity for their sacrifice."

As I stared in silence, Michelle touched my arm and looked

at me with a pained expression. "Do you want to talk about anything?"

"Not now. I'm fine. Just so happy to be here with you."

Michelle forced a smile. "Me too. When are you going to get your back looked at again? You've been dealing with that for over a year, you need to heal and not mask the pain with medication. It could be serious."

I paused, arching my back into the chair.

About a year and a half earlier I'd herniated two discs falling down a stairwell during a combat deployment. After finally seeing a specialist, I did a series of epidural injections. They helped for a couple weeks but the only thing that really took the edge off was my prescription for oxycodone.

"I dunno. Soon, I guess. Those injections helped a little but didn't last that long. It takes so damn long to be seen I've just been taking the pain meds for now. I'll schedule something with the VA in the next week or so. I promise."

We finished the pizza and polished off the bottle of wine. Michelle headed upstairs, and I locked the doors and looked out the window. All was calm, the streetlights illuminated the road, and all the families were secure in their homes, not knowing that thousands of miles away soldiers were working to protect their freedoms.

I went upstairs and brushed my teeth.

"So, I gotta make my rounds and see everyone. I can't believe it's been ten months already.… I'm happy to say it flew by."

Michelle was moving decorative pillows off the bed. "Maybe for you. It was the longest deployment of my life. Every time I saw something on the news, my heart stopped. Those calls you made to me were the only things that kept me sane."

Michelle sat on the edge of the bed. I put my arms around her and kissed her. We made love again and I listened to her rhythmic breathing before falling into a coma-like sleep.

I hadn't slept like that in forever, but unfortunately it was short lived. I shot up in bed, feeling sudden fear rush through my head, hyperventilating as I looked around the cool blue light of predawn. My temples were pounding. The bed was damp with cold sweat as I grasped the sheets. I had been yelling in my sleep. I took a deep breath; tears were streaming down my face. I didn't know where I was.

Startled, Michelle put her arm on me, "Jake! Jake! It's OK… shhhh, it's OK, everything is going to be OK. You're home."

I breathed deeply, trying to gather myself.

"I'm sorry. Had a bad dream."

"Talk to me. What were you dreaming about?

"We were pinned down by enemy fire in some bombed-out house. We couldn't escape. There was no way out and we…"

I fumbled for words.

Her eyes fixated on me with concern. "Shhh…it's OK, slow down…I'm here. Talk to me."

"I can't. You just wouldn't understand."

Michelle brushed a teardrop from my eye as I turned away and sat on the edge of the bed.

"Jacob, I don't understand…but I want to. I want to know what happened."

"I'm fine. Go back to sleep. I'm going to get some water."

I headed downstairs and got a bottle of water out of the fridge. I held the bottle on my head and wiped away sweat. Reaching into the liquor cabinet, I took a long swig of Jack Daniel's and exhaled in relief. I was home and that's all that mattered. Upstairs I found Michelle was still sitting up in bed. She was crying and trying to hide her tears.

Frustration filled my thoughts. I didn't know how to explain to her the haunting memories of my deployment. "I'm sorry. It's going to be OK. Just had a bad dream. Everything's gonna be OK."

Wiping her eyes, she looked up at me. "I know, but I can't help you if you won't talk to me. It's not good for you to keep this bottled up inside."

I knelt next to the bed and put my head in her lap as she ran her fingers through my hair. "I know you want to help. We can talk about it in the morning. Let's just try to get some sleep."

This was a common occurrence my first few weeks back. Sometimes the only way I was able to drift to sleep was by listening to Michelle breathe. I loved the feeling of protecting her in our home. It gave me purpose. Her slow, methodical breathing changed intensity as she dreamed. It was my ultimate reprieve from war. There is a feeling of vulnerability and satisfaction when you are consumed by someone. As I held her in my arms, I could forget the horrors of the desert and eventually I too would drift away.

Sleeplessness had plagued me in the desert, and I hoped being home would return things to normal. During my many months of deployment, I had slept with my arms and legs covered in panty-hose to protect me from sand fleas, M4 and .45 at my side as I listened to the sounds of explosions, gunfire, and Humvees.

Now that I was home, I tried to adapt to the supposedly calming sounds of the fan and air conditioner but couldn't. I began to have some serious issues. Sometimes I would drink Jack until I finally passed out, and if that didn't work, I'd take pain or sleeping pills. It got so bad I pissed the bed once after drinking all night and taking an Ambien. It really worried Michelle but I dismissed it as getting used to reality and trying to find a way to sleep. I contemplated going to therapy to appease her, but was certain I'd adjust after a few weeks. After all, last time I went to the VA they just medicated me and said to talk to a therapist about my PTSD. I really didn't see the need to wait a month for the same diagnosis.

CHAPTER 3
CIVILIAN LIFE

As I SLOWLY put the pieces of civilian life back together, I tried to gain perspective on how lucky I was to have returned home to my wife and family. I remembered Kandahar, the dilapidated housing and the villagers who lived each day in fear of bombings and rebels. The villagers survived without clean water, proper nourishment, or even the promise of another day. Yet they never complained. At home, all I heard Americans do was complain—*my team didn't win, my phone doesn't get a signal*. It all seemed so trivial. People sat in front of their TVs, hypnotized by so-called reality shows as life passed by with each minute of fake controversy and commercial interruption.

For me, being back home with Michelle, was a dream come true. Sometimes I felt as if she were an angel that had been put on earth just for me. Even the most subtle things, those only a man in love would notice, brought me such elation.

The next morning, we were getting ready to get groceries. In typical Michelle fashion, the fifteen minutes she said she needed to get ready was going on forty-five.

I sat at the table, fumbling with my pocket watch, and looked at the clock on the microwave. Frustrated I playfully yelled up the stairs, "What on earth are you doing, woman? It's gonna be dinner time when we finally get there!"

The hairdryer ceased, "What?" Michelle yelled back.

I rolled my eyes, repeating myself.

Before I could finish, she shouted back, "Oh calm down! Always with the drama. I'll be down in a moment."

I headed upstairs to check on her "progress." I snuck through the hallway to the bathroom so she couldn't hear me. There she was brushing her teeth, unconsciously dancing in the mirror like a little ballerina. I smiled and watched her for a moment before she saw me.

Toothbrush in hand, she defiantly pointed. "You! Sneaking up on me, huh, boy? My breath is minty fresh, come over here and give me a kiss."

I headed over and as she leaned in to kiss me, she quickly moved away and splashed water from the sink all over my shirt.

"What the heck, babe?!"

"Serves ya right. Now give me that kiss." She leaned in and kissed me as we both embraced the moment.

On our way to the grocery store, Michelle was researching baby nursery ideas on her phone. Prior to my deployment we'd decided, upon my return, it was time to start trying for a family. While I was a little apprehensive about fatherhood, the idea of Michelle wanting to have sex all day every day certainly appealed to me.

Looking up she said, "If we have a boy, I think I like the name Jackson. Jackson Bedford."

As the reality of having children set in, my stomach began twisting. I hadn't the first clue about raising a child and was terrified I'd screw things up.

"I don't know, hun. I'm…it's just. I don't know how to be a dad. I'm afraid I'll mess it up. I'm just really nervous that…"

Michelle interrupted me and held my hand, intertwining her fingers with mine

"Don't be so hard on yourself. Kids don't come with instruction manuals. You learn on the go. I know you will be an amazing father, I just know it."

I stared off in silence, trying to imagine our lives with children. I could disassemble an M4 rifle in under a minute but couldn't change a diaper if my life depended on it. To say I was nervous about the unknown was an understatement.

Michelle on the other hand was calm and confident. I suppose it came to her naturally; she had a soft temperament and plenty of experience working with babies. Michelle worked in the neonatal nursing unit at St. Francis Hospital and took great pride and satisfaction in nursing sick babies back to health. I still remember the first time the unit lost a baby, shortly after she had started her job.

I'd come home from running errands to find Michelle crying on the couch. She was holding her knees, tucked in a ball.

"What's wrong? What happened?" I asked, putting my hand on her shoulder.

Brushing aside tears, she quietly spoke. "Some days just really, really suck."

I stood in silence, awaiting more details.

"We had a baby with a serious heart defect, poor little soul weighed only four pounds.… All the care and treatment in the world, all the amazing doctors and technology, and we simply couldn't do anything for him.… It just hurts."

I didn't know what to say without being insensitive. As polar opposite as our careers were, I too had been at this crossroads. But instead of sorrow, I'd felt anger.

Andre Simms, or Dre as we'd called him, always had a way of making our platoon laugh. We'd all loved him, and he was one of my best friends. Even as I'd held him while he'd bled out from a bullet wound to the abdomen, he'd looked up at me and said, "I'm gonna be really pissed if the last thing I see is your dumb ass staring at me. Get me to the medic, I'll be fine…"

It was my first deployment, and the first time someone died in my arms.

We'd shed no tears as we mourned Dre that night. His memory had fueled anger amongst us and we'd vowed to take revenge for his death. We waited anxiously for our next mission briefing, relishing the opportunity to kill in his memory.

As the flashback resided, I gently pulled Michelle into my arms, trying to console her. She tucked herself under my head and cried while I rubbed her back.

"Honey, no one ever said this was going to be an easy job. Like anything, there are good days and bad days…and even on this bad day, you can look back knowing you gave that little boy the best care and the most love possible before he went to heaven."

Still holding me, Michelle brushed her tears aside. "I know. It doesn't make it any easier though."

In that moment, Michelle had seemed destined to be a wonderful mother, while I was destined to be a marine. Coming from a large military family, I knew early on that I wanted to be a solider. After three years of deployments, I was trained to become part of a special operations team within the 22nd Marine Expeditionary Unit. I was honored to be a part of a Special Ops capable unit as I'd worked my ass off to graduate training.

While I loved the camaraderie of my brothers in the 22nd MEU, the deployments had taken a serious toll on me mentally and physically. I was finishing my eighth year in the service, and knew in my heart I couldn't leave Michelle again. Being with her was my only stability and I feared what I could become if I didn't have her in my life. It was time to focus solely on my transition back to civilian life, which was proving to be a much larger obstacle than imagined.

CHAPTER 4
INNER DEMONS

THOUGH OUR RELATIONSHIP seemed like a fairytale at times, like all couples we had our issues. Well, I had issues. I'd always had a temper, which was exacerbated with drugs and alcohol. While I was *never* physically abusive, there were times I completely lost it when drinking. It'd never been an issue prior to my first combat deployment, but ever since then I had my moments.

During my first couple of weeks home, after drinking all night, I noticed the stove was left on after Michelle had cooked breakfast.

"Dammit, Michelle, you can't leave the stove on. You're gonna burn the whole damn house down!"

"Oh shit, I'm so sorry. The phone rang and I completely forgot. Sorry, hun."

"Forgot? How can you forget the stove is on? You've gotta be more careful! Fuck!"

"I don't know…I just did! I'm sorry.… What else can I say?"

The flood of anger rushed through me. I didn't feel like myself.

"Fuck this! The whole place is gonna burn down and then what? Are we gonna live on the street?" I roared.

I grabbed the coffee maker and threw it against the wall. Glass shattered everywhere and the remaining coffee pooled against the kitchen floor between the tiles. Michelle was in shock, her face red with confusion. She burst into tears.

Immediately, I felt horrific guilt. Seeing her cry gave me a feeling unlike any sensation I'd ever had. I felt subhuman. I wanted to apologize and tell her it was going to be all right, to console her in my arms and stop her crying. But I didn't. I was helpless and didn't know how to fix things.

Storming upstairs to the bathroom, I took a few Xanax and shamefully stared at my reflection. When I came downstairs, Michelle was sitting at the table, trying to calm down, overcome with tears.

Putting my hand on her shoulder, I whispered, "I'm so sorry, honey…I'm so sorry. You're right, it's not a big deal. I didn't mean to lose my temper."

Looking up at me through teary eyes, Michelle sighed. "I just don't know what to do. You won't talk to me, you won't talk to a therapist, and I have no clue how I can help you. I'm scared, Jake."

Something had to give. Seeing the pain and confusion in Michelle's eyes was unlike anything I'd ever experienced. I could see how helpless she was in the face of my tirades. Healing our relationship became my top priority.

Through sheer will power, I made significant progress in reducing both my alcohol and controlled medication use. While Michelle would have liked me to give up all my vices, she compromised on some.

I packed a tin of Skoal straight and put a big pinch in my bottom lip. Before heading outside, I turned my head upstairs. "Michelle, I'm gonna be outside washing the cars."

"What?"

Shaking my head, I shouted, "I'm gonna be outside…"

"Why are you talking like that" she said, peering down the stairway at me. "Ugh, seriously, I thought you stopped that disgusting habit."

I rolled my eyes. I'd been trying to keep it from her as best I could

"All your teeth are going to rot out and you'll look like some swamp critter."

"Swamp critter?" I asked, amused at the imagery.

"Yep, don't get near me until you brush your teeth."

"Yes, dear," I said with the highest degree of sarcasm before heading outside.

While I still drank, took pills, and dipped in moderation, I felt entirely in control of my actions for the first time since arriving home. I spent a couple hours a week at the shooting range, harnessing my concentration, and started working as a personal trainer at a friend's gym.

In the evenings, I worked on preparing a resume and gathering referral letters for a future in civilian life. My confidence in a potential future outside the military was growing and there were some strong career options I was pursuing.

I had a good laugh while working on my resume. There was nothing more illogical than comparing life as a civilian to that of a combat marine. In the desert, the focus is to survive a harsh environment while locating and often killing adversaries. In a civilian setting, this would lead to multiple life sentences and psychological case studies. I figured I'd focus more on leadership qualities and discipline, probably a better interview topic.

Having a structured routine allowed me to flourish and I warmed to the idea of raising children. The thought of becoming a father invigorated my spirit and I felt ready to accept the challenge. Relinquishing my fears, I began reading books about parenting and started picturing our lives with little ones running around.

I thought so much about the future…looking past the sleepless nights and diaper changes. I couldn't wait to go to ballet recitals or little league games. Parenting to me seemed like a salvation that could replace the jarring images of combat with those of our beautiful family.

As I looked to the future, I used the past to fuel my desire to heal. In my military career, I had been on multiple combat missions in extremely hostile territories. I had thought that these experiences had prepared me for any obstacle that could occur back in the states, that my training had hardened me to overcome anything.

I was wrong. There are some things which the mind cannot fathom…things which will break a man down well beyond his depths of perseverance.

CHAPTER 5
A TYPICAL TUESDAY

MICHELLE HAD ALWAYS worked twelve-hour night shifts at the hospital. While it was necessary for us financially, I hated not having her around for three nights. Sure, I liked to grab a few beers and bullshit with my buddies from time to time, but being around her was the only thing that ensured my mental stability.

After packing a quick dinner, Michelle walked into the office, where I was putting some finishing touches on my resume.

"I'm heading to work. Whatcha up to?"

I turned my office chair toward the doorway. Michelle was wearing blue scrubs, balancing her keys, lunch bag, and hospital ID in one hand.

"Just working on my resume, hun. Will you take a look tomorrow after you wake up?"

"Sure, you have any ideas of where you might apply?"

"A couple. Just want to get this thing ready so it's perfect. You know me…failing to prepare is preparing to fail."

Rolling her eyes, Michelle laughed. "Is that a quote from your high school football coach?"

"You know it!"

Michelle gave me a kiss. "OK, love you. I'll see you in the morning." She smiled as her long dark hair swept back.

"Love you too. Have a good night."

I watched from the office windows as the car pulled out of the driveway. After I had put the finishing touches on my resume, I got a yellow notepad and started making a list of all the home projects I'd be starting in the near future. As I started writing, the phone rang.

"Hello?"

"What's up, brotha? You enjoying being back in Flawda?"

"Dave! What's up, man? Yeah, it's great being back.... What-cha up to?"

"Gonna go grab a couple beers and shoot some pool with a few of the fellas. You free?"

I glanced at my watch, it was ten till six.

"Sure, I'll come hang for an hour or two."

"Good deal. Won't be long…I've gotta drive back to Clewiston tonight. I'll swing by in fifteen."

"Sounds good. Thanks."

I threw on a T-shirt and checked my phone for Michelle's text. We had a routine, she would always text me both when she got to work and when she was heading home.

5:54 p.m. "Safe at work. Luv U!!!"

Once I got the text, I felt secure and could get on with my evening…counting the minutes till I saw her again.

I heard the diesel engine of Dave's truck pull into the drive-way and headed downstairs.

Dave was a good buddy of mine that I did a lot of hog, deer, and turkey hunting with. He lived on a large farm out in Clewiston, Florida, which is about an hour or so west, in the middle of the state. He came to the coast often to work construction projects. As we played a few rounds of pool at Palm Beach Billiards, we picked up right where we had left off, harassing one another and talking about the good old days.

Dave chalked up his pool cue and took a swig of beer. "Man, you gotta come see the kids! They're getting so big.… It's crazy how time flies."

"I know, man. Michelle and I will come visit you and Lee soon. It's been too long. Maybe we'll plan a camping trip or something. Michelle is dying to do a digital detox and put the phones down for an entire weekend."

Dave lined up a shot. "Corner pocket. Well, come on out. I'll be done with this Palm Beach project in about a month and should have some more free time th—"

Dave's phone began buzzing and he looked down.

"One second Jake, gotta take this." Dave picked up the phone with a look of concern and answered. "Hey man, what's up?"

I sipped my beer and watched, hoping everything was OK.

"The big bull? Hercules? Shit…that sunuva bitch does this every few months."

Dave held his finger up as if to say he'd only be a moment

"Okay. No, it'll be fine but you're gonna have to sedate him if he's kicking and being aggressive. No, you won't need that, it's too strong. Go to the barn, in the top drawer look for a brown bottle with blue writing, it says Rompun."

Dave rolled his eyes and took a sip of his beer. I felt at ease knowing things were under control.

"Yep, that's it, Xylazine. About 200 Mg." He held the phone up to his ear with his shoulder and chalked up his pool cue.

"Sounds good. Thanks man. Let me know if you have any issues. I'm heading back soon."

Dave hung up and put the phone back in his pocket.

"Sorry about that, Jake. One of the big bulls was acting up. It's always something. My shot right?"

I smiled. "Yeah, man, you're up."

Dave drained the shot and walked around the table with a little swagger. "Old man's still got it! What were we talking about man?… Completely forgot."

I packed a chew of Skoal. "Picking a weekend when Michelle and I could come see you guys."

"That's right. My bad. Well, as I was saying, anytime next month probably works great. The kids would love to see you guys. They are so much fun. You won't even recognize 'em."

"Can't wait, man. I'll get you some dates and we'll plan it."

I laughed as Dave missed an easy shot to win the game.

"Got a little too cocky, huh, ol' timer?"

Slightly blushing Dave laughed. "Damn right I did. Say, when are you guys gonna start a family? You better hurry up, you're gonna be an old-ass man with balls dragging at your ankles soon."

Laughing, I set my beer down on the table. "Yeah, Yeah. We actually just started talking about it before my last trip to the desert. We're practicing now…. I'm just nervous, man. I don't know anything about kids."

"Neither did I." Dave took a long swig of his Bud Light. "But you learn. The first six months it's all about mama…lots of sleepless nights, diapers, crying. But then they start interacting and laughing. It's so cool, man. Well, you'll know when you have one. Your shot, Jake."

I nodded and focused on the jukebox in the corner, taking it all in. I was drifting in thought, smiling as I imagined Michelle at the hospital holding one of the swaddled babies in the neonatal unit, singing it lullabies. She was going to be the best mother in the world, the perfect mom. She loved those babies so much.

As I lined up my shot, Dave kept talking about the virtues of fatherhood. Smiling and trying to catch a word or two of Dave's conversation, I tried to imagine what life would be like as a father. I wondered what we would name our baby and if it would have Michelle's beautiful brown eyes.

Afterward, Dave drove me home. I thanked him and headed inside. The silence of the house always unnerved me. I closed my eyes and pictured Michelle reading gossip magazines on the couch, eating a bowl of strawberries.

Turning off the lights, I went upstairs to shower.

As I dried off, I sent Michelle a final text for the night.

"Going to bed, see U in the a.m., Luv U!"

Then I took an Ambien and a couple pills for my back. I'd been starting to sleep a little better and was increasingly optimistic about overcoming some of my PTSD baggage.

At 10:27 my phone vibrated. "Sweet dreams, busy night. See U tomorrow, Luv U!"

I climbed into bed, breathing deeply, and closed my eyes. All was well in the world and I waited for the medicine to help me drift away.

CHAPTER 6
COLLAPSE

As SOON AS my alarm clock went off at 6:30, I began my routine. I woke up and checked my phone for Michelle's morning text. Nothing yet, must still be finishing up. After a quick protein shake, I showered and brushed my teeth…still no text.

She should have been on her way home. I called, but the phone just rang and rang. I texted and there was no response. I started to get a bit concerned but thought nothing of it, after all, a busy night in the NICU is exhausting and there is plenty of paperwork to complete before the incoming shift arrives. I figured I'd give it another couple minutes and then I'd text her mom. Maybe she stopped at the house, after all it wasn't that far away.

I attempted to check my emails but it was futile, I couldn't focus. I texted Michelle's mom, Linda. She responded that she hadn't heard from her. I said I'd let her know as soon as I heard anything, and she would do the same.

About thirty minutes later my phone rang.

I'll never forget that sound. As soon as I answered, my whole world collapsed and fell into slow motion. It was a surreal displacement of truth filled with overwhelming disbelief and confusion.

"Hello?"

"Yes, Mr. Bedford? This is Sergeant John Petrillo of the Palm Beach County Sheriff's Office. I have some bad news. I need you to liste…"

It is at this point I knew that something about life was about to irrevocably change for the worst. I had this instant feeling, like getting hit in the stomach so hard you have to vomit…but there is nothing in your stomach.

"What happened? Where's Michelle? Is she OK?"

I lost my sense of reality in the moments following my response…. I don't remember the details or if I even said anything else. I remember not knowing exactly where I was. Tears were streaming down my face so heavily I couldn't see…my nose was dripping…my lungs felt heavy as I struggled to breathe…the light faded, and I collapsed on the cool tile.

Ringing…

Ringing…

My eyelids fluttered as I lay on the kitchen floor. My phone was ringing. It had all been just a nightmare…

Where is Michelle?

Ringing…

My phone was next to me. I didn't recognize the number. I stared at the phone, and answered, "Hello?"

"Jacob, are you OK? It's Sergeant Petrillo, I lost you…. Are you at your house right now?"

Barely able to speak I muttered, "Yes."

"OK, listen…I'll be there in five minutes."

I was in a daze…. Nothing seemed real.

"Uh, OK."

There was a knock on the door. I got off the floor and opened it to see a Palm Beach County sheriff.

"Jacob, I'm Sergeant Petrillo. May I come in?"

"Sure."

We walked into the kitchen. I could see in the man's face he was flustered and extremely uncomfortable.

Sergeant Petrillo looked to be in his midforties, solidly built and tan.

The sergeant struggled for words, looking at the ground while speaking. "Jacob, I have some terrible news. Your wife was killed early this morning leaving St. Francis."

I ran to the sink and began dry heaving but was unable to vomit. Petrillo put his hand on my shoulder.

"It's OK. Take your time."

My voice echoed in the sink. "I don't understand. I just talked to her last night, she was there…"

"I know…this is going to be difficult. But I'll be transparent and tell you all I know. We are just now gathering details on your wife's death.

"Based on early conversations with coworkers, Michelle was busy all night, as the hospital had multiple admissions during the day. The last contact her colleagues had with her before her shift ended was in the break room. They were all having a snack, laughing and talking.

"Michelle clocked out at 6:07 a.m. and headed to her car. We believe, based on initial evidence, she was approached by four men in their late teens to midtwenties armed with guns and a knife. They may have tried to take her away but she refused and tried to grab a can of mace from her purse. A struggle ensued. We found the mace on the ground but it was never used."

"They opened the car with her keys, bound and gagged her with duct tape, and drove behind a medical office building next to the hospital. No one was around, though the tenants in the building pay for twenty-four-hour security.

I was sick. "Wait…why would anyone want to hurt her? I don't understand."

"We've gathered some identifiable prints and run them through our database. Our initial belief is that that Michelle was a random target of a gang initiation by a violent local gang called the 8th Street Kings. Early findings from our homicide department indicate she was raped and murdered, likely as part of that initiation."

I leaned against the sink unable to talk. Petrillo stared at me and continued.

"Early speculation is that Michelle succumbed to blunt force trauma and multiple stab wounds to the chest. The attackers left Michelle in the parking lot, then drove off, leaving her car near a dumpster. It appears she put up one hell of a fight. The coroner believes she suffered a broken wrist and multiple abrasions from attempting to deliver blows to her attackers. She gave everything she had trying to escape but didn't have a chance against four armed men."

I stood in silence and disbelief. There was no way this could be happening. It couldn't be true. Sergeant Petrillo tried to continue, but fumbled his words. He lowered his head and let out a long shaky breath. I slumped on the ground, leaning against the cabinet below the sink. Sergeant Petrillo took a knee next to me and waited in silence.

Putting his hand on my shoulder, Sergeant Petrillo spoke. "Jake, there is nothing I can do to bring your wife back…but I'm going to do everything in my power to make these bastards pay for what they've done."

I started crying. I didn't care that he saw. The sergeant had never been through anything like this…I could tell from his expression. There was nothing he could do. Petrillo tried to stay strong but tears streamed down his face and we cried together in my kitchen.

"I am so sorry, Jake…I am so sorry for your loss."

This man, a man I'd never met, helped lift me to my feet and hugged me. I was in shock, putting my arms around him, feeling his badge against my chest. I cried like a newborn. I cried until all the tears in my body were drained and I was an empty shell. Petrillo loosened his grip and looked at me.

"Jake, I'm so sorry to deliver this news. It's the hardest thing I've ever done in my life. I will get justice for you.… You have my word."

I didn't know what to say or how to react. I just stared at the refrigerator in silence.

"I'm leaving my card here on the counter with my cell number. Call me if you want to talk. I'll be free twenty-four seven for you."

As he prepared to walk out, he looked back at me one last time.

"May you find peace in this time of need. With God as my witness, we will find these animals, and your wife's murder will not go unpunished. There will be justice."

Petrillo walked out the door as I stood shaking in the kitchen.

CHAPTER 7
CLOUDS OF DARKNESS

In the days following Michelle's murder, our families scrambled to find some semblance of purpose or reason behind her untimely death. They turned to God in seeking clarity and understanding…. I turned my back.

As we made funeral arrangements for my twenty-five-year-old wife, we were told that we needed to have a closed-casket funeral because of the swelling and disfiguration on Michelle's face. The coroner's report said she passed away from arterial blood loss and suffered severe head trauma from being hit repeatedly prior to the stabbings. It is likely she had drifted out of consciousness a good time prior to passing, so the hope was that any suffering was minimized.

I was in a haze. It took some time for the true realization to hit me. I would never hold her in my arms again…our dreams of having a family were gone forever.

During the funeral, I tried so hard to be strong and fight back tears. Everyone was crying. Michelle's mother was hysterical and my mom did the best she could to console her outside. Clutching my pocket watch, I looked at the photograph of

Michelle next to the casket. I began shaking as tears blurred my vision and I struggled to breathe. I felt a pounding in my temples and raced away, gasping for air. My father rushed out and held me, gently rubbing my back until I was able to calm down. The fading sun and trees reflected on the casket as it was lowered into the ground. As friends and family continued to pay their respects, I walked along the cemetery grounds, seeking isolation from the crowd. Our friends Pete and Mary slowly approached me with bated breath, though Mary stayed back at the last minute, weeping into a handkerchief.

"Jake, I don't know what to say.… I'm so sorry."

I stood in silence. Pete gave me a hug. Still holding my arm, he looked back at Mary. "We love you, man. We're here for you. I'll be by to check in later. I'll give you some time."

As they walked away, I stared from a distance at funeral attendees mourning next to the casket. I felt a venom course through my veins and every muscle felt like it was going to burst. I desperately needed a drink…just to calm myself. I had no intention of moving on with the passing days. Time could not heal these wounds and prayer could not save me. I swore vengeance, knowing salvation could not cure my loss.

As I gazed at the funeral procession crying and saying their goodbyes, my anger intensified. My hands clenched tightly and my jaw locked as I fought back more tears. My brothers and some friends came to my aid, walking over and embracing me in silence as they walked me back to the casket. I took a Xanax given to me by a friend and gently placed my dog tags and a bouquet of tulips on Michelle's casket. I waited silently until most of the people had left, my friends and family standing behind me as if not wanting to disturb my final moments with her. When I had seen enough, my brother drove me home. I stared out the window as the radio played softly, my brother leaving me to my thoughts. As we pulled into the driveway, I saw that a few friends had already arrived at my house. My family wanted someone to stay with me, as they feared I wouldn't do well alone.

CHAPTER 8
THE PROCEEDING HOURS

INSIDE THE HOUSE, the tables were covered with floral arrangements, and someone had ordered food for everyone who came back to comfort me. I poured a large glass of Jack and tried my best to numb the discourse of emotion. As friends and family came, my brothers sat with me, drinking in silence, echoes of a televised baseball game hanging in the air. I tried desperately to keep myself together but wanted to release the rage I felt inside.

I got off the couch. "I'll be back in a few."

My brothers looked at me with concern and nodded their heads.

Heading upstairs, I looked at Michelle's closet. The clothes were arranged meticulously but her workout shoes had been tossed next to the hamper as she'd undoubtedly rushed to get ready for work. I looked around the closet, the surroundings now so seeming unfamiliar.

I washed a Xanax down with a gulp of whiskey and headed back downstairs.

My brothers were the last to leave and after I had hugged them goodbye, I stumbled to my empty bed around 1:00 a.m., hoping to pass out. Instead, I buried my head in my pillow and sobbed uncontrollably...putting my face so deep I hoped to suffocate. I cried until I passed out, leaving behind a twisted reality only to awake to a certain Hell.

While the rising sun signaled the reality of a new day...my nightmare hadn't ended. I sat on the edge of the bed buried in an abyss of depression. I struggled to breathe—the air seemed so heavy that just inhaling was laborious. Another bottle of Jack lay half empty on the nightstand, I hadn't been sober since the funeral.

As the days passed, my family and friends slowly drifted back to their mundane lives. I sought isolation, waiting for the seemingly endless arrivals of flowers and cards to subside.

People pitied me, not knowing how to act. They had this facade of understanding as they acted out their routines on their sick little stage. It is said that time will heal sorrow, but I couldn't begin healing. Cold sweats haunted me as I replayed over and over how Michelle had been murdered. I considered suicide but felt responsible for ensuring justice for Michelle's death. Without justice, I simply could not pull the trigger.

CHAPTER 9
THERAPY

OUR PARENTS KEPT trying to get me to go to church and pray…
but I couldn't. I couldn't face *God* now—I had no faith that
everything is part of his plan. Family and friends begged that I
talk to a psychiatrist…. They insisted, saying it would only help.
I agreed just to appease them but honestly I just wanted to be
left alone.

My mother arranged for an appointment with a psychiatrist
that specializes in post-traumatic depression. She was optimistic
because he had experience in helping soldiers cope with the loss
of team members. Driving to the appointment she explained how
important this could be in the healing process. I was agitated that
she tried to sell me on this but I nodded in agreement. She too
was suffering and I supposed, more than anything, this would
put her at ease, so I humored her.

I walked into the psychiatrist's office. There were two large
brown leather chairs facing his desk. On the wall were diplomas
from various universities and awards from various pharmaceuti-
cal companies he'd likely received for pushing their pills and
numbing the minds of the mentally disturbed.

The psychiatrist was reading paperwork in a manila folder. He looked up, removing his reading glasses, and put his hands on the desk. "Jacob, what you've gone through is perhaps the most traumatizing event a human can experience. There is nothing I can say or prescribe that will take away your pain. The only thing we can do is work together to help you through this."

I didn't want to be here, and he knew it. Crossing my arms, I stared out his window into the parking lot below. "I have nothing to say. What can I say? I've lost the only thing I cared about."

We sat in silence. He leaned back in his chair, resting his chin on his hand, waiting to see if I'd respond any further. Breaking the silence, he said, "Jake, I can't imagine the range of emotions you're going through. The pain, anger, and sorrow…I just want to help you work through this."

I gripped the leather chair. "I don't know that I can work through this. I just don't know what will happen."

He furrowed his brow, perplexed or concerned. Maybe both. He leaned closer to his desk as if he wanted to say something but instead he waited.

I spared him the agony. "I just don't get it."

"Talk to me. What don't you get? That Michelle was murdered?"

"Yeah, I don't get it. She was such a wonderful person…she was perfect. She didn't have any enemies…. Why her? Why not me?"

He was making headway. This was his breakthrough on reaching out to a troubled soul. His fucking culmination of years of medical school training.

"It's completely understandable to ask these questions. The hardest part about what you're going through is that there really aren't any answers for what happened."

He joined me in looking out the window. The bougainvilleas were in full bloom, dropping flowers on the pavement.

"Jacob, we live in a wicked world and horrible things happen to good people. Every day, horrible things happen.… It is our ability to cope with those things that make us human. It is your ability to work through—"

"I don't feel human! I don't feel anything."

A pained expression came over him. I could see fear in his face. He feared pushing me to the brink and treading too heavily on my emotional state.

Our remaining time was spent bantering about my feelings and what I've been doing since the funeral. His strikingly calm demeanor sickened me.… I wanted to kill him for even mentioning my wife's name. He put me on Seroquel and cautioned me about drinking with the Xanax and oxycodone I'd been taking. I wanted to put a bullet in his head right there, painting his smug diplomas with brain matter. Fuck him! I was just another sob story to tell his peers about on the golf course. He'd never seen the look on a man's face as he lay there mortally wounded, gasping his final breaths thousands of miles from home, and he'd damn sure never buried his soul mate. Needless to say, it would be the last time I ever sat in that posh leather chair, having some civilian asshole analyze what concoction of medications would "cure" me.

CHAPTER 10
POST-THERAPY NIGHTCAP

THAT NIGHT, I drank by myself on the couch, reflecting on my visit to the psychiatrist's office. Numb from the combination of booze and pills, I pondered my ability to cope with the loss of Michelle. I was naïve to think that my combat experience could help me persevere through emotional loss. Even having been exposed to death many times, I'd never felt anything like this.

Soldiers understand their service may bring about the ultimate sacrifice; death was an occupational hazard we accepted. This was far different because in the end I didn't *lose* Michelle…she was taken from me in cold blood by a bunch of fucking animals.

The more I thought about Michelle's murder, the more the anguish turned to anger. It seemed to intensify with every moment I spent not doing something about her death. No matter how many pills I took, no matter how much I drank…I couldn't escape. My thoughts became blurred, like my brain was infected by an incurable virus. I started thinking about finding the killers and what I could do to them.

Shaking my head, I finished my glass of whiskey, trying to rid myself of these irrational thoughts. I was, I *am* a reasonable man… not a killer, right? I just needed closure for myself, and our families.

We deserved justice, and I could no longer stand on the sidelines anymore while the police investigated. I knew what had to happen, the only real peace I could ever possibly experience was coming face-to-face with her killers. I needed to find out *why* they had killed Michelle.

As I poured another glass of Jack, I couldn't help but wonder how I'd react coming face-to-face with these men. Of course I wanted to rip them apart, but I was drunk, not some tyrannical murderer. I felt this compelling urge to find these monsters, and learn how they could so freely destroy the life of a beautiful, vibrant woman. Did they feel remorse?

I became obsessed with finding the killers. Believing that by confronting this evil I could somehow understand why my world had been ripped apart. I sobered up as best I could, forced down some food, and went outside for some fresh air.

Sitting on our porch in a picnic chair, my thoughts drifted away to our family dinner before my last deployment. I closed my eyes, hearing the sounds that had surrounded our home that night.

The laughter of my nephews, Caleb and Ryan, chasing each other filled the room. My mom, Janet and Michelle's mom, Linda, were discussing the floral centerpiece on the table while my brothers and Michelle's dad debated a call in the football game on TV.

Michelle was opening a bottle of wine in the kitchen and caught my stare. I smiled, heading outside to fire up the grill. I closed the lid and packed a chew of Skoal.

My dad, Art, came outside and we silently watched a magnolia tree swaying in the breeze. He put his hand around me and squeezed my shoulder. "Son, I know this is hard for you… and being nervous is expected. Just promise you'll be safe, take care of yourself."

"I will, Pop."

"We love you so much and will be with you no matter how many miles away you are. Just get home safe. You and Michelle have such wonderful things to look forward to. Keep your wits about you and be smart."

I gave my dad a hug. "Love ya, Pop."

We stood in silence for a moment before Michelle leaned out the sliding door. "Chicken and steaks are ready for the grill when it heats up."

"Thanks, hun. Almost ready."

My dad ruffled my hair and we headed inside to prep dinner.

A lone tear fell to the pavement as reality crept back in. What next? What was there to look forward to? In all of the clouded cognition I had, the one realization that stood firm was that I did not want to live my life without Michelle by my side.

I refused to accept that she was the target of random violence, that she had been taken from me because of nothing more than mere chance.

CHAPTER 11
THE DETAILS UNFOLD

I STARED AT Sergeant Petrillo's card but somehow wasn't able to muster the courage to make the call. As much as I wanted to know more, I couldn't bear the reality that Michelle was gone forever. But as the silence of the day droned on, I finally made the call.

"This is Sergeant Petrillo."

"Hey, Sergeant Petrillo, it's Jake Bedford."

The sergeant's voice softened. "Hey, Jake, call me John if you'd like. How are you holding up? I wanted to call but didn't want to disturb you."

"I appreciate that, I'm used to addressing folks by rank. Military habit I suppose. Any details on the case?"

"Yes, from fingerprints and DNA samples at the crime scene, we've identified two suspects associated with the 8th Street Kings. As I mentioned before, we believe this was a gang initiation carried out by four men. We have prints on two other suspects, but they weren't in our database. We are actively pursuing all these men and getting some intel from all sources at our disposal."

I paused to let the information sink in. I took a deep breath, suppressing my tears, and responded, "Is there anything I can do to help? Anything at all?"

Sergeant Petrillo calmly responded, "What I need you to do is take care of yourself. Spend time with your family and friends and work through this. You've gone through enough already. It's up to us to help bring you justice."

The sergeant paused. Feeling the tension of the moment, I gave him a reprieve.

"Yeah, I'm doing all that. Thanks. I'll be in touch soon."

"Jake, I can't begin to tell you how much respect I have for your service to our country and for how you are handling this. Don't hesitate to call me if you think of anything…or even if you just want to talk. OK?"

"OK. Thanks, Sergeant Petrillo. I appreciate it."

Sergeant Petrillo and his men were genuine in their convictions and I could tell they truly felt invested in solving this crime. Over the coming days, I thanked them when they called or stopped by the house. They updated me as best they could and gave me as many details as allowed.

The 8th Street Kings were one of the most violent street gangs that operated in Florida. They had a loose hierarchy but, for the most part, were disorganized due to greed and dissent within the gang. They were primarily financed by robberies, prostitution, and a large portion of the marijuana and cocaine sales within the lower counties of South Florida.

One suspect was a twenty-five-year-old named Carlos Zentillo. He went by the name C-Lo. The second suspect was nineteen-year-old Shane Tidwell, or Shay T, as he was often called. Both had criminal records as juveniles and adults for multiple assaults, possession, trafficking, firearms possession, and more. It was likely the other two individuals hadn't yet built a rap sheet. It was Petrillo's hope that their intel would soon allow them to identify the suspects for arrest.

I listened intently as the officers asked me questions and updated me on case developments, but their investigation became a secondary focus. Based on the intel they gave me, I knew enough to begin my own case. I needed to locate the 8th Street Kings and I had some names to start my mission.

CHAPTER 12
IT BEGINS

IN PLANNING FOR the execution of this task, I needed to check my weapons cache. Knowing that my mission would take me deep into enemy territory, I had to be prepared for the worst. I had installed a large gun safe in the closet to keep our insurance policies, passports, and, most importantly, my firearms. I am an avid shooter, hunter, and sportsman; my gun collection is something I take great pride in. I kept the following weapons and ammunition at my disposal:

Tactical Rifles:

› 1 Rock River Arms AR-15 semiautomatic assault rifle with 4–16x50 sniper scope

› 1 Colt AR-15 A3 tactical carbine semiautomatic assault rifle with laser/strobe and EOTech XPS3 Holographic sight

› 1,000 rounds of Brass Lake City 556 mm cartridges (NATO)

Small Arms:

> › 1 Glock 21 (.45 ACP) with flashlight mount
>
> › 1 Springfield XD-9 with Crimson Trace laser sight
>
> › 1 SubCompact Beretta PX Storm 9 mm
>
> › 1 Sig Sauer 380 ACP pistol
>
> › 250+ rounds for each of the above listed weapons

Shotguns:

> › 1 Benelli M4 tactical shotgun
>
> › 200 shells (12 gauge) assorted

Hunting Rifles:

> › 1 Smith & Wesson model M&P 15–22 .22 LR with scope
>
> › 1 30/06 Springfield rifle with Leupold 18x40 scope
>
> › 200 rounds (7.62x63 mm)

My collection of firearms grew from my love of shooting and belief that one should be prepared for any situation that may arise. Some of my weapons were gifts from my father, who would gift me a new weapon every few years when I was growing up. I also had the following items on hand should the need arise.

> › 50 government-issued MREs (Meal Ready to Eat)
>
> › 10 rolls of duct tape (100-mile-an-hour tape as we called it)
>
> › $5,000 cash (most of this was from wedding gifts, and from savings that we kept on hand for an emergency)

As I looked over my firearms, I couldn't help but think of the sickening irony of it all. I had a personal arsenal at my disposal that could outfit a small SpecOps team...yet when the rubber met the road, I couldn't protect my own wife. I stared at the gray interior of the safe, feeling powerless...shamed in knowing that I had failed as a husband. Suppressing my emotions, I persevered knowing that tactical precision was the only chance I had to make this work.

CHAPTER 13
FRESH AIR

I HAD PROMISED my friend Mike I'd grab dinner with him that evening. My friends and family had tried to reach out but I'd been distant and unresponsive. While grieving was to be expected, I'd been consumed by darkness. I was worried it would spread to others like some disease. Mike had called multiple times and I knew I had to get out. Hell, I had to eat something.... I was becoming emaciated. I reluctantly met Mike at Belle's Cafe down the street.

We ordered some dinner, and Mike stared at me in an awkward silence I'd become accustomed to.

"You haven't been eating much, have you?"

I picked up a menu and pretended to study the contents.

"No, I haven't. Why?"

"'Cause you look like you got eaten by a wolf and shit off a cliff. Man, I'm gonna sit here till you finish whatever the hell you order."

"I know. Just haven't had much of an appetite lately."

Mike's blue eyes softened.

"Don't want to sound like a broken record, but me, your

friends, and family…we are all here for you. You're gonna get through this. Jake, you're the toughest sonova bitch I've ever met. It's just gonna take some time…and food!"

As we sat and talked, I looked at the families and couples around us. I paused briefly, focusing on an elderly gentleman, probably in his '80s, sitting by himself in a booth. He had a tan jacket, gray slacks, and white Reeboks with Velcro. He looked down at his coffee through his thick glasses and just radiated a sense of loneliness; he was wearing a wedding ring but looked completely solemn. I could tell we shared the loneliness of being without our soul mates. This was the life I had to look forward to without Michelle. In a panic, I got up from the table, telling Mike I needed some fresh air. I went outside and sat on a bench near the newspaper boxes. I looked past the palm trees into the distance.

Mike came outside. "Hey, bud, you OK?"

He sat next to me on the bench and we watched the fading sun cast shadows behind a large palm.

"Yeah, I just needed a minute. Ya know, sometimes I just see things…and it sets these memories in a tailspin."

"Like what?"

"That old man inside…sitting by himself."

Mike looked through the window.

"That guy? He reminds you of Coach Barry wearing depends?"

I laughed.

"No, he just looks so lonely. I know I sound pathetic."

Mike put his arm on my shoulder and squeezed me tightly. "Look at me, Jake. There isn't a goddamn thing about you that's pathetic and don't you ever forget that. If me or my boys are ever half the man you are, I'll consider myself the damn luckiest guy around. What you've been through…shit, I don't think I'd have it in me."

Taking a deep breath, I exhaled long and slow.

"Thanks, brother. I'm all right, I guess. Let's go get some chow."

As we ate, I started feeling a bit better about what I was going to do. I had found my calling; it felt right. But I didn't want to talk about me. I wanted to talk about Mike. We talked about his kids and I looked at pictures of them in their baseball uniforms. An hour passed and as I looked at my empty plate, I thought to myself that I was lucky to have surrounded myself with such wonderful people. When we finished dinner, I gave Mike a hug.

"Thanks for getting me outta the house and spending some time with me. I needed it."

"Any time, Jake. You call me if you need anything at all. We're all here for you."

"Thanks, man. Love you guys."

Heading home, I called Michelle's phone as I'd done every night since her death. I liked to listen to her voicemail…to hear her voice just one more time.

CHAPTER 14
PREPARATION

Arriving home, I locked the door behind me. The house was so quiet and dark, I paused for a moment to take in the silence. I flipped on the lights and turned on the TV to have some background noise. I grabbed a pen and a notebook from the kitchen drawer. It was time to get to work. As I closed the drawer, I saw a blinking light on the answering machine.

"Hi, Jake, it's Sergeant Petrillo. We caught one of the men and are in the process of a full debriefing to get any information we can. Just wanted to let you know. Was hoping it might bring some good news. Call me any time."

I listened to the message twice more. This was not good news. It meant that I would not be able to find this man myself. And likely word would get out and make the other murderers that much more difficult to track. I had even less time than anticipated. I needed information.

I went to the bedroom dresser where I'd left Sergeant Petrillo's card. I glanced at the picture next to Michelle's jewelry box. It was a picture of us on the Juno Beach fishing pier the first year we started dating. I couldn't get over her smile and how young she looked. She was wearing a blue sundress and we were on our way to dinner. I had been lucky to spend the best years of my life with her. I looked back at the card in my hand, took a deep breath, and dialed.

"This is Sergeant Petrillo."

"Hey, Sergeant Petrillo, it's Jake Bedford. I got your message."

"Hey, Jake, we apprehended Shane Tidwell a few hours ago."

My mind raced. Tidwell, aka Shay T, one of the four men from the reports. Petrillo was excited and I tried to keep up with him.

"We had a tip from one of our undercovers who busted one of them on drug charges. He was hiding out with some fellow bangers near Lake Worth. We took in four individuals total but he's the only one who seems to have any connection with Michelle's murder."

"OK. Has he said anything that might be helpful in catching the three others?"

"He's not saying much yet, at least not anything helpful. We'll see what we can get out of him."

Frustrated, I acknowledged their success. "OK, thanks again."

As I hung up the phone, the complexities of the judicial system weighed heavy on my mind. I wondered if some attorney would work on a plea agreement for Tidwell. Would it be realistic to fathom this dirtbag might get leniency for giving up the other three? Knowing little of the judicial system, I went to my office to research Florida's handling of convicted murderers. I found that Florida had been an electric-chair state, but in 2000 the legislature allowed for lethal injection as an alternative execution method. The major precedent behind the change was that the electric chair was considered "inhumane."

Inhumane? I didn't give a shit about humanity, I wanted justice for myself, for Michelle, and our families. What closure would we have knowing they had drifted away under the peaceful concoction of pentobarbital. Michelle's life was stolen from her in the blink of an eye and society was worried about the humanity of murderers?

I learned that there is a gap of over fourteen years between offense, conviction, and execution in Florida…fourteen years! I couldn't physically survive knowing her killers would be eating and breathing under the umbrella of that justice system.

Heading downstairs, I went to the patio for fresh air, piecing together the hypocrisy of American justice. It didn't make sense how a free society could so readily accept such bullshit. I felt sorrow for those who took any comfort in our legal system. Though I had turned my back on faith, I felt some sick comfort in the verse of Exodus 21:24. I vehemently felt that the only justice for Michelle's death was an "eye for an eye."

Looking at the clock, I saw there was little time for distraction, I was going head to head with the police in locating these men

It was assumed there was little loyalty among gang members. Most lowbrow organized crime cells are all about self-preservation. There is no code of honor among these men. Even the fiercely loyal rebel zealots we faced in the desert would give each other up under certain questioning tactics. If it was possible to make people betray their entire religious ideology, then I could certainly force these pieces of shit into giving each other up.

I was confident that I could get one of the 8th Street Kings to give up information on Michelle's murder. With the police already interrogating one of the suspects, this might be my only chance for target acquisition and interrogation.

CHAPTER 15
THE PLAN

I WISH I could say my planning was meticulous, down to the very detail…but this was not the case. I had very little time for recon prep, and the detectives had more information than I did. I finally decided that I needed to find any member of 8th Street Kings and do my own interrogation. With minimal time to scout out the area, research my targets, and study their routines, I was up against the eight ball.

This process would require extensive surveying of a localized perimeter. I needed a vehicle that would keep my identity protected and could be ditched if necessary. I called a cab and had the driver drop me off just south of Riviera Beach on Dixie Highway where there were some small shady car dealerships. Tropical Auto had fewer than a dozen total cars on the lot, but I found a hidden gem among them. A black '89 Honda Civic CRX hatchback with 126,435 miles on it. It was inconspicuous and already tinted out… perfect for zipping around and blending in. I bought the car for nineteen hundred bucks cash and headed out. Quick and easy. I parked it at a Wal-Mart not too far from my house and took a cab home so my neighbors wouldn't notice my new car.

I knew the 8th Street Kings primary source of income was drugs, so I could make contact through a narcotics purchase. But I still needed to capture the target and bring them to a discreet location for interrogation. Fuck! Sweat started beading down my temples and I felt a tightness in my chest. A single misstep could leave me dead, and failure was not an option.

I could utilize my garage for questioning, but any loud screaming could definitely get my neighbors attention. I took a deep breath and looked out my back window. The butterfly bush was in full bloom. I thought of Michelle…how much she loved to sit outside and read. I wondered if she could see me, if her spirit were here with me. But I only felt the same emptiness that anchored my every breath.

I sat down at the kitchen table with a glass of water and mulled over my options. The entire mission was reliant on my ability to remain clandestine. How the hell could I pull this off? Burying my head in my hands, I let out a long sigh.

"There's gotta be a way," I said to myself.

The only feasible option was to incapacitate my victim quickly and quietly during the transport phase of interrogation.

"Wait a minute. A tranquilizer!" I said, finishing my water and pacing around the kitchen.

I remembered the conversation Dave had on the phone at the pool hall. I knew Dave had access to various veterinary tranquilizers for farm emergencies, getting access to them…well that was another story.

CHAPTER 16
THE FARM

I HADN'T TALKED to Dave since Michelle's funeral, but he'd left a few voicemails to check in on me. Clewiston was a bit of a hike and I didn't have time to burn. This was my only shot. I got in my truck and headed west.

I called Dave about forty-five minutes out. He was clearing trails on the swamp buggy and said to just hang out at the house for an hour and he'd be back. His wife and kids were at the in-laws for the day, so it'd be a good time to catch up with "D&B"—that's what Dave called dip and brew.

I pulled into the drive, opened up the swing gate, and headed down the gravel path to the house. It was a beautiful piece of land…lots of old trees covered in Spanish moss, an old creek trickling through the pasture, and palm trees of all varieties as far as the eye could see. It had an old Florida feel and was very quiet, except for the sweeping winds and occasional cow. My head hurt as I tried to recall the details from Dave's conversation while we'd played pool. All I remembered was that he kept a tranquilizer in the top drawer of the barn, as for what I was looking for I was clueless. I knew my way around from our hunting trips so I parked on the gravel path and headed inside.

The barn was full of tractors, tillers, bailers, and other equipment. It was near a stable where Dave kept horses and feed. I went to the large toolbox in the corner and opened up the drawers, pleased to see a variety of bottles and vials. I quickly shifted through the contents. Acepromazine, Nuflor, Adequan, Banamine…I didn't recognize anything. As I kept sifting, I slowly felt time slipping away and I became woozy. Maybe I had just wasted a day and hope had gotten the best of me. I pulled out my phone and Googled "large animal tranquilizers" as I sat down outside on a wooden bench. As the screen populated with various veterinary medicine websites, I heard the buggy pulling back to the farm.

"Shit," I muttered, putting my phone back in my pocket and walking over to the buggy.

Dave climbed down the ladder and smiled when he saw me. He gave me a handshake and a quick hug before we headed up to the house. He handed me a cold Bud Light and a pouch of Red Man Golden Blend.

Dave leaned against the counter and adjusted his hat. "How ya holdin' up?"

"As best as I can. I'm thinking of getting away for a bit…just doing some hunting or camping. Spending some time in the woods to get my mind off things."

I was thinking off the cuff, trying to lead into some way to set myself up to get a tranquilizer. While I knew Dave had access to tranquilizers, justifying my need was tricky. We sat for an hour, talking as the sun slowly began to fade. I was tired, but I clung to what seemed like my last resort.

"Dave, you know a lot about large game animals, right?"

Dave gave me a puzzled look and said, "I know a bit, why?"

"I need to get access to a strong tranquilizer for my trip, figured you might be able to help me out."

The look on his face was one more of surprise and interest than shock.

"A strong tranquilizer huh. What the hell do you want it for?"

Trying my best to shield my frustration, I lied, hoping he'd at the very least share some insight. "Well, if I end up taking a trip out west alone, I'm just not sure my rifle will be enough. It's for an emergency, ya know…just for peace of mind. I'd like to be prepared for the worst."

I sensed that Dave realized that I was full of shit. After all, if a rifle doesn't do the trick on a large game animal, you're pretty much fucked. I was going to try to save face but knew that it might be best to just shut up and see what happened.

Dave raised his eyebrow and was silent for a minute. Finally he shook his head and looked me square in the eyes.

"Well, I have Xylazine, which is what we use most of the time around here. The only thing stronger than that is M99, etorphine hydrocholride."

I gazed at him for a moment before breaking the silence. "M99, huh? Do you have that?"

Dave took his hat off and wiped the sweat from his forehead. The evening humidity hung thick in the air. He looked flustered and took a moment composing his thoughts.

"Yeah, I have it. Keep a small kit in the house for farm emergencies. You'd need a tranquilizer dart and dart gun to use it. You planning on taking down a rhino?"

"Maybe."

I sensed his discomfort as we sat for a moment in an intense silence.

"Jake, etorphine can easily kill you if you're not careful. I need to know this is not for you. Don't make me regret helping a friend."

"Dave, I swear to you I'm not trying to kill myself. It will only be used for animal emergencies, you have my word."

Dave nodded, got up, and headed into the house. He came back and handed me a small Styrofoam box with a Novartis Pharmaceuticals stamp on it. It had an orange side stamped "Large Animal Immobilon" and then a blue side stamped "Large Animal Revivon." As I held the box in my hand, my mind raced. I became shaky.

Dave interrupted my thoughts. "Jake…Jake! Listen, I don't know where you got that, do you understand?"

I nodded.

Putting his hands in his pockets, he cautioned, "That stuff is strong enough for elephants. The one vial is etorphine and the other is diprenorphine. It's an opioid antagonist that can reverse the effects of the drug. Think of it as an antidote if you will."

Wide eyed, I nodded.

"Dave, I don't know what to say other than thanks, man. I love you guys."

Dave nodded and spit out his Red Man in the gravel.

"Lee and the kids will be back soon. You wanna stay for dinner? They'd really love to see you."

As much as I wanted to stay, I knew it was not possible. I had to start planning.

"I'd love to but I really ought to head back."

Dave seemed genuinely concerned, but he let me off easy. He simply gave me a hug and let me go on my way.

"If you need anything from us, anything at all…we'll be here. Our thoughts and prayers are with you."

As I headed out to my truck, my eyelids felt heavy. I couldn't let Dave see me cry. But as hard as I tried, I couldn't help it. I closed my truck door and sobbed uncontrollably, resting my head in the palms of my hands. The tears slowly trickled down my face and found their way to my forearms. The emotional strain of loneliness and anger had worn me thin. I had no one to turn to for emotional support. I wanted so much just to have someone put their arms around me and tell me things would be OK, but I knew that was impossible.

I hid the small tranquilizer box under the passenger seat and headed home. I turned the music down so it was barely audible and I began planning in my head. Finally, about forty-five minutes into the trip, a calmness swept over me. After crying so heavily, I was relaxed and full of confidence. The storm had passed and the horizon was clear. The sun faded away into orange as I passed through fields of sugar cane. I had already overcome a potentially impossible task. After all, who the hell has a buddy they can call out of the blue and get elephant tranquilizer from? I laughed to myself for the first time in forever.

It was still relatively early, only 9:27 p.m., when I got home. My attitude had changed and my body felt invigorated by the evening's victory. I went inside and made a quick protein shake. I had three messages but decided not to play them. No time for distractions.

I went to the garage, gathered tools, and set my work station. I duct-taped a large painter's blanket to the garage floor. It had a plastic bottom to prevent any fluid leakage. I removed the bottom of an office chair so just the seat and armrests remained. I set the seat on the painter's blanket. I had a minimum of three feet of blanket overlap on each side.

For noise prevention, I ensured that a small Kong dog toy could be utilized as a gag and the hollow boring through its center would allow for breathing if necessary. My tools were primitive at best. I wasn't planning an extravagant operation, so basic items would hopefully work…hunting knives and a grill torch. I was not worried about the repercussions of the law. I had a clear objective. It seemed so much easier without planning for a complex escape. It was like going into combat: protecting your men and civilians is a top priority even when deadly force was required. It was my duty, my job, to locate members of the 8th Street Kings.

With my workstation completed, I had to research the proper amount of etorphine to use. I found a website dedicated to zoo medicine with a dose rate for species of large African wildlife. I was now proficient in calculating the appropriate takedown amount of etorphine for an African elephant, black rhino, springbok, warthog and zebra...just no 8th Street gangsters. In planning, I assumed that the target weighed between one hundred and seventy and one hundred eighty pounds. I felt this was a safe bet for an average adult male. Based on that estimated weight ratio, the closest comparative species on the size-range table was the warthog. Unfortunately, my table gave me a range of three to seven milligrams of etorphine. Not that I'm familiar with tranquilizers, but that seemed like a broad spectrum. I decided to go a bit higher on the range. I had read on the etorphine package that the formulation was 2.45 milligrams per milliliter...so, in planning, I figured three milliliters would equal 7.35 milligrams. I felt comfortable about a possible overdose since the tranquilizer kit included the morphine agonist, Revivon.

As I opened the small box, I removed a vial containing exactly 10.5 milliliters of etorphine. I had syringes at the house and was meticulous in filling a twenty-gauge, one-and-a-half-inch needle with three milliliters of the lethal, bright red liquid. The interrogation location was prepared, the Honda Civic would serve as discreet transport, and the tranquilizer would help capture the target.

Now I just needed to plan my evening. As much as I wanted to scout the area, my window of opportunity was steadily decreasing. It was time.

CHAPTER 17
THE MISSION

It was just past eleven when I started loading my truck. As I gathered my supplies, I mentally charted the details of my plan. It was a strange paradox that my military training had essentially prepared me for this *exact* type of mission. Within the past three years alone I'd attended SOTG (Special Operations Training Group) to complete urban recon and surveillance, urban sniper, and dynamic assault courses.

I did my best to strategically prepare for any and all variables that might occur from departure to return. I wore olive-green cargo pants and a T-shirt underneath a thin, black hooded sweatshirt. The sweatshirt was great because it had a front pouch that was perfect for storing the syringe.

I placed my AR-15 and the Benelli tactical shotgun in a large black duffel bag. They were unloaded and I didn't intend to use them. I tucked my loaded .380 Kel-Tec pistol in my hip holster and walked into the house, my heart beating rapidly. The adrenaline had begun to kick in, and, as in combat situations, I needed to refocus my thought process. My mind tried to tell me that this was too risky, and I might spend the rest of my life behind prison bars. But there was no time for that—the mission was proceeding. Besides, I'd go in a body bag before I went to prison.

Closing my eyes, I breathed deeply, exhaling slowly to regain my bearings. I walked through the living room and looked at a picture from our wedding. I was lifting Michelle up, cradling her in my arms. I smiled, looking at her light-blue shoes. She insisted on being nontraditional and wearing these pretty blue shoes that she loved. She clutched a bouquet of tulips, smiling radiantly as we began our lives together. The bouquet reminded me of the one that was placed on her casket the day of the funeral. I thought of the family we would never have and the emptiness that now filled my black heart. I shut the light off and left.

CHAPTER 18
IT BEGINS

THE WAL-MART PARKING lot where I left the Civic was less than seven miles from the house. I suppose one of the greatest benefits of Wal-Mart is that, for some reason, even late into the evening, there are many bizarre characters shuffling in and out. I assumed that even with twenty-four-hour security, my truck parked for a few hours would be the least of their concerns.

I pulled up and parked toward the back of the lot, where the lighting was dim at best. It was far enough away to stay out of the main focus of patrons but not so far back it was isolated from overflow traffic. There were security cameras on the main pillars of some of the light posts. I would have to take a chance. If things went according to plan, there would be no reason authorities would even review the security tapes.

After sitting in the car with the lights off for ten minutes, I headed over to the Civic. It was 11:47 p.m. as I started my journey toward Dixie Highway. The intersection of Dixie and Palm Lakes was my target area to locate an 8th Street King. I had heard about drug busts and gang activity at this location. Though there was a major risk it was heavily patrolled by law enforcement, I had no other options. I hoped there was some luck on my side.

Heading eastbound I passed a multitude of run-down houses with yellow grass and broken rusty fences. It was unlikely gang members would be near the main road due to the higher volume of traffic and people. Many of the homes were over fifty years old and their aging owners were fighting a losing battle with the crime around them. Much of the neighborhood seemed to have been relinquished to gangs.

Getting closer, I saw a small bridge that covered a spillway. Either side of the bridge was an ideal location for drug dealers. It was dark, out of sight, and you could see a patrol coming in either direction. I turned before the intersection, passing a liquor store that I decided would serve as my target point. It was a two-story brown building with apartments on the top floor. It was a shit hole. Its screen windows were falling out, and air conditioner condensation had dribbled a green mineral streak down the brick to the sidewalk. There were multiple no-loitering signs outside but these seemed to be just a formality as there were already three people drinking on the side facing the bridge.

There were some people standing around but I felt my best bet would be near the liquor store. After all, I hadn't a clue what these guys looked like…. My search was entirely based on police reports, arrest documents, and gang-related news articles. Intel reported that members of 8th Street Kings were males, aged eighteen to twenty-five, displaying dark-green gang colors or a green bandana hanging from the front right pocket. I had to say I appreciated the 8th Streets assisting with the colors and bandana. Those were really my only saving grace…. Talk about not staying under the radar. Fucking idiots.

I pulled the Civic into a parking spot about forty yards from the liquor-store entrance. There was just enough light to make out activities on the side of the building. I cut the engine and waited about twenty minutes, just watching and surveying the surroundings. Luckily, I didn't see a single police cruiser. I thought this strange, but at least it proved beneficial in not scaring away any potential targets. The same three people continued drinking on the side of the building and foot traffic to the store was steady. A lot of people fit the target description and I couldn't clearly make out any gang colors. While time was limited, I wasn't ready to throw a Hail Mary.

It was 12:37 a.m. The car was getting hot, but I was afraid to roll the windows down and lose the cover of my tinted windows. At around 1:00 a.m., I saw a prospect leave the store. Nearly six feet tall, wearing a dark-gray windbreaker jacket and a tilted Oakland A's hat…dark green with the yellow *A*. He had baggy jeans and unlaced Timberland-style boots, helpful in the unlikely event I would need to give chase.

I assumed, watching him leave, that he had rented an apartment upstairs. After all, the likelihood of him being in the store for almost thirty minutes seemed slim, as I never saw him enter. He walked around the building and joined the individuals on the side. I hadn't planned on this. I couldn't exactly stay stealth by approaching a group and trying to lure him away with a potential drug deal. I needed to get him alone or far enough away to ensure the safety of the mission. My patience was slipping. Even if I got this guy alone, I still didn't even know if he was a member of the 8th Street Kings.

My palms began to sweat and slide down the edge of the steering wheel. My mind raced with uncertainty, my anger grew, and I thought about how simple it would be to just start shooting. But I needed to know this was an 8th Street King and use him to find Michelle's killers. The target lit a cigarette and started walking east, away from the group, and around the corner of the building.

I started the car and passed the bridge, turning right on a side street heading to the other side of the liquor store. Target acquired—he was on a cell phone, standing behind a trashcan. As I came within fifty yards, I rolled down the window a bit and breathed slowly, my face flush and sweaty. I spoke softly to myself. "Blessed Father, watch over my family with a drawn sword, whisper that I may live to hold my loved ones again." As I approached, he noticed me and put his hand to his backside, possibly reaching for a handgun. I cautiously rolled down my window. This was my only chance.

I leaned slightly out the window. "What's up, man?"

Hand still on his backside, the target cocked his head. "Sup?"

"You got anything, man? I'm kinda fiending right now—you got any blow?"

The man squinted and took an aggressive stance.

"Who the fuck are you? You a cop?"

I held my hands up to ease the tension.

"Naw, man…if you can't help…no problem…. Thought you might be holding."

He looked around scanning the vicinity.

"What you need? Twenty bucks min and don't waste my fucking time."

"Just a twenty or something. You got me?"

He took his hand away from his back and reached into his front pocket.

"Show me the money."

I took a twenty-dollar bill out of my pocket and handed it to him. He handed me a small Ziploc bag about an inch in diameter. It had a small white rock…. I didn't even know what the hell it was…cocaine, crack…could've been rock candy for all I knew.

I quickly placed the bag in my pocket, but he was already walking away.

"Look man, I gotta get rid of some guns. You interested?"

He turned back. "What you know about guns, mother-fucker? You out of your mind. Better get the fuck on up the street before I smoke your ass."

Losing patience, I became defiant. "All right, man, no big deal. I have a bunch though…need to get rid of 'em."

I quickly reached into my pouch and grabbed the .380 pistol. Without hesitation he pointed a 9 mm straight at me. Panicked, I set the gun on the seat and lifted my arms into the air.

"Whoa, man, chill out…just showing you some of the stuff I got."

He nervously looked around and reholstered his gun back into his jeans.

"Easy, man. I need to get rid of it. Just showing you. Fifty bucks, man, it's yours… C'mon, I need the cash."

"I'll give you the twenty back for the gun…that's it. Take it or leave it."

I took the twenty back and handed him the .380.

"I also got an AR and a shotgun. You want them too?"

He gazed at me with a deafening intensity. Did he know something was up? Was he going to shoot me? I couldn't even defend myself. I just gave him my only loaded weapon! I wanted to get out of here.

The man nodded toward the overpass behind us.

"Meet me under the bridge, and don't try anything stupid… you a long way from home."

"All right, I'ma turn around. Meet you there."

Great, Jacob, now you'll get blasted under a bridge by one of the same fucking criminals that killed your wife. As I pulled under the bridge, I parked to the left side and turned off the car. This was it, he was going to come out of the shadows, put a 9 mm bullet in my skull, and I'd die here, under a fucking bridge! I had to think quick.

He strolled up, holding his gun.

"Where the guns?"

I opened the hatchback and unzipped the duffel bag. I saw from his expression I had a chance. I was guessing it wasn't every day a car rolled up and offered eighteen hundred dollars' worth of firearms in a back alley for cash or drugs.

He put his gun back in his waistband and took out the AR. My hand in the sweatshirt pouch, I steadily loosened the cap on the syringe. My heart was beating so hard I could feel the pulse in my temples. My mouth was dry to the point I couldn't swallow. My existence essentially came down to this moment.

My voice trembled. "Take a look at the scope, man. That's the same one the military has."

He lifted the AR and pointed it through the tunnel to look at the scope.

"Five hundred…for both."

As he closed his left eye to peer through the EOTech, I uncapped the needle and struck. I aimed for the side of his neck but hit him in the trap area and injected. He swung around, the needle still in his neck, and reached for his gun. I grabbed him in a bear hug until his body went limp in my arms.

I sighed a heavy sigh…one that can only be understood by someone who has been in a life-and-death situation. I immediately glanced to both sides. It was clear. I threw the syringe, his 9 mm, the AR, and the Kel-Tec pistol into the trunk. I lifted him over my shoulder and belted him in the passenger seat. Another quick glance at my surroundings—dim light and no people around. I started the car and headed out.

My mind was completely clouded as I tried to recall my plans. I knew this could be an unpredictable disaster and I had no precise method for dealing with it. I was working against time in so many ways. He was asleep in the passenger seat, head slumped onto his right shoulder and drooling. His breathing was slow and deliberate. I put my blinker on and pulled off the exit. It had been only about fifteen minutes so I was hoping I had at least another fifteen before he regained consciousness.

I drove through my neighborhood. It was pitch black except for the pale yellow glow of a streetlight at the end of the road. I appreciated the safe darkness that cloaked my entry as I pulled into the garage, closing the door behind me.

CHAPTER 19
THE GARAGE

I PLACED HIS slumped body onto the office chair and secured his arms and legs with duct tape. Each arm was taped twice to the armrests. Once just below the elbow and another exactly at the wrist joint. I then secured the waist and the chest of the target, and then a final wrap around both the chest and arms to prevent lateral movement. Resistance was futile.

The lower body required more security. I chose six wrap points starting at the upper thigh and finishing at the lowest part of the ankle. Once secured, I placed the small Kong dog toy in his mouth. I wore Kevlar gloves in case he suddenly woke and bit me. His breathing remained heavy and I monitored the passage of air through his nostrils.

The Kong was perfect, large enough not to choke on but small enough that it could fit comfortably in the mouth. Well, comfort is a relative term. I secured it with half a roll of tape. I used a knife to cut through the tape and ensure free breathing passage. I could stuff this with a rag to muzzle sound if necessary. As I took a step back, surveying the garage, I felt in total control.

I waited. It had been forty minutes and I was getting

impatient. I wondered if I should get the other vial of medicine to counteract the effects of the etorphine. I had it nearby in the tranquilizer case. As I waited, he began coughing. I panicked at first, worrying he might vomit and choke before I started my intel, but he soon stopped. He dragged his eyes open with a dazed look. He surveyed the garage, passing from paint cans in the corner, to picnic chairs on the wall, to an old set of golf clubs. He hadn't even looked down at the knives and torch carefully laid near my feet.

Slowly he came back to full consciousness. As the glaze lifted from his eyes, he stared at me with uncertainty. He was mumbling through the muzzle, but I couldn't understand and didn't care. He tried desperately to fight the restraints but could only fall on his side. He looked down at my tools and then back at me, panic overwhelming him as mucous ran from his nostrils. This was the reaction I had expected.

CHAPTER 20
INTERROGATION

INTENTLY GAZING INTO his eyes I spoke. "You will take directions or I will fucking kill you."

He tested the restraints again unsuccessfully, tears streaming down his face as he gasped for air through the hole in the Kong.

I waited.

"I want to tell you why you are here. You will give me information regarding the 8th Street Kings. If you comply with my requests, you will live. If not, I will put you in so much pain you will wish for death. Nod your head if you understand."

He nodded and mumbled something. There was no more eye contact. It appeared he had given up the struggle.

"I am going to remove your gag so you can talk. If you raise your voice, yell, scream, or do not comply with my requests, I am going to cut off your hands. I advise you to listen, as your life is not worth anything to me. If you want to live, you will listen very carefully and do everything that is requested.

"Do not panic. Comply and you will not get hurt. Nod if you understand me."

My experience had taught me sometimes a simple expression will let you know if you have a compliant subject.

He nodded aggressively and I began my work.

I pulled a razor knife from my pocket and he began to panic.

"Shhh, I'm removing this.... It will not hurt. You wanna breathe, don't you?"

I needed to carefully cut the tape to remove the Kong. As I cleared his mouth, he gasped for fresh air. People feel a sense of immediate freedom when no longer breathing in a confined manner.

He spoke, but softly. He knew I was serious. "What do you want from me? I don't know shit...I swear. Please..."

"I need information. I brought you here because I already know you have the answers I need. If you give me the correct answers, you live. If not...if not...well, you know how this goes. How long have you been a member of the 8th Street Kings?"

The man gasped.

I lifted him slowly by the arm so he was sitting up. "Shhh, it's OK. Catch your breath and speak slowly."

"Since...since I was fifteen, man. I'm twenty-two now. Look, man, if this is about drugs or money you can have whatever you want. Please let me go...please!"

He was mine. He'd already begun conceding defeat.

"What's your name?"

"Rashad Maxwell."

"Are you a 'shot caller'?"

He had calmed down enough that his voice was confident and coherent.

"Yeah, I run the block."

"Who do you answer to in the 8th Street hierarchy?"

"C-Lo...but he's hemmed up."

I knew Shane Tidwell was in custody so I wanted to check

this information within the 8ths. I wanted to see what type of alert they had and what they had been told.

"Do you know Shane Tidwell?"

"Yeah, he's locked up…got picked up recently."

"Did you know him well?"

"Yeah, I ran with him back in the day. Not as much now. I just see him around the block."

"What was he arrested for?"

"I think rape and assault, but it could have also been drugs or weapons. I swear, man, all I know is he was picked up about a week or so ago."

"He was arrested for rape and assault. There was a gang initiation that took place at the hospital. Shane Tidwell and Carlos Zentillo were involved."

Putting his head down, the man shook a bead of sweat from his face.

"Yeah, I heard about it."

"Me too. Were you there?"

"Naw, man. Look, what's this got to do with me? I didn't do shit, OK?"

I walked to the corner of the garage and grabbed a bottle of water.

"Are you thirsty?"

"Yeah, I'm dyin'…"

I held the bottle up a few times, he gulped from it. Part of interrogation is taking advantage of truth by distorting the reality of the situation. I needed to start taking advantage of this.

"Good, I appreciate your cooperation. It will keep you alive. I want to tell you what will happen if you don't cooperate. You have been very honest with me and that is good, so I'm hoping I don't have to do this to you."

Placing the bottle of water near his feet, I began.

"First, I will slit your throat and you will die, painfully, within minutes. Next, I will spray your entire body with a combination of alcohol and ammonia and remove your hands, feet, and teeth to destroy any DNA evidence. These are burned and crushed into a powder that is spread down a storm drain. Your body is then burned and the ashes are spread in a field in Okeechobee on a cow pasture. You will disappear."

I had never done any of this, but it sounded just crazy and realistic enough to make him choose life over loyalty and truth over bullshit.

His eyes started tearing up and he started hyperventilating. "Fuck, man, I don't want to die."

"Where is Carlos Zentillo?"

"I don't know!"

I grabbed a rag and duct-taped it into his mouth with three wraps around his head.

"Wrong answer."

I grabbed the torch and began heating the blade of the knife. It glowed red in the dim garage light. He tried to scream but it was no use with the gag in place. I took the smoldering knife and placed it under the neckline. This is an extremely sensitive area that can cause excruciating, long-lasting pain. It burned into the skin for five seconds in a six-inch line just under the neck. The distinct and sickening smell of burning flesh filled the air. He screamed, then stopped, breathing heavily as mucus ran down the tape.

"I asked you to be honest with me. I am going to take that gag out of your mouth. If you scream, or even raise your voice, I will gut you like a pig."

I removed the gag. He started gasping. I knew in a couple minutes he would experience a calm as his adrenaline faded and endorphins overcame the trauma.

"Where is Carlos Zentillo?"

I waited for his breathing to calm so he could form a coherent sentence. Holding the gag in my hand, I waited.

"I heard he's down in Miami…staying with a cousin. He also stays with his girl at nights…he's got her car."

"Where is his girl and what car is he driving?"

"It's a black Nissan Altima, rimmed up and tinted. He goes there late at night…around midnight or later. She lives in Lake Worth."

I put the rag down and wrote the details in small notepad.

"Shane Tidwell. How much will he say to the police?"

"He probably won't say shit; he's been locked up before and can operate inside. He'll probably get off that rape charge.… It was the other two that did most of the work. He's no snitch."

A nauseating rush swept through my body. I would have vomited had anything been in my stomach. The words felt heavy as I tried to form coherent sentences. "W-w-who were the other two guys that were with them at the hospital? What are their names and where can I find them?"

"Angel Araujo. Goes by 'A-Dog.' And Mario, he goes by 'Shaggy.'" They run together. I think they've been in Delray a lot. I don't know the house, but they're pushing up near the gas station two blocks south of Linton."

"How will I recognize them?"

The man shook his head, closing his eyes.

"Man, if they find out I'm talking, I'm dead anyway. Fuck this, if you're gonna kill me, just fucking kill me.… I don't fucking care anymore."

"They will only find out if you tell them."

"A-Dog has a green bandana tucked in his jeans or around his leg. The new guys always flaunt colors. Fuck man, I gotta piss…c'mon, let me go."

I refused to break focus.

"What does Shaggy look like?"

"He's short with dreads...probably five-six. He's usually wearing a green shirt under something."

"We are not done yet. Piss yourself if you want. You're not leaving until I get answers."

I walked to the corner to get another bottle of water. I hadn't expected to get this much information off one interrogation. Had I not still felt so sick I might have been impressed with myself.

"Rashad, tell me how you knew that it was A-Dog and Shaggy who did most of the work at the hospital. How would you know? I mean, you said you weren't there."

"Man, we all knew about it. It was their initiation."

"So you knew about the rape and murder of an innocent woman and did nothing about it? It's how someone joins the 8th Street Kings?"

The man looked at me as if I was stupid to even question their street code. "Yeah, man, that's the game. I gotta fuckin' piss."

Closing my eyes, I was frozen in my tracks. I could feel my blood run cold, piercing my heart. I repeated the words under my breath, trying desperately to comprehend their meaning.

"That's the game...that's the game...that's the..."

I tried taking a deep breath, but couldn't. My eyes welled up, and I began shaking. Brushing away the tears, I closed my eyes, picturing my final moments with Michelle. I remembered her leaning down to kiss me in my office chair moments before she left for work. My final kiss and I didn't even get to hold her in my arms. I felt cheated.

My hands balled into fists and I slowly turned to face the man bound in my garage. He looked at me with a vacant, remorseless expression.

As soon as our eyes locked, I felt the uncontrollable rage I'd kept at bay flood my body. I growled, baring my teeth like some rabid predator. There was no turning back. In a quick, fluid motion, I stuffed the gag in his mouth and started taping heavily. He started to scream but it was no use, nothing could stop me.

"That woman that was raped and murdered? That was my wife! You ripped me apart so you little cowards could wear a green bandana? You're going to die, you worthless piece of shit!"

He immediately started thrashing sideways. I pushed him on his side, placing all one hundred and eighty-seven pounds of my weight on his neck to pin him to the floor. He shook with desperation and made wild gasps through his nostrils, his body demanding air. Using all the strength in my body, my right hand clasped his nose shut and held him down so he wasn't able to move. I snarled through my gritted teeth as he struggled to breathe. His eyes were wild, darting around the garage and finally focusing directly into my eyes. I watched him, looking into the darkness of his pupils. His resistance lapsed and his eyes slowly turned glassy. Collapsing on the floor, I sobbed, burying my head between my hands.

"What have I done? Oh God, what have I done?"

I stared at my hands in shock. They were shaking uncontrollably. My eyes drifted to the body, slumped over, fluid coming out of its mouth and nostrils. I felt no remorse, or vindication. I thought of my wife and felt an overwhelming shame. The thought of her watching me from heaven left me petrified. Michelle would have never wanted me to take vengeance into my own hands.... She would be disgusted by my actions.

I had forsaken her, but what did it matter anymore? I had just committed a murder in my garage and might spend the rest of my life in prison. In the blink of an eye, my uncontrollable rage shredded any shell of existence I had left to live. The killing didn't bring me any peace, it only magnified the infinite feeling of loneliness that consumed me.

Twenty minutes later, my adrenaline finally began to dissipate. I wanted to believe this all was just a result of a terrible lapse in sanity, but perhaps it wasn't. Perhaps it was never just about vindication for my wife's murder. This was ensuring that the wolves could no longer hunt without fear of retaliation. I had now come too far to turn back. My only salvation was in the suffering of the wicked.

CHAPTER 21
DIRTY WORK

It was approaching 5:00 a.m. My time was limited. I had to dispose of him. I drank a cold beer and took a Xanax to ease my nerves. The adrenaline surge had drained me and I hadn't the slightest clue about what to do with the body. It was too risky to dump it, I might be seen. I didn't have the time or the stomach to dismember him, either. I had no other choice but to go back out "west" and bury the body in some farmland.

With my Kevlar gloves on, I wrapped the body from the head down with a heavy-duty contractor's trash bag. I tightly wound the body in a large blanket. This was the most reasonable method I could think of to prevent leaving any additional forensic evidence. I placed the body in the back of the Civic. I would have to hurry – as it would be daylight soon, I couldn't use the Civic for the job.… Its dark tinted windows drew too much attention.

I drove carefully and, with the last bit of darkness fading, put the body on the rear floorboards of my truck. Luckily, the Wal-Mart parking lot was huge and at this hour there was significant space between my vehicles and anyone else. Again, I would have to hope that nobody had reason to check the security footage.

There was no foolproof way of hiding the body on the floorboards so I'd have to be careful driving. I had some old towels, wood scraps, and newspapers to cover the body. This would hopefully simulate enough clutter to draw attention away from the blanket. I had two large gas cans, a shovel, and my other tools, which I placed in the truck bed.

It was just over an hour drive. I finished two Red Bulls and drove in silence. I studied the lines on the road, thinking of what I'd done and where I'd go from here. It was 6:09 a.m. when I pulled up to the entrance of a cattle farm. While it was a huge risk trespassing on someone else's land, it was one I had to take. Luckily, I estimated the land had around twenty-five hundred acres of undeveloped pastures and forests, with multiple entry points. Most farmers carry their day-to-day responsibilities around crops and cattle, none of which were in this section.

I followed a dirt road toward a three-way split off the beaten path. Much of the land had not been cleared, and, even with four-wheel drive, I could get stuck if I didn't pay attention. The daylight was actually good for my cause. Had it been dark, I would have needed headlights, drawing way too much attention. As for the fire I would need, that was another impossibility at night. As the sun rose, I put on work gloves and began digging.

The hole needed to be at least four feet long by two feet wide. I figured this was just enough to fold the body inside and light the fire. I dug feverishly, the lack of sleep combined with the heat was making me delirious. The size of the hole was not the issue… it was the depth…. At least four feet would be required. The ground was dry but very soft, making the labor tolerable. I finished digging and filled the bottom layer with dry grasses and sticks. I pulled the body out of the truck and carefully placed it in the hole, dousing it with gasoline. Next came another layer of sticks, leaves, and grass.

I looked around. Nothing. It was safe. I removed my gloves, carefully lit a match and tossed it in hole.

Whoosh.

Instantly the combustion engulfed the hole, flames rising above the dirt line. The heat was so intense I ran back to the truck, hoping that the fire wouldn't spread. The dry ground was a major risk and I didn't have an extinguisher…only water.

Dark smoke billowed from the pit, and ash scattered in the light breeze. I stood under a large royal palm, nervously watching the black clouds dissipate into the blue sky. I hadn't planned on the smoke being so overwhelming. The sickening smell of burning flesh filled the air, making me sick to my stomach. I tried to forget what was actually going on, but couldn't. I didn't feel human.

Exhausted, I wiped away perspiration with my sleeve and used the shovel to break up the remaining embers that filled the hole. Unfortunately, it takes some time for a body to completely burn; it is not an instantaneous process. I again doused the remains with gasoline and set fire to it. I hoped the breeze would carry the smoke away quickly and provide me some relief from the overbearing Florida heat.

I scattered the remaining ashes in the hole and poured water over the site. I filled the dirt back to the top and was pleased with the way it looked, as undisturbed as possible. I hoped some rain might assist in the near future and allow weeds to fill the spot in. Luckily, one thing Florida had was plenty of afternoon showers. The dust would hopefully settle and keep my secret buried without notice.

The ride home was nauseating, I found myself grateful for the solitude. Cloaked behind the steel coffin of my truck, preventing others from seeing the hideous creature I'd become. I pictured myself in a courtroom, being sentenced to death. The irony of facing the same charges as Michelle's killers infuriated me, knowing that I could have any similarity to those animals. We were a pathetic culture of slaves depending on an incompetent hierarchy of politicians and a broken system of justice to set things right. I could let neither judge nor jury dictate the justice of Michelle's murder.

I felt no remorse for my actions. I knew in my heart what had to be done. There was no turning back.

CHAPTER 22
RECOVERY

It was 9:40 a.m. when I finally crawled into bed. I set the alarm clock for 3:00 p.m. and instantly fell asleep.

My slumber abruptly ended to some pop song on the radio. Rolling over, I turned it off and sat up in bed. I was woozy but able to collect myself, doing my best to suppress the reality of my actions. I went downstairs to get some food and prepare for the second phase of my mission. My refrigerator was empty, except for a few bottles of water, some beer, and expired condiments. As mundane as the details of a vacant fridge seemed, it was yet another realization at how much my life had changed. I hadn't even considered grocery shopping since Michelle's death.I mixed some oatmeal, water, and protein powder in a blender and sat at the table in silence.

My interrogation had proven unbelievably successful. I now had intel on two gang targets directly affiliated with Michelle's murder. I studied my notes from the questioning and realized that I actually knew more about the killers than the police. They were still looking for details and I had in my possession a road map to see this through. With the absolute exception of remaining undetected, the only obstacle I faced was Father Time. The police themselves were no longer allies, but obstacles in my race to locate the killers.

It was nearly 4:00 p.m. I needed to quickly utilize my intel. Hoping a cold shower would heighten my senses, I turned the water to full blast. As the cool water fell on my body, I thought about telling my story, as a warning to those who intended to inflect harm on the innocent. I laughed to myself. Jacob Bedford, author of an American tragedy. I tried to dismiss the idea, but the more I thought about it, the more reasonable it sounded. Lt. Col Dave Grossman had a theory on combat psychology. As a society, we are almost entirely comprised of "sheep," productive individuals with no capacity for violence. There are two minorities among the sheep, "wolves" and "sheepdogs." Wolves prey on the sheep. They lack empathy and have a high capacity for violence. Sheepdogs, on the other hand, have a capacity for violence but also possess a deep love for their fellow citizens. They live to protect the flock and will confront the wolves when needed.

I wrapped a towel around myself and headed to my office. Glancing at the notepad with my target descriptions, I found myself transfixed by the notion of a brutally honest warning to those who preyed on the innocent. I stared at the notepad, considering the sheer insanity of it, a detailed self-incrimination for the world to read. There may come a time, but as of now, there was no story to tell. The tide of vengeance had yet to rise.

CHAPTER 23
THE MISSION

If ANGEL AND Mario were potentially in Delray, I'd have to run a recon mission to determine their likely locations…but then what? Was I going to attempt to drug, murder, and hide these bodies as well? It just didn't add up. The next phase in planning would require a new methodology. It brought a new appreciation for the simplicity of my days in the Corps. Planning this mission was unlike anything I'd ever done, but I started thinking about what the best approach would be using my combat experience.

With the development of MARSOC (Marine Corps Forces Special Operations Command), the intelligence we received regarding special reconnaissance, foreign internal defense, and direct action was so clear that we were almost always assured of finding our targets. The only question would be what type of resistance we would encounter and how we could promptly eliminate any "static" detrimental to our objectives.

There was a night mission outside of western Kabul. We had been tasked to capture or eliminate a Taliban leader who had been planning suicide bombings targeting embassy and foreign agency offices. Our command briefing determined the target's location to be a heavily guarded safe house about ten klicks outside the city. Based on this intel, it was certain we'd encounter direct hostile forces, requiring an air support team. That team was the 160th SOAR or "Night Stalkers," a bunch of badass motherfuckers who could mow 'em down from above if we got in the shit.

Well, by the time we were knee-deep in it calling for air support, they had to stand down due to high levels of civilian activity around the safe house. We improvised by shooting our way out through a maze of concrete to a back alley to join our rescue team.

I killed four men on that mission. People always ask if you become desensitized to killing, but as I've said before, it's not difficult to fire at someone shooting at you with an AK-47. Half the time you simply react. You don't even see the enemy (or what's left of them) until you've secured the area with patrol. As our Humvee convoy rumbled back to base, I noticed the magazine of my M4 was down to two rounds. I breathed a sigh of relief; today we were the lucky ones.

I digress. I had no tactical support, no key location intel, and absolutely no fucking idea of what to do when I located the targets. Also, as a civilian, I now had to worry about the authorities investigating the multiple felonies I was about to commit. My only hope was finding Mario and Angel while the police tracked Zentillo.

Operating as a civilian conducting urban warfare operations was severely hampering my mental stability. I sat at the table and had a few swigs from a bottle of Crown Royal, rolling my pocket watch between my fingers. Pondering the logistics of the mission, I reached for the bottle again and paused, thinking of Michelle.

We'd come back from my nephew's T-ball game and she was unpacking a cooler. I'd washed down an oxy and a Xanax, struggling to suppress the anxiety looming for my deployment next week.

Michelle had a pained look in her eyes. "I'm worried with

you taking these pills all the time. We are meeting Pete and Mary for dinner in a couple hours. You're gonna pass out at the table."

I tried to keep my composure. "I'm fine. My back is killing me and I just need to take the edge off. You have no clue what this feels like inside."

She put her hand on mine, gently squeezing.

"I don't. I want so much to help take this pain away from you, but you have to let me…you have to let your guard down. I love you so much."

My face felt flush and heat rushed through my body. "Fuck, I'm fine, just leave it alone, babe. I try so hard to fight it, but I can't! It's like I'm suffocating. This tightening feeling comes over my whole fucking body. Did you ever think…what if, what happens if I get blown up over there? Are you still going to love me?"

Michelle's eyes welled up with tears. "Baby, look at me."

I struggled to turn away but she gripped my arms firmly.

"Look at me…look at me. I will *always* love you, no matter what."

I wiped a tear away before it could land on the table. Taking a quick swig of Crown, I dumped the remaining bottle in the sink. I splashed water on my face then went upstairs.

Her memory fueled me, and I was due for a little good luck. After all, no matter how tactful or cautious I was in my approach, the perfect plan didn't seem to exist. Time was limited, and I'd need to prepare for multiple scenarios. The etorphine had worked perfectly on my first victim, but I didn't have enough to make mistakes. After target one was eliminated, I was down to 7.5 milliliters. I filled another syringe with exactly three milliliters of the tranquilizer, carefully capped it, and prepared for the evening. I put on jeans, a long-sleeve tee, and drove to Wal-Mart to pick up the Civic.

CHAPTER 24
CRIMINAL ESPIONAGE

As I BEGAN the thirty-minute drive to Delray, I pieced together potential plans for the evening. The intel I had gave me a starting point for my search, but I knew it might take a while to locate members of the 8th Street Kings, particularly my targets. Though I was no expert on gang activity, I knew that they had to protect their territory from rivals and this meant not being stationary.

Needing a sense of comfort, I plugged my iPod into the Civic's auxiliary cable. Michelle and I had a travel playlist, and the song "Red Dirt Road" brought back memories of driving to the Keys for weekend trips. For the brief duration of the song, I was reminded not of pain and sorrow but the incredible joy my wife had brought me. Smiling, I thought of my recent flashback of Michelle saying, "I will *always* love you, no matter what." I wiped my eyes. "I'll always love you too baby, now and forever."

The realization that a perfect plan didn't exist allowed me the autonomy to improvise a bit. Once I located the targets, I'd need to take them out while minimizing my risk of discovery. This was tricky—there weren't many ways to proceed without immersing myself in close-range interaction. The firearms-sale tactic had worked to perfection but it was just too risky to try again.

South on 95, I saw a large Best Buy sign. I pulled off the interstate and headed inside. There was a forty-inch Samsung LED flat screen on sale for under five hundred bucks. My mind mapped out the intricacies of the plan. This idea would give me some cover. I loaded the TV onto the pushcart and headed to the counter.

I paid for the TV, put it in the hatchback, and headed back down 95. As I pulled off the exit to Delray, my senses felt heightened. There was no room for failure; my mind and body needed to be sharp. I scanned my surroundings and began heading just south of Linton Boulevard.

As in most neighborhoods in Florida, it is pretty obvious when you are getting into the wrong side of town. Though many people are quick to judge, I firmly believe that ninety-nine percent of people are just trying to get through the day and make ends meet. Overall, Delray was a pretty nice area with only a few rough spots just west of the highway. I think these areas served to protect the outskirts of gang turf between Lauderdale and Miami.

I pulled into a small plaza with a run-down liquor store and parked the Civic. It was still daylight so there was minimal activity, allowing me the time to examine one of the waypoints gathered from my interrogation. It was eighty-four degrees and the sun was just starting to fade a bit.

I saw a few guys hanging near a gas station across the street. I pulled the Civic up to the air compressor on the opposite side of the gas pumps. I left my wallet, took the iPod, and exited the vehicle.

I walked up to where the guys were hanging out. It was obvious that I was out of place, and they looked alarmed that I was approaching them.

"What's up, fellas? You guys interested in an iPod…brand new, ten bucks."

The man replied without hesitation. "Nah, we're good."

I was undeterred. After all, I hadn't expected gathering intel to be easy.

"C'mon, man. I'm short on cash, ten bucks…. It's brand new, sells for a hundred and fifty bucks."

The second man lit a cigarette and looked up. "Where's it at?"

I pulled the silver iPod from my pocket. It wasn't *technically* brand new but it didn't have a scratch on it. I handed it to the guy who looked around suspiciously.

"I just need ten bucks quickly. You want it or not?"

The men scanned the parking lot. Visibly agitated, one of them snapped at me. "Man, we don't want an iPod, what is this? What are you doing here, you fucking pig?"

"Chill the fuck out. I'm not a cop. You want it or not?"

As fate would have it, one of the men eased up. "For ten bucks, I'll take it."

He pulled a roll of money out of his pocket. I estimated he had about three hundred bucks in twenties and tens. He handed me a ten-dollar bill and we made the exchange.

"We straight."

"Thanks, hope you like country."

He scoffed, "Yeah, I'm gonna have to do something about that."

I started to walk away, but then turned around again casually.

"Hey, I have a TV I was supposed to drop off for a guy named Mario, goes by Shaggy, you know where he's at?"

The two men looked at each other before responding. "What kind of TV?"

I strolled back toward the men. "It's brand new, in the box. A forty-inch LED, top of the line. I was told to ask for him. You know him?"

"Yeah, I've seen him around. What you want for the TV?"

"Listen, I've got a lot of merchandise. I don't have that much time right now but I can come back. Whatever you need—TVs, computers, iPads...anything. Do you know where I can find him? I was told he'd be interested."

They hesitated...and I thought about the terrible miscalculation I'd made exposing myself. The brief seconds of ensuing silence lasted forever.

"Might try around L Street, but he don't want no TV. You looking for drugs?"

"Nah, just selling merchandise...trying to earn a dollar. You want me to come back down sometime with electronics, just let me know."

Visibly annoyed, both men walked back to the gas station. One of them muttered, "Sure, whatever, man."

Getting back to my car, I quickly drove away. L Street wasn't even in Delray, it was about twenty minutes north, back in Lake Worth. I knew L Street because it had been the scene of a fatal stabbing about a year ago. It received a lot of press because of the public outcry to stop gang violence. I drove into a McDonald's parking lot to collect my thoughts.

My best chance to capitalize on the location was to act tonight. For the first time since I had started my mission, I had compromised my identity. If people started going missing, I'd have shot callers searching all over for a black Civic and a white male patrolling the area.

It was now 6:26 p.m. and I had been sitting in the McDonald's parking lot for a half hour. I needed to eat something, and I really needed a drink. I figured I'd grab a quick bite and head to L Street to look for Mario.

I went inside for some food and headed back to the car, where I ate and calculated how this could go down. A cold sweat kept running through my body, making me nauseous. I took a Xanax. When working any reconnaissance mission, it is one of the most critical elements to blend in with the environment. It would hurt my credibility if I didn't look calm and collected, particularly since I was out of place to begin with.

Even though I was ready to get moving, I felt drowsy. The Xanax might not have been the best idea, regardless of my anxiety. I really needed sleep. Unfortunately there wasn't time to waste. I closed my eyes and sighed heavily, looking at the clock. It was still early, though the drain of the last couple days weighed heavy on my mind, and my body was starting to crash. The inherent risk of proceeding while groggy was unbelievably dangerous and would certainly get me killed. I knew that I couldn't rest here and headed to a nearby shopping plaza, where most of the stores were open until 9:00. I felt comfortable enough to close my eyes for a moment. Setting my phone alarm for twenty-five minutes, I cracked the windows and let the weight of my eyelids carry me away for a brief escape from reality.

CHAPTER 25
NO REST FOR THE WEARY

I AWOKE BEFORE my alarm to the crack of thunder, it was around 7:10 p.m. Peering out the window, the gray rainclouds hovered in the sky as the winds whipped the trees. I washed down some Advil, watching the downpour collect on the paver tiles. Still exhausted, I collected my thoughts in the car as I drove towards L Street. The dim streetlights cast eerie reflections on the rain-soaked streets. I passed some liquor stores and a pawnshop before pulling into a Texaco to grasp my bearings. I'd narrowed down a location and figured my best opportunity was driving around to look for gang colors.

I went inside the Texaco and grabbed a sugar-free Red Bull. The store was empty except for the clerk, who was encased in bulletproof glass, watching TV. The clerk barely looked at me as he muttered, "Two fifty." I handed him a five-dollar bill, gathered my change, and left.

I went back to patrolling in the Civic, feeling the comfort of anonymity behind the tinted windows. Shortly after turning near L street, I saw three men standing just outside the shadows of a gray duplex, leaning against a broken chain-link fence that ran beside a trash-littered sidewalk.

Since drive-by shootings plagued this area, an unknown car pulling up could cause a stir…or so I thought. I parked on a side street about forty yards away, preparing to go on foot. I would be walking right into the lion's den. While I could get killed, I didn't see any other method of approach. I decided to put my 9 mm under the driver's seat because if, for any reason, they found me armed, it would compromise my identity.

I took three deep breaths and exited the car, then slowly walked down the street. Sweat seeped through my shirt in the muggy Florida air. I wiped my face, trying to mentally compose myself. This side of the building seemed eerily dark and I saw only the embers of a cigarette under a cloud of smoke. I was within thirty feet when one of the men walked out of the shadows.

He was wearing jeans, a black long-sleeve T-shirt and a green "561" hat—the area code in Palm Beach County. As I approached, the three men put something down at their feet and aggressively started toward me, fists clenched.

The man in the hat looked up. "Yo, you lost, son?"

I kept walking and made contact. "Nah, hoping you can help me out."

They were within ten yards, and I quickly assessed that all the men were members of the 8ths. One man wore a green bandana under a Miami Hurricanes hat and the other had one hanging from his front pocket.

"Can't help you. Get out of here now."

I stopped in my tracks, keeping my hands visibly at my sides. "Easy, fellas. Be cool. I was told that Mario wanted to see me. Is he around?"

Immediately they surrounded me. This tested the limits of my fight-or-flight response. The men sized me up, one smoking a black cigar and the other a cigarette, which he promptly threw out. I put my hands up in the air, trying to look as defenseless as possible. I formulated my words carefully. "Look, fellas, I have a television for him, was told to stop down here. I really don't want any trouble."

The man smoking the cigar took a long drag and exhaled. "Start talking before I make you disappear."

Adjusting the brim of the green 561 hat over his short braids, the man looked me up and down. "Motherfucker, who the fuck told you to come down here and look for Mario? Start talking."

I slowly moved my hands back to my side. "I unloaded electronics to some guys earlier. They didn't have the cash for a TV and said Mario might be interested. They looked about your age…that's why I'm asking."

The man kept a steady gaze on me as the other men looked for him to make a move. He nodded casually to the man with the bandana in his jeans, who took a semiautomatic handgun out of his waist and cocked it.

The man raised the gun and pointed it directly at me, waiting for direction. A wicked grin came over the leader's face as he lit a cigarette and spoke. "You better start making sense, motherfucker. Who the fuck told you to look for Mario?"

I knew that in these shadows no one could see us. For the first time in weeks, I felt alive. I felt fear…true, overwhelming fear. I knew I would be killed. My heart was racing and I had the sudden urge to urinate. Visibly rattled, I summoned the courage to speak, wiping the perspiration from my hands on my shirt.

"Chill out, man," I stuttered. "It was jus…just some guys at a gas station. They didn't have money for the TV. I'm trying to get some cash quickly and they said he might be interested. If you don't know him, it's no big deal…just let me go."

I paused, awaiting my fate. My mind raced, contemplating a way to defuse the tension.

The man in the Miami hat broke his silence. "What guys? What gas station?"

Visibly agitated, the men moved closer and I stared directly into the barrel of the 9 mm being held by the man with the bandana. Keeping a slanted gaze on me, he turned to the men. "What you think, Wax? This motherfucker a cop?"

The man with the Miami hat, Wax, turned to the leader. "Dunno, man. I don't trust this fucker. What you think, Shag? Put two in this fool's head?"

When I heard him say Shag, a chill ran through my spine. It had been Mario, aka Shaggy, all along. This immediately explained their apprehension in talking to me. Something beyond anger overcame my body and my eyes fixated on the man. He had a thin mustache and goatee. Light brown skin and a tattoo on his neck that appeared to be a series of Roman numerals. I was face-to-face with Michelle's killer. The moment was paralyzing.

Hatred seethed through me as I looked into the bloodshot brown eyes of the man who had destroyed everything I had ever cared about. I needed to tactfully reengage. Every ounce of tactical training and restraint came down to this very moment. I would either elevate or fold.

Raising my trembling voice, I pleaded, "Wait, wait…I'll leave. I have a brand new forty-inch LED TV I have to unload. No big deal, I'll leave. Sorry. Please, just let me go, man… I'm sorry."

I knew I had to come up with something quick, even if they didn't see me exit the car, they might shoot me and find it anyway. I needed leverage.

I wiped the sweat from my forehead.

"Look, just let me go. I just got a shipment in and need to

unload these electronics quickly. I have a lot of stuff…just have the TV right now. I need cash and can't exactly have a yard sale, if you know what I mean."

The man slowly put the gun down and holstered it in his jeans. Slowly regaining clarity, I felt I had a chance to survive.

"Listen, I don't want any problems. I'll leave now. A couple of guys said you might be interested. I'm not a cop. I need to go—I can't get caught with this shit. Fuck, I'm outta here."

I slowly took a step back when Wax grabbed me by the shirt and lifted it up. I guess he wanted to see that I didn't have a wire or a gun on me. I knew I couldn't fight back against three armed men. Resistance would be pointless.

As soon as he let my shirt go, I focused on defusing the situation.

"Listen, I have a brand-new TV in my car. It's worth five hundred bucks. I'll sell it now for one hundred. I also have eleven car stereos, receivers, and more TVs in a storage unit. I have to unload all this stuff soon before I catch heat. You feel me?"

Shaggy poked me hard in the chest. "Who told you to look for me?"

Taking a step back, I didn't miss a beat. "A couple guys down south. I sold them some iPods."

I had slowly started easing my way back. "Look, I'm sorry. I'm outta here, no worries, man. If you're not interested, then let me go. I can't deal with the cops. I've got a warrant out already."

The men looked at Shaggy for direction, their hands readily placed on their weapons.

"Get the TV."

"Huh?" I blinked as the drops of sweat hit the pavement.

"Go get it."

"It's in my car, right there," I said, pointing to the Civic.

"Come take a quick look. If you like it…I can get you all the other stuff, just let me know what you're looking for."

Quickly glancing at one another, the men nodded in unison. Shaggy lit a cigarette and for a brief moment the situation seemed a bit less tense…or so I hoped.

Shaggy flicked ash on the pavement and pointed at me. "If you are fucking with me, I'll fucking bury you. You hear me, son…word is bond. I'll put five in you where you stand."

Slowly backing up, I nodded to him. "Just check it out. If you're not interested…then you'll never see me through here again. Just remember, I can get you tons of stuff if you're interested."

What immediately went through my head, which luckily wasn't the bullet of a 9 mm Glock, was that they'd hold me at gunpoint, have me take them to the storage unit full of goods (that didn't exist), rob me, and kill me on the spot.

Silence.

The men looked at each other. I waited.

Wax laughed, turning to his friend with the Miami hat. "Yo, Stacks, Shag, let's check it out." As he smiled, the streetlight reflected off the gold fronts of his teeth. "This crazy motherfucker right here. Aight let's see it then."

We walked to the Civic. I wasn't sure if I should keep talking or just keep my mouth shut. As of now I had a slight glimmer of hope that I'd at least make it out of here alive. I was thinking about the irony of dying at the hands of a man who had raped and murdered my wife. It couldn't happen.

I opened the hatchback, the three men behind me. I saw two of them position their hands on their backs and I prepared for them to draw down on me. Unarmed and vulnerable, I exhaled and closed my eyes.

"Here it is, a brand-new Samsung. Top of the line, still in the box. One hundred bucks. Like I said, if you want more stuff, then I can be here as soon as you need me. Just let me know."

The men pushed me aside and examined the box. Shaggy turned to me and pulled out a knife. I jumped back.

He laughed. "What, you think I'm gonna stab you? Jumpy motherfucker, huh?"

He opened the box top and looked inside to ensure the TV was inside. It was pristine and new with the protective cover and Styrofoam protectors.

I stood a couple feet back so they had full access to the trunk. "What you think? You want it or not?"

Ignoring me, Wax turned to Shaggy. "Shag, you want it? If not, I'll take it…need something at the crib to watch the games on."

The men looked pleased. I was just hoping at this point they would not proceed to rob and kill me.

As they removed the box and set it on the pavement, Shaggy turned to me, his eyes barely visible under the low-brimmed ball cap. "Who'd you say told you to find me?"

Wiping my face on my shirt, I'd had enough. "I didn't, but if you don't want it, I won't waste your time."

I needed to deflect any information about who sent me there or who I was to maximize my chances of self-preservation.

Amused with himself, Shaggy spoke without the slightest hint of fear. "You're a crazy motherfucker coming around here, but yeah, we'll take it." Wax and Stacks grabbed the box and headed toward some parked cars. Shaggy reached in his pocket and I jumped back again. "Relax. You wanna get paid, don't you?"

He unwrapped a wad of cash with all fifties and twenties, and counted the money.

Relief swept through my body. I might just live through this. I was here talking to the man that had murdered my wife and it was taking every ounce of strength to not just say fuck it, and go after him. I wanted to pin his skinny ass to the concrete and gouge his eyes out.

He handed me one hundred dollars.

I was stunned. I took the money and put it in my pocket, wiping my sleeve against my face.

I was intensely focused on getting away, barely paying attention to the men.

"Where's the rest of it?" he said, lighting a thin black cigar.

"Rest of what?"

"The merchandise, motherfucker. Where's the stereos and stuff."

Focus, Jake…you must focus.

"Oh, they're in storage. I can have them here tomorrow night if you want them…but I'll need cash on the spot. I'm not fucking around."

The gray cloud of smoke plumed, covering his face. "Get it tonight."

I was drained. There was no way I could get back here.

"I can't, too much heat around here. You'll have to wait."

Wax and Stacks walked back to join Shaggy in his interrogation. They looked at each other and a sense of uneasiness crept through me again. Maybe they thought I was trying to set them up somehow.

"Listen, if you want the stereos and stuff, I can be here tomorrow at eleven…but it has to be quick. I don't have time to fuck around. This is already taking too long."

Shaggy fired back at me. "You're a cop, I knew it."

He was trying me. They knew I wasn't a cop coming in here unarmed.

"Yeah, I'm wasting my time setting up misdemeanor charges for stolen merchandise. I'm not a fucking cop. I have plenty of buyers I can find for top-quality electronics. You want this shit or not?"

Putting his hands in his pockets Shaggy smirked. "All right, meet us tomorrow around eleven. We'll be around."

"OK, I'll meet you guys behind the building."

I pointed to where they were hanging out by the spotlight.

It was getting dark and I knew that nothing good could come from hanging here too late.

"I'll meet you exactly at eleven. If I don't see you, I'm not stopping by, and I don't want anyone else with you. There is too much heat around here."

Closing the trunk, I opened the door. "Stereos are one hundred bucks a piece, retail for five hundred. I'll bring some other stuff also. We'll have to be quick. If there is any heat in the area, I'm not stopping. Got it?"

The three men stared at me in the uneasy silence of darkness.

Shaggy broke silence. "Aight, bet. Tomorrow night. Don't do anything stupid. I'll blast your fucking head off."

I gazed at him for a second, struggling to keep my composure amidst a sea of hatred. The other men silently waited behind him before they all walked away.

"OK, see you then," I said, closing the door.

As I pulled away, my whole body shook uncontrollably and my eyes welled up. I could barely see the road ahead. I was in no shape to get on the interstate and quickly pulled into a Wendy's parking lot, hoping to regain my composure.

I could feel my pulse racing through the veins in my wrist. I took another Xanax and waited. I pulled out my pocket watch, rubbing the etchings with my thumb, and placed the cool brass to my forehead, focusing on breathing slowly and methodically. Three seconds in…seven seconds out.… My whole body shuddered. It was the calming shudder of a child who had just finished crying and was idle in the loving arms of a parent. Wiping the remaining tears from my eyes, I glanced at the skyline. I'd made it through.

CHAPTER 26
BACK TO THE WAR ROOM

I HEADED BACK to 95 North toward the house. I certainly hadn't expected to get so emotionally distressed. Then again, I hadn't expected to come face-to-face with Michelle's killer. There was nothing that could have prepared me for that. Heading to Wal-Mart for my truck wasn't an option. I didn't care about the repercussions, I needed a drink. Speeding through the neighborhood, I felt comfort in the darkness. Opening the garage, I quickly snuck the Civic inside. The night was quiet, belonging only to the endless chorus of crickets.

I immediately went to the cabinet. Grabbing a bottle of Jack, I chugged nearly a quarter before I gagged. The Xanax-and-alcohol-induced dizziness. I stumbled to the kitchen table and collapsed into a seat. I could feel myself fighting the urge to drift away. Death seemed so easy.

I couldn't get Shaggy's face out of my head. Every vivid detail branded into my mind…about five foot six and lean…couldn't have weighed more than a hundred and fifty pounds soaking wet.

His eyes haunted me. Those lifeless, brown eyes. It was an evil I'd never seen…mocking me without a hint of remorse.

I tried standing up but fell down over the chair. My legs were heavy. I crawled on the tile floor, struggling to pull myself to the cabinet. Where were my pills? Scouring the counter and cabinets, I searched for my oxycodone.

My vision became increasingly blurry, to the point I saw trails of light as my pupils failed to focus. Unable to find my pills, I launched an empty beer bottle against the wall. The shards of glass crunched under my shoes as I shuffled back to the bottle of Jack. I tilted the bottle up, just wanting it all to end, unable to shake the vision of Shaggy.

I wanted to see Michelle just one more time, to hear her voice and see that beautiful smile. We were supposed to have kids together, to grow old together, like everyone else. I'd always done good. Why had this happened to me? Was this God's plan?

No…no fucking way…. There is no God! There is nothing but hate and darkness. My eyelids grew heavy, the room around me fading under the soft glow of the kitchen light as I collapsed on the table.

CHAPTER 27
THE NEXT MORNING

THE REPETITIVE BEEPING of a garbage truck backing up made my temples pulse with pain. I lifted my head off the kitchen table and rubbed my eyes. It was 9:21 a.m. A broken bottle of Jack lay at my feet pooling on the tile. Standing up, fighting the dizziness, I headed to the cabinet for some Advil as I surveyed last night's wreckage.

I pulled a barstool over to the sliding door and sat down with a glass of water. It was sunny outside and the palm trees swayed gently, casting shadows on the pavement. The brown palm fronds sagged slightly over the new lime-green trunks.

Staring outside, glassy-eyed, watching chameleons race across the porch, I felt the heavy weight of loneliness. I didn't want to keep living without her. Revenge was the only motivation strong enough to snap me out of the lethargic, coma-like state that consumed me. I went upstairs to shower. I'd need to sober up and get a plan in place for the evening. I had to be in Lake Worth before eleven and I still had no idea how I would carry out this execution. Once again, I was a complete mess. I had let alcohol interfere with what had become the most important mission of my meaningless life.

The frigid water shocked my body awake and I gasped as the water hit my face. My cold body dripped water on the tile while I stood naked, staring into the mirror, not recognizing the reflection. I'd lost so much weight, and the color from my face was gone. I looked like a corpse with my raggedy beard clinging to the pale skin. I searched the room for clean clothes, not remembering the last time I had done laundry. I piled the clothes into a large contractor trash bag.

The Advil fought off the hangover but I still felt cloudy and lethargic. I needed to drop off these clothes at the laundromat and start my day. Forcing down a granola bar, I knew time was working against me each moment I sat in the kitchen, feeling sorry for myself.

The Civic sat quietly in the garage, resting like a black chariot of death. It was likely I'd need access to this car for the evening and I didn't want to use it during the day. I decided to call Pete to see if he could give me a lift.

Pete had called a few times since the funeral but I just never had called back. Add that to a long list of unanswered messages on the machine. I dialed his number.

"Hello."

My voice quivered under the dryness of my throat. "Hey, Pete, it's Jake."

"Hey, man. I've been hoping to catch up with you. Mary and I have been thinking about you a lot, it's good to hear your voice. How are you holding up?"

"I'm doing as best I can. Some days are good, some bad…to be expected. Just waiting for a call from the sheriff's office telling me these pieces of shit are in custody."

It took a moment for Pete to respond.

"I can't imagine how hard this is, Jake. I don't even know what to say…just that I'm sorry and we are here for you if you need anything. Anything! I mean it."

"Thanks, Pete, I do appreciate you guys being there for me. How's the family doing? The kids?"

"We're doing good. Lots of back-and-forth to practice and summer camp. Mary has been wanting to stop by to check in but I told her to give you some time. I didn't want to keep calling if you were with your family or something. So, now that I've finally got you, when can we catch up?"

"Soon hopefully. I'd love to get together with you guys. Actually, I'm calling because I have a favor to ask, if you're in the area."

"Sure, anything. What's up?"

"My trucks getting some work done and I have to run some errands. Would you mind driving me to the cleaners to drop off some clothes and swinging by Wal-Mart? I have a ride home, just no way of getting there. Figured if you were around, might be good to catch up for a short bit."

"Yeah, that'd be great, I'm off today. I can be over there in like fifteen minutes…is that cool?"

"Yeah, that works. Thanks man, I'll see you then."

As I hung up the phone, I came to the realization that my reality and the real world had been drastically out of touch. That is serious coming from someone plotting a series of murders. I had great family and friends to help me cope and ease me through the loss of my wife…I just resisted their help. I had kept in touch with my family sporadically throughout the past few weeks but for the most part all calls and letters remained unanswered and unopened.

I had voluntarily shut the world out and resisted help without even realizing it. I thought for a moment about gaining some clarity and sense of reason behind this but my head was pounding. I didn't want to think about it, but I had to. There was some overwhelming burden of knowing why I had a total disregard for my support system of family and friends. As I sat, staring at the magnolia tree dancing in the wind, I came to the realization that because of how Michelle was murdered, there was simply no way I could live without revenge. If Michelle had passed from an illness or perhaps a car accident, I would have been devastated but, I think, able to cope…over time, with the help of friends and family. This was different. A beautiful, vibrant woman…so full of life was savagely murdered without reason…and there was just no way to heal these wounds. I suppose by resisting the help and company of those trying to support me I could focus on my mission and not get caught up in a world of bullshit sympathy. I was as dangerous an enemy as you will find…because, simply put, there is nothing more dangerous than a man with nothing to lose.

KNOCK! KNOCK! KNOCK!

I couldn't let Pete in the house, it was a mess…broken glass, liquor bottles, and pills everywhere. I grabbed my laundry bag and went out the back door to meet him around front. He gave me a hug and looked me over. Though he didn't say anything, I could tell from his expression he was concerned. We started heading out to the cleaners down the street.

We sat in awkward silence before Pete interrupted.

"Hey, Jake, I know I sound like a broken record but if there is anything Mary and I can do to help, you know we're here for you. We've been worried because no one's heard from you, ya know?"

Looking out the window, I leaned back in the seat, gently thumbing the case of my pocket watch, my thumbnail tracing the etching on the back. "Thanks, Pete, I'll be fine…just need some alone time. I'll get back to everyone soon but I may get out of town for a little while to clear my head."

Pete looked over, taking off his sunglasses.

"Where ya goin'? You sure you don't need some company?"

"Nah, I'm good." I paused for moment and looked out the window as we pulled into the strip mall. "I'm not sure yet where I'm going. May go out west to do some hunting or shoot over to the Bahamas for some tuna fishing.… Hell, maybe I'll even get the old surfboard out for a quick trip. Just not sure yet. The only thing I know is that I wanna get away from this place for a while."

Pete smiled, perhaps content to have his friend back if only for a moment.

"Maybe that's a good idea, clear your head and do something you really enjoy. Hey, you want to go get some food? You look like you could use a good meal."

That was Pete's gentle way of saying I looked terrible. With my pale face and black, sunken eyes, I probably looked like death. I was starving but there was no time.

"No, I'm good. Just had some lunch a little bit ago, thanks though. I just want to start getting back to a routine. Hadn't done laundry in forever. Figured I'd drop this off and then get a few things at Wal-Mart."

Pete looked dismayed. "All right, man, but don't think I won't force you to come over for a steak and a cold beer as soon as your ass is back."

I laughed, turning to him. "All right, Pete. Thanks, man. You're a good friend. Appreciate ya."

After dropping by the cleaners, we stopped by Wal-Mart and Pete dropped me off at the entrance. I said goodbye and promised to give him a call soon. It was 10:27 a.m., time to get planning.

Walking in, I felt the gravity of life weighing heavily on my mind. I missed my friends and family so much. I longed for the life Michelle and I had had together and regretted taking things for granted. I couldn't help but wonder if I'd see everyone again. Did things really have to be this way? The doors opened and the chill of the air conditioning hit me.

Making a quick lap to the end of the first aisle, I figured I'd pick up a few things that might be necessary for the evening.... Unfortunately, since I didn't have a plan, I had no clue what to get. I grabbed some Gatorade, Advil, and a box of PowerBars. By the time I got back outside, Pete was gone, so I walked out to the truck. I had to get a game plan now. I started up the truck and sat looking around at the palm trees in the parking lot.

I opened a Gatorade and started to think. I knew the exact time and location in which Shaggy would show up. What I didn't have was any way to lure him to my vehicle alone, incapacitate him, and take him out. Since I was unable to utilize my key advantage of having animal tranquilizer, I would have to utilize sniper tactics to eliminate my target and operate under the cloak of anonymity. Thus my planning began.

CHAPTER 28
BACK TO WORK

As I BEGAN planning, I realized that this was a logistical nightmare. In essence, I had to find a way to show up undetected, establish a clear sight point, and take out my targets. The most efficient method would be to fire a quick, precise kill shot on Shaggy, all with the hope of an opportunity to repeat fire on the other one or two gang members. I now considered all members of the 8th Street Kings disposable, direct target or not. After all, they had to be eliminated as they might potentially reveal my identity. Maybe that was just my excuse. Part of me felt that if I let them live, another family might just be ripped apart by their sickening disregard for humanity. Either way, there was no time ponder my moral code. I had work to do.

I was planning a complex sniper mission in public and could not risk capture, detection, or injuring innocent civilians. I didn't own a silencer, known in the military as a suppressor, but I would need a method of gunfire suppression. I had never needed or considered purchasing one. There is really not much need in deer or hog hunting. In order to purchase a firearm suppressor, I would have to be approved in advance by the ATF, which takes up to six months or longer. Then, once approved, I would have to pay a two-hundred-dollar transfer tax when the suppressor changes hands from a class-three firearms dealer to me. I had neither the time nor the patience to deal with the red tape.

The only solution at my disposal would be to create some type of suppression device. I would need to be cautious just buying materials so as to avoid suspicion. I believe that in Florida, manufacturing and carrying an unlicensed suppressor is subject to a $250,000 fine and/or ten years in prison.

I had seen home-made suppression devices made from a two-liter water bottle filled with newspaper clippings and sponges but I had never trusted them. That was the shit you see in movies. I always had trouble believing that the gas discharge wouldn't blow the bottle clear off the rifle. A suppressor is a means of reducing firearm noise by slowing the escaping propellant gas emitted when firing a bullet. Since I was pretty fucking sure a bottle wouldn't be able to do this, I decided to go on to Plan B, figuring out how to create *something* that would.

I headed home, pulling back into the driveway around 11:00 a.m. The day was still young. I opened my gun safe, looking for the proper rifle that would service as the blueprint for the suppressor build.

My eyes were drawn to an unfamiliar handgun. It was the Taurus 9mm I'd collected from my previous 8th Street encounter. There were fifteen rounds in the magazine and the serial number had been shaved off. It was a major tactical advantage having a firearm that couldn't be traced to me. Unfortunately, one that served me no use in a sniper mission.

I knew exactly what I needed: my 30.06 Springfield rifle with Leupold 18x40 scope. I'd had quite a few great hunting trips with this gun. Just looking at it brought back memories of carefree days in the woods. I was confident in the scope and in my shooting abilities from distances of over one hundred yards. From a distance and muzzle-velocity perspective, this was the closest thing I had to a sniper rifle.

As I held the rifle in my hands, I thought carefully about the location I would be shooting from. A black cloud swept over the entire plan as things unraveled before my very eyes. I stood motionless, leering into the gray cloth interior of my gun safe. Paralyzed by a frustrating roadblock that came to mind.

This was a hunting rifle, meant for wide-open shots in the great outdoors, free from any concern of law enforcement or detection. The 30.06 was extremely loud and carried a report of around 160 decibels. There were two factors, large factors, that made this gun logistically impossible for use on the mission. First and foremost, the rifle was simply too loud to go undetected. Even with a real military-grade suppressor there was simply no way to reduce the decibel level to avoid immediate detection. The second issue was it, as a long rifle, couldn't be disassembled. It would be the ideal choice if I could shoot from a fixed position, such as on top of a building where I could lay down and carefully aim, but that wasn't the case.

I just couldn't think of any way that could work, after all this isn't some fucking movie where I can slide down a fire escape and leap into a getaway car. In order to maximize my ability to evade detection, it was likely I'd be shooting from a vehicle or within a confined space so a small compact rifle would be a necessity.

I needed a combination of quiet, compact, and lethal. I looked at my .556 and .223 AR-15s. They were simply too damn loud, probably not a hell of a lot quieter than the .30-06. The only logical choice was to utilize my Smith & Wesson model M&P 15-22.

My true comfort level with this gun was around fifty yards with dead accuracy. The accuracy of this weapon was predicated on utilizing proper ammunition, specifically Aguila .22 super-maximum hypervelocity hollow points.

Though the .22 was the most conducive rifle I had to adapting a suppressor, it was meant for small game like gophers or raccoons. A kill shot on a human would require precision and leave little to no room for error.

A sniper approaches each target with one objective in mind: one shot, one kill. I knew that the major disadvantage of the .22 was I would need to completely calm my nerves and ensure a perfect kill shot. This was much easier said than done since I was not operating in a combat zone. Carrying out my mission in a civilian setting would risk capture by authorities.

I didn't have time to worry. I took the rifle along with two thirty-round magazines and headed downstairs.

CHAPTER 29
ENGINEERING ON THE FLY

My objective was simple, maximize the reduction in rifle sound with minimal time expenditure in creation. Having limited knowledge in manufacturing a firearm suppressor, I used Google to locate detailed instructions for a home-made. 22LR suppressor.

I found a multitude of options, but there was no time for due diligence. I knew how a suppressor worked and identified the most logical manufacturing plans available. While I couldn't get all the build items, I was damn near close enough to make due. I made a list of what was needed:

› 12" 1 1/2 PVC pipe tubing and end caps

› 12" heavy-duty metal tubing

› fiberglass resin

› lithium grease

› wood screws

› 1 package of steel wool

› heavy-duty sandpaper

I headed to Lowe's, paid cash, and exited the store. It was time to play MacGyver. I parked the truck in the driveway and brought my rifle to the garage. It was 12:15 p.m. I scarfed down a PowerBar while meticulously reviewing the diagram showing the fit and finish of the suppressor.

Small holes were to be drilled into a twelve-inch section of metal tubing to serve as a gas release. A drill rod kept proper alignment to the gun while heated fiberglass hardened the pipe to the gun barrel. It was sanded smooth and covered by a twelve-inch PVC pipe cover. The internal workings were packed tightly with white grease and steel wool to assist with spreading propellant gasses.

Dealing with fiberglass resin and hoping for a clean project is like calling the cable company and expecting a helpful customer service agent…. It just doesn't happen. Luckily this wasn't a beauty pageant. I just needed something that would serve a one-time purpose. Once completed, I just needed to let the fiberglass cure for a couple hours.

CHAPTER 30
RECON 101

IT WAS JUST after three. I had determined my method of taking out hostile threats but needed to do a significant amount of recon in order to determine my placement for the mission. I'd be heading down to Lake Worth to do some reconnaissance.

I needed to take a breather to compose myself.... I had only one chance to get this right. I took three Advil with a bottle of water and sat at the table. Prior to leaving, I thought of what objectives were necessary:

› Monitor the weather for the evening. Even at close range, I wanted to ensure I knew what the conditions would be like for shooting, in case any adjustments were necessary.

› Ensure that no activities were planned in the surrounding areas. Though 11:00 p.m. is certainly not a time for peak activities, it was imperative I make sure that there were no local activities or concerts that might lead to increased traffic in the vicinity.

› Determine my tactical shooting point to give me a

fifty-yard sightline to where the targets would approach. This had to be a clear, precise path that allowed a clean shot and immediate exit from the scene.

Based on this research, and for my own safety, I assumed the mission would be carried out from a vehicle.

While I had experience executing urban warfare in combat, my urban recon and surveillance and urban sniper courses never prepared me for operating in the US. The dynamics of operating in Florida were drastically different from anything I'd ever done, so naturally I began to sweat the details of the mission. Most notably, which vehicle would serve as my command post. I wanted to use the Civic, but since the targets recognized it, parking hours before the meeting could arouse suspicions. Fuck, what would I do? It was far too risky to use my truck as I didn't have time to tint my windows. I would have to use the Civic. My only hope was that I could find an inconspicuous spot to park.

A quick glance at the clock. 3:19 p.m. No matter how many details I tried to account for, there was simply a tremendous amount of risk and uncertainty in this mission. I would consider it a success to just kill my targets and evade detection...even for a few hours. I knew at the minimum I'd have an opportunity to kill Shaggy and the other 8ths...but actually evading any authorities over the course of the evening was a stretch. The bottom line was they needed to die. I could worry about evasion later. I would not be taken alive by anyone...authorities or criminals. I would die in a shootout before that happened.

It was time to move. I wore a hat, sunglasses, and a hoodie. I'd drive my truck around, scouting potential shooting locations. I put in a pinch of Skoal, hoping the nicotine could quell the knots of panic in my stomach. I was utterly paranoid about being caught and knew that I was going on a suicide mission, what with modern law-enforcement technology. I started wondering if I should plan an alibi, or if it would even matter.

I came to the decision that I should call Sergeant Petrillo to check in. He was my only pipeline that could give me police intel on the ongoing investigation.

CHAPTER 31
CHECKING IN

SOME MIGHT CONSIDER calling the lead investigator just prior to killing one of his prime suspects one of the most insanely idiotic actions in the history of criminal behavior. On the other hand, it could help me gain valuable intelligence. After all, I was not yet a suspect in anything. The first murder hadn't shown any connection to the case and, as far as anyone knew, some 8th Street gang member was missing, and that typically doesn't make Palm Beach Post headlines.

As I approached 95 South, I took five careful breaths and made the call.

The phone rang a few times before I heard the familiar voice. "This is Petrillo."

"Hey, Sergeant Petrillo, it's Jake."

The sergeant's voice softened. "Hey, Jake. How are you doing?"

"As best I can, sir. I wanted to follow up with you guys. Any progress on the case?"

His voice was unwavering as he spoke. "Well, yes, we have made some progress. I wish I could say we've got all the guys in custody but we just don't. I know you want these guys bad. Between you and me, I wish we could settle this ourselves and get these pieces of shit off the street.

"The guy, Shay T, that we took into custody gave up some info on Zentillo's whereabouts but nothings turned up. We believe he is at his cousin's house in Miami, lying low because he knows there's a lot of heat on him. We've got a full-scale manhunt and surveillance team looking for him and should hopefully get him to turn up any day now."

Looking for answers I started in. "Well—"

Petrillo interrupted. "We also found out the names of the two lower level guys involved and we're actively searching for them. We've had to be careful not to spook them."

"Any idea where they're at?"

I immediately regretted saying that—would I reveal my position? How much would he read into this?

Petrillo spoke confidently without pause. "Well, our intel says these guys are based locally, but many deal drugs or stay in Broward County, so we've had to get multiple law enforcement operatives involved. Don't worry. I promise you we're throwing everything we've got into this case."

I processed the details as his words hung in silence. "Yes, sir. I know. Keep me posted if you find anything."

Sergeant Petrillo's voice again softened and his pain was evident. "You know I will, Jake. Please keep your head up and don't hesitate to call if you need anything. I can't imagine what you're going through. All I can say is that I'm doing everything I can. We'll get these guys, and I can assure you that they will pay for what they did."

I appreciated his conviction and for a moment felt the bond of justice with this man I barely knew. "Yes, sir. I may get out of town for a few days to do some hunting or fishing.… I really just want to clear my head."

"I hear you. You're a strong man, Jake."

Taking a deep breath, I exhaled into the phone. "Thanks, that means a lot."

"My pleasure, man. Call me any time you want…day or night. I mean it, you always have someone to talk to. If you're OK with it, I may stop by from time to time just to check in, make sure you're doing all right."

Unannounced visitors were the last thing I needed but I let him off easy, knowing he was doing everything he could. "Thanks, sir. That would be fine. I really appreciate all you are doing."

"You got it. Enjoy some time off…clear your head. We'll talk soon."

"I will. Thanks."

As I pulled off the exit, I breathed slowly, maintaining focus and clearing my head to remember all the details that would become critical for the evening. I carefully surveyed the area, monitoring any activity that might compromise my mission.

I took a left turn down Avenue K, about three streets west of where I had made initial contact. I would complete a perimeter drive around the gray duplex that would serve as my target point. There was minimal activity during the day, just a few elderly people sitting on their porches, taking shade behind the ragged fenced-in yards.

As I turned down each street, I examined parking options and traffic patterns. Finally, I passed the chain-link fence where I had parked the night of the meeting. There were some cars parked outside but plenty of spots with enough room for the Civic.

Turning left at the end of the street, I noticed a dead-end sign up ahead. This was a key recon note. While planning the execution was important, it was of equal importance to observe the path for escape routes. While driving, I saw mostly residential housing and abandoned lots overgrown with foliage, but I took notice of two commercial properties in the vicinity that could play a major role in the planning of the mission.

One of these properties was a Texaco gas station. It had moderate vehicular and foot traffic.

The second property was a small convenience store below some low-end apartments. There were three rental units above the store with small overhang balconies. Though the viewpoints were minimal, I knew I would have to shoot south of where it was located. This would allow me to remain out of sight, giving any witnesses only a clear view of the targets and the street.

I parked on a side street, watching the store activity for ten minutes. A Ford Focus pulled up and a middle-aged male went inside and returned with cigarettes. A homeless man with a shopping cart was near the dumpster behind the building, appearing intoxicated and disconnected with his surroundings. As I prepared to leave, two men came outside onto the porch of one of the rental units. They sat in chairs outside, drinking beer and enjoying the weather, seemingly unconcerned with the outside world. I estimated the balcony was fifteen feet above the pavement, which gave them a clear vantage point of the target zone but not enough to view my shooting position. Critical mental note as my planning ensued.

Driving away, I'd gathered enough baseline recon on my operating environment. I knew the area would likely be busier as the evening progressed. Traffic was slow to moderate on side streets all day but never to the point that I would have concern about escaping.

In remembering my initial meeting with the targets, I knew that there were two options in setting up a firing point.

Option One:

Utilize the same parking where I'd originally met the targets. From this vantage point, at forty to sixty yards, I would be parallel with the men, allowing a clean shot. Firing parallel could allow the closest target to shield the men, preventing clear shots to the head. This was a major tactical disadvantage as it could eliminate the possibility of making multiple kill shots. I also felt that the suspects were more likely to be aware of my vehicle if it was parked in the same vicinity as the initial encounter. The only advantages to this vantage point were the ability to easily escape and avoid detection from the corner store blocking my line of sight.

Option Two:

Park perpendicular to the street where the targets would be located. The key advantage to this would be the ability to take multiple clear headshots on all targets. The major issue was a street in the firing lane between my position and theirs. I needed to ensure that cars were clear in both directions prior to shooting. It seemed like a major concern but I figured that with minimal traffic at 11:00 p.m., I could be assured a small window to check, aim, and fire.

Reviewing the intel details, I decided to utilize option two, based on the ability to fire multiple head shots with minimal time expended. I'd be relying on some luck with traffic but felt that the odds were in my favor.

It was 5:13 p.m. and the sun slowly began fading beyond the South Florida clouds. I drove twice past the strip that would serve as my shooting point, using landmarks to gauge yardage to the target and to ensure that no one could park in front of my sight-line. Everything looked in order. I paid additional attention to the location of streetlights. Obviously it would be imperative to be located in as inconspicuous an area as possible.

Slowly cruising down the street, I saw the gray duplex ahead. To the right stood two tan residential duplexes, to the left was a vacant coin-operated car wash. If I could park on the opposite side of the street near the abandoned car wash, I would be within target range and hopefully out of view.

What may be the most fucked up part about all of this was that no matter how organized I seemed to be, dumb luck played a huge factor in my mission…. Running a one-man sniper team among civilians was damn-near impossible.

Making a turn, I pulled past the car wash to examine the parking options. There was a fire hydrant on the far corner that I assumed would be clear, based on the yellow curb and the no-parking sign. The spot directly behind this would work perfectly in providing clear sight lines and a quick exit from the scene. The only drawback was its proximity to a streetlight and, of course, the lack of assurance that it would be available. If this position were secured, my mission was completely viable. At the very least I was out of the direct overhead spotlight that would likely be glaring down around 11:00 p.m.

I'd hope to utilize this position, otherwise my only option was near the no-parking hydrant zone. It was unbelievably risky but there were no alternatives…. This was it. I'd hopefully arrive early enough to secure the spot and prepare myself mentally. With my intel secure, I continued toward the interstate, heading home to focus on the remainder of the plan.

CHAPTER 32
GEARING UP

Back home by 6:30 p.m., I gathered a couple bottles of water and went to the garage. The suppressor materials had completely hardened. I set the rifle on a towel in the garage and put my work gloves on. Without the slightest clue if it offered any forensic protection, I cleaned each bullet with the quick wipe of an alcohol swab, hoping to remove any DNA lingering on the shell cases. Perhaps there was a deeper meaning, the faint hope of wiping away my relation to the ammunition before the evening was set in motion. It faded to an afterthought as I loaded the magazine with the Aguila .22 ammunition.

The next step was creating a firing position from the Civic. The windows were blacked out already and I had one of the cardboard sun blockers for the front window. This would allow me to work within the vehicle without outside detection.

Firing position from the hatchback would prove somewhat tricky. The position that provided a stable base for sniper fire was lying down and bracing my legs between the passenger and driver seat. Once the rear seats were folded, this could be accommodated.

As a shooting platform, I'd need to have an opening from the rear of the vehicle large enough for scope clearance. Opening the trunk, even a little, would draw unwanted attention to the vehicle. After all, who parks a car at night and leaves the trunk partially open? The CRX Civic hatchback is unique in that it has an opaque glass insert in the rear of the vehicle that could be perfect if I could remove it properly.

To do so, I simply taped the window center-piece with clear packing tape and smashed it with a hammer. The glass removed easily and it left a clear rectangular section underneath the fully intact main hatchback glass.

Repeatedly I practiced my body position with the rifle. This would work perfectly. Though it was possible to keep most of the rifle within the vehicle, the additional space added by the suppressor needed to extend out of the trunk space for the most favorable firing position.

Using a black contractor trash bag, I tightly secured the vacant centerpiece of the Civic with duct tape. The next item of business was masking the license plate temporarily. I created two false number stickers with computer paper and a sharpie that could be secured before I parked as an extra precautionary measure and then quickly peeled when needed.

By 8:00 p.m. the weapon and ammunition were prepared. The vehicle had proper concealment measures in place. The weather looked as if it would be overcast with a twenty percent chance of rain that evening. There were no events taking place and I had hoped that Shaggy still had intentions of showing up on time.

My intense preparation gave me distinct confidence that nothing could stand in my way. I admired my rifle with the home-made suppressor. Sadly, I would've never thought my personal firearms would be used in this manner. As a hobbyist, I focused on precision and concentration…not killing.

I remembered the first time I took Michelle shooting. She had always wanted to try it, so when we started dating, I took her to the West Palm Shooting Center.

An older gentleman named Tom checked us in. "What targets do y'all want?"

Not paying much attention, I placed my gun cases on the counter. "We'll take whatever is the cheapest."

Looking at the options, Michelle chimed in. "We'll take two of the zombie targets!"

I smirked sarcastically turning to Tom. "OK, two zombie targets, please."

We headed into the shooting lane. I spent time explaining the proper use of the .380 pistol she was holding. As I stood behind Michelle, I placed my hands over hers, explaining proper hand placement and what to expect from the recoil.

Her shooting goggles fogged up and the earmuffs were so oversized she looked like an air traffic controller.

"You ready to give this a shot?" I asked.

Nervously she nodded.

"OK, take a deep breath and as you exhale, gently pull the trigger."

Boom!

Michelle fired repeatedly, shooting with confidence at the snarling zombie thirty yards away. She emptied the magazine, set the gun down, and turned to me with a brilliant smile, exhaling in relief. "Wow, that was awesome!"

She was empowered and her confidence was so unbelievably sexy.

I smiled. "You did amazing, hun. What do you think? Wasn't so hard, was it?"

She wiped her goggles. "No, it wasn't. It was such a relief. I was so nervous and I feel so badass right now!"

As we cased our weapons, we walked out of the range into the gun store.

With a bit of pep in her step, Michelle tugged at my sleeve. "I really liked that .380, it was very smooth. Can we take a look at some?"

With admiration, I nodded and we walked over to a gun case.

She immediately pointed to a Tiffany-Blue Ruger LCP .380 pistol. "Look at that one. I didn't know they made them in different colors."

"Sure they do. Maybe Santa will bring you one for Christmas…but if I know you, there's some other stuff you'd rather get in Tiffany Blue."

Michelle blushed and held my hand as we walked out.

Smiling, I allowed myself a brief moment to reflect before turning back to my rifle. I had work to do. Thinking about post-mission procedures had me focusing on four critical objectives:

> Safely and quietly evacuating mission sight without detection.

> Locating a safe place to return post mission.

> Ensuring firearm suppressor is destroyed and firearm barrel patterning is destroyed or undetectable.

> Destroying or removing vehicle from my presence.

I mulled through these concerns. The factors that lay before me this evening were just too unpredictable to have a single evasion plan…or that's what I told myself.

Even with my newfound confidence, my nerves prevented me from being able to focus on post-shooting details. I was just too wired to contemplate the finite, precise details after the mission.

Everything came down to the simple seconds when I could exhale and slowly pull the trigger. Shaggy's lifeless, cold eyes haunted me...seemingly looking right through me, without remorse for having ripped my world apart. I yearned for this vengeance, like a drug, biding my time until I ended his meaningless life.

CHAPTER 33
ANARCHY

I WOULD LEAVE the house around 10:00 p.m. That would give me enough time to set up and run through my protocols. At 8:30 p.m., I managed to get through a PowerBar before taking three Advil. My body wanted a drink so badly I had the shakes.… Just one, I thought, to ease my nerves. I resisted the urge. For the first time in a while, I felt empowered by something other than blind, uncontrolled rage. Even a small glass of whiskey would impair my judgment. I couldn't risk it.

Surveying my closet, I gathered clothing that provided comfort and above all the ability to absorb sweat. I packed two bottles of water and two handguns with extra magazines.

I would fit my rifle with a shell catcher to ensure the discarded bullet shells remained in my possession until I decided when and where to dispose of them. These are easily made with the proper mesh and some long plastic zip-ties.

The clock approached 9:00 p.m. I put the rifle in the backseat, covering it with a blanket. I loaded the passenger floorboard with my toolbox, a power drill, and an annular cutter. Tossing my duffel bag in the passenger seat, I glanced briefly at the stars and headed toward Interstate 95.

The night was eerily dark and had the uneasy feel of a late Halloween evening. Wind swept the trees as I drove in silence, gently flipping the pocket watch through my fingers. Exiting the highway, I pulled off on a quiet side street, carefully affixing my numeric decal across the license plate for disguise. The coast looked clear. I pulled near the target location.

Many of the streetlights were not functioning properly and those that were cast softly glowing shadows. Looking ahead, I saw that the last parking space was open. Luckily, there was still plenty of spots and it didn't look like too many people were in the vicinity.

Turning off the lights, I slowly parked behind an older gray Toyota Corolla. It had not been there earlier but that didn't cause me concern. I had a good four feet of clearance in front allowing me to escape quickly without backing up. I put up the sunshield to provide cover from any passersby and sat quietly in the driver's seat.

It was 10:41. Because it was a side street, traffic was minimal. The only cars passing were those on the main street perpendicular to the Civic. There was no traffic light at the intersection and it was highly unlikely that traffic would back up into my shooting lane.

I crawled into the backseat, pulling the rifle from under the blanket. Removing some duct tape, I prepared my sightline through the scope. The shot was clear, the working streetlight above helped provide additional light for the scope. A scope will not function properly in complete darkness, at least not mine. It needed some light to properly illuminate the optics and ensure that I could gauge the target in the crosshairs.

I positioned myself in the rear of the hatchback and focused my vision through the scope. As I sought my distances to the target area, things looked good. This was a very close-range shot in an urban area. I'd have to be quick and efficient with my killing. Luckily, the shots were at minimal distance and I was extremely confident in hitting the targets.

10:52 p.m.

With the car off and no AC on, the South Florida humidity lay thick in the air. I wiped my palms on my pants, and sweat steadily beaded down my face. I pulled the charge handle to chamber a round. We were live. All that I needed was a couple pounds of trigger pull and the rest was history.

The first activity I saw was a man likely in his midtwenties walking by on the opposite side of the street. He was smoking a cigarette and looking at his cell phone, no concern as he walked south and passed the car without hesitation. I had removed a foot-and-a-half section of the duct tape from the Civic's hatchback. My window was large and secure, I just needed an opportunity.

10:58 p.m.

A Chevy Malibu with bass tubes sped down the opposite side of the street. It was becoming slightly busier. I kept an eye on the target area. Still nothing but the occasional car, passing without knowledge of my existence.

11:08.

Three men slowly walked up the perpendicular street toward the target location. This must have been them. My heart raced, sweat profusely dripped from my brow. I breathed slowly, three seconds in, seven seconds out. My vision would be entirely through the scope from now on, both eyes fixed on the location.

It was them. I saw a green bandana hanging outside one of the men's pocket. Unfortunately, they were in the shadows ten feet from my target zone, away from the direct light of the streetlamp. I wanted to wait, but I knew that if they left and went the other way, I couldn't get a second chance for the kill.

Two of the men were smoking and I could see the embers glowing in the shadows. The men were talking, very animated and moving their hands. I simply couldn't make out their faces to see which one was Shaggy.

11:12 p.m.

As the men talked, one of them took a few steps up the street to look for something. I clearly saw a neck tattoo, though couldn't tell if it was Shaggy's roman numerals. He looked under six feet tall but was wearing a black baseball hat low down to his face. He walked back to his friends, pulling a pack of cigarettes from his pocket.

Breathe…three seconds in, seven seconds out. Three seconds in, seven seconds out.

I checked to ensure the safety was off. Headlights flashed down the street and a black sedan passed by. The men all slowly followed the car with their eyes for a few seconds and resumed conversing.

The man with the hat pulled out his lighter and reached to light his cigarette. I had him dead to rights, the crosshairs just under the brim of his hat. I saw the firelight and the embers of the cigarette. I exhaled and pulled the trigger slowly.

POP! POP! POP! POP!

The sound was like an M-80 firecracker. The man fell immediately to the pavement, and the others froze, looking around in confusion.

I sighted the man to the right in the darkest shadows. I fired four shots toward his head and he slumped to his knees. The third man looked almost straight at me.

POP! POP! POP! POP!

Four more shots. Shit, I hit him in the chest, possibly the

neck. He started to take off running. I was terrified he might have escaped alive.

Fuck…it was happening! I could feel every vein pulse as the adrenaline rushed through me like a freight train. The clock was ticking.

The target to the left had fallen against the fence and lay face up. The second target was facedown on the concrete, blood pooling beneath him.

I left the rifle in the backseat, starting the car and throwing the sunshield in the passenger seat. I estimated that sixteen seconds had passed since my first shot and I knew that the noise would bring attention. The stakes of survival were now at their highest point. My nerves were unhinged.

I kept the lights off and slowly exited the spot, seeing lights come on in two of the duplex apartments. No one was outside yet. I didn't even see anyone come to the window.

My suppressor had definitively worked. The report sounded very similar to a small firecracker and didn't have the same distinct sound of gunfire. I estimated it was possible that I had reduced the firearm noise by about thirty decibels, which was plenty for the limited preparation I had. This is why the report sounded much similar to that of an M80. The noise was quick and brief without the hanging echo usually associated with any rifle round.

I drove to the end of the side street and headed west before turning on the lights. Focusing on maintaining a slow speed was difficult, as my heart rate and breathing were critically elevated.

I heard sirens blaring in the distance, but they wouldn't be taking side streets. When I was about seven miles away, I pulled into a residential neighborhood and removed the sticker on the license plate. I also fixed the tape so the empty glass panel was covered.

While I needed to get rid of the Civic, destroying the gun was my top priority. It was critical to reduce the ballistic finger-printing of the rifle. Provided there were no witnesses, this could buy me some serious time to evade detection.

I headed south on Military Trail for about ten miles and monitored the radio. I had assumed I might hear about the police presence on a local station and that freeway exits near the crime scene might be closed.

So far, I had heard nothing. I approached Lantana Drive and headed toward 95 South. Adrenaline was still coursing through my body and maintaining the speed limit was arduous.

CHAPTER 34
THE AFTERMATH

I'D BEEN ON 95 South for forty-five minutes. The monotony allowed me to gather my wits. I left the freeway past the first Fort Lauderdale exit, looking for a hotel to begin my mission debriefing. There was a Motel 6 off State Road 84 that would work. I parked along the outside of the building as far out of the lights as possible.

My ability to survive was predicated on maintaining composure. I put on a fresh T-shirt from my duffel bag. I'd need to do some basic prep before check-in. I put the toolbox in the duffel bag with my clothes and disassembled the rifle. All of my items were in my green camo duffel; I'd be able to check in without arousing much suspicion.

I closed my eyes unable to shake the image of a SWAT unit breaking down my hotel door and ending my life. It would have to be that way. I could not go to prison.

The lobby was empty. News played in a small lounge area, and there was a young girl working solo at the check-in desk. I gave a credit card for incidentals. She seemed annoyed that I had interrupted her text messaging and handed me my key.

I got a six pack of Bud Light from the grocery section and headed to my room. I turned the deadbolt before putting my duffel on the bed. As I set the beers on the counter, I caught my reflection in the mirror and started to cry.

I thought of Michelle's smile and the morning that had ripped my life apart. I thought about the fact that in the eyes of the world I was nothing but a cold-blooded killer. The few pounds of trigger pull on that rifle had brought forth the crushing weight of reality on my shoulders.

I cried hysterically, burying my face in a pillow so no one could hear me wailing. As my tears soaked the pillow, I pulled it tightly to my face. No matter how much liquor I drank, no matter how much oxycodone or Xanax I took, Michelle's smile was a haunting reminder of my infinite loneliness. I wished to hold her, if only for a moment, to touch her skin and smell her hair. I wondered if she was watching me, in heaven, looking down on me.

Heaven wouldn't hold a place for a man like me. I could pray and ask forgiveness but I had committed the sin of murder many times over. I had never considered my actions in combat as sins but this was different.... I had taken the lives of men who weren't actively trying to kill me. This was in cold blood. In this life or the next, Michelle was a memory that would slowly fade from my tired mind. There were so many things left to tell her, so much I had taken for granted.

I rinsed my face with cold water. This journey was far from over. I took a pinch of Skoal and opened my first beer. The air conditioner hummed in the background as I stared at the duffel bag on the floor. Snapshots of life panned through my mind like cinema and tormented me with visions of Michelle holding the child we'd never have. I remembered the very first time I saw her.

Michelle had worked part-time as a bank teller at SunTrust

while she was in nursing school. It was a Tuesday afternoon on a hot July day and I needed to make a deposit to my IRA. It may sound cliché but for me it was lust at first sight. She had a dark-blue dress on and her black hair swept behind her as she smiled at an elderly gentleman at the counter. I was captivated, standing in line, praying that I'd be lucky enough to have her assist me.

"Sir, I can help you right here," an older teller said to me two stations down from Michelle.

"Uh, what? Oh, I'm good," I said as I allowed the lady behind me to cut the line. I didn't even remember what the hell I came to the bank for. What should I say? How should I act? I didn't know if I'd have a chance with a girl like this…after all, she'd see I wasn't a business tycoon as soon as she pulled up my account.

My mind raced…what to say, what to…

"I can help you right here." Michelle looked up casually and smiled.

As I approached her station, I stood there not saying a word, wide-eyed like a deer in headlights.

Michelle stared at me bewildered. "Can I help you?"

It was as if I had crammed twenty saltine crackers in my mouth. I couldn't talk. All I could muster was, "Sure, yeah, uh… deposit please."

She smiled. "OK, I'll need to see your ATM card and ID so I can pull up your account."

"Oh, umm…I need to make a deposit to my IRA. Can you help me with that please? Thank you."

She stared at me like I was wearing a squirrel costume, before laughing and again saying, "Uh, sure but I'll need your ATM card and ID for that."

Well done, Jacob, you idiot. "Oh, yeah. Sorry about that," I said as I slid my cards and my IRA deposit check over the counter.

She punched some buttons on a computer and I knew my time was limited. C'mon, man, think.

I looked on her name tag. OK…here goes. "Michelle, may I have a deposit slip please as well?"

As she looked up, we locked eyes for only a moment. "Sure."

I took the pen and scribbled furiously across the slip in barely legible cursive, "May I call you sometime?"

As soon as I handed it back, I regretted it. What a clown move!

She looked at it and gave me a quick glance, rolling her eyes. It was settled…even Babe Ruth struck out over a thousand times. What did you expect? She's probably dating a pro athlete or something.

She handed me my receipt and the folded-up deposit slip back.

Her smile was out of this world. "Thanks for banking with SunTrust. Have a nice day, Jacob."

I smiled back sheepishly and nodded, putting the papers in my pocket. We locked eyes once more. "Thanks, Michelle. Have a nice day. Thank you."

As soon as I got outside, I opened the deposit slip…a phone number! The feeling of elation was indescribable. Well, at least until I called the number and realized she'd given me the number to the SunTrust branch.

I refused to give up so easily. Over the next couple weeks I scrounged up every dollar I could find, even selling a couple of my surfboards, just to have an excuse to make a deposit. Finally, with a few nervous smiles and some persistence I got her real number. Michelle and I spent a week talking on the phone before she agreed to come bowling with some friends and me. After that…we were literally inseparable.

I caught myself smiling for a brief moment before glancing back at the duffel bag. I had to get moving. Maybe there would be time later for reminiscing. As I removed the gun, I placed all the parts on a towel laid over the bed. The gun was legally registered in my name so I couldn't just get rid of it. That would lead to more suspicion. I had a plan but really wasn't sure if it would work. I removed the suppressor I had created and attached an annular cutter drill head to a ten-inch drill attachment. I had hoped that by destroying the rifling pattern in the barrel a ballistics analysis of the firearm would prove futile.

I drilled inside the barrel repeatedly with the annular cutter, slowly grinding away at the steel lining. When this was done, I wrapped steel wool on the attachment and manually ground back and forth on the barrel. Since I had attached a mesh shell collector, I had all of the fired shell casings, which I would dispose of with the suppressor.

I would also destroy the firing pin and scrub the entire weapon down with bleach, then alcohol. I had no clue if these would help remove any DNA but I supposed it couldn't hurt. I turned on the news and went to work. About three beers in, the story came up on the news. I froze, turning to the small flat-screen on the dresser.

A young reporter, stationed near police cars, lights blaring behind yellow tape, stated that the victims had been identified by police and that someone speaking under the condition of anonymity believed it could be gang related. As of now, police were not releasing any details, as it would be an ongoing investigation. Many people were standing around the murder scene along the perimeter of the yellow tape, like patrons at a play. It sickened me.

My mission was accomplished. The men were dead. And yet I felt no feeling of triumph, just emptiness and shame.

CHAPTER 35
A FRESH START

With each thrust of steel wool, the rod pushed out more shavings from the gun barrel. I cleaned the weapon and placed it carefully on the towel.

I would need to immediately get rid of the shell casings, suppressor, and any articles of clothing I had worn that night. I grabbed a plastic laundry bag from the hotel closet and put all the clothing, including my shoes, inside it.

I wanted to go to a coin-operated car wash to clean the Civic, but figured this should be done in the morning. It was too late, and it would be best to stay hidden and carefully plan for tomorrow.

Opening the last beer, I took two Xanax that would hopefully put me to sleep. I wondered if I'd even make it through the night. The thought of the door busting open and authorities rushing in had me on edge. There was just no way to monitor police progress. I had to rely on good fortune to get through the next five hours.

I was so paranoid that I brought both handguns and extra magazines into the bathroom with me while I showered. If ambushed, I'd draw down and make them take my life. I had always thought suicide was for cowards but now I realized that in my situation it loomed not only a possible but also an ideal conclusion.

It was my only choice.

While there was no way I'd risk sitting behind bars, I wouldn't kill anyone who didn't deserve it. It would go against everything I stood for, if that even mattered anymore. I wouldn't leave families to mourn the death of an innocent man. It couldn't happen.

I loathed the killer I had become but there was no turning back. I had put into motion a plan that had only one way out. There were no happy endings.

The drugs hit me hard and I became dizzy. Still covered in soap, I managed to stumble out of the shower and collapse on the bed.

At 6:27 a.m. I awoke, a pounding in my head and a tightness in my stomach. It was the feeling you get when preparing to go back to work after a long vacation, only immeasurably worse. I felt like hell.

As I urinated, I saw my two handguns and extra magazines lying on the bathroom counter. I placed both hands on the sink and looked in the mirror. For the first time in my life, I had what felt like an out-of-body experience. I wasn't looking at myself; the man in the mirror looked dead. My lifeless eyes were bloodshot and my pupils reduced to small circles reflecting the bulbs from the bathroom vanity.

Dressing quickly, I scanned the room. My duffel bag was packed. I set myself in motion to focus on my agenda.

Before leaving, I gave the room a final once-over, ensuring the removal of even the slightest hint of evidence. There was nothing but an empty dip can, some beer bottles, and a toothbrush. No point in hiding these, my check-in was on record.

I left out the hotel's side exit and went to the car. The sun peered through the clouds on the tall royal palms. Squinting, I wished for rain. The sun just didn't feel right. I wanted a driving rain with thick gray clouds misting over South Florida, the smell of ozone in the air after a fresh lightning strike.

CHAPTER 36
EVIDENCE REDUCTION

FORT LAUDERDALE HAS many storm drains that feed into deep underground pipes leading to local waterways. I anticipated that the weight of the suppressor and shells would sink until a rainstorm flushed them into the intercostal waterway or some other waste area. It seemed like the most opportune method of immediate disposal. I hoped that once discharged, the saltwater would further damage the evidence.

I pulled into a neighborhood and parked next to a storm drain, dumping the suppressor and shells. Now I needed to burn my clothing. It was the only way to eliminate any trace of existence. While it was risky driving around with evidence of a triple homicide on me, I didn't see any other options.

As I drove, I cautiously monitored my surroundings, scanning for a car wash. Uncertainty hung over my head and I couldn't help but think about my friends and family. For weeks, my answering machine had filled with messages that I'd neglected to return. This simply heightened their concern for me, increasing the risk of a surprise visit. I couldn't have that. It was becoming impossible to get through the day and continue planning.

I saw a coin-operated car wash off south Federal Highway and went to work. I got five dollars' worth of quarters. Almost all of which went to vacuuming every possible carpet fiber. Then I used the alcohol to towel off everything else. After a quick rinse, the Civic looked like…well, it looked like a piece of shit 1989 black Civic with well over 100,000 miles on it. Good enough.

Anyone who has been around Fort Lauderdale knows that there are a ton of shady cut-rate car dealerships next to tire stores and mechanics. I was in luck because I really didn't need to haggle, I needed to unload evidence. I had carefully considered what a colossal mistake this might be. Certainly some type of evidence might tie me to this car…but then again what choice did I have? I could sell the car for scrap metal but they still verify title information and sometimes wait months to disassemble vehicles.

I stopped at the first dealership I passed, walked in, and asked for one thousand dollars. I got five hundred and was on my way. The paperwork took less than fifteen minutes. I must have looked like a complete junkie, my pale ghostly skin and sunken eyes. The guy must have thought I was so desperate to get a quick fix that I'd accept anything. Which was true. Money had little meaning to me—I just wanted to get home. With my duffle bag in hand, I walked two blocks to a Jiffy Lube and called a taxi.

I could have rented a car but didn't feel like having to deal with the hassle or paper trail. Yellowcab, Fort Lauderdale to West Palm Beach…one hundred and fifty dollars, done. My cab driver picked me up and eyed me, probably wondering if I had the cash. I showed it to him, told him the exit, and we were on the way.

The cab smelled like vanilla and we listened to some Creole news channel—it was the perfect white noise for me to drift away for a forty-five-minute nap.

CHAPTER 37
REALITY

My eyes crept open passing Boynton Beach Boulevard. It took a moment to gather my bearings and I directed the driver the last twenty minutes home. Without a word, I handed the driver one hundred and seventy-five dollars and sent him on his way.

I felt immediate relief as I walked through the door. I'd made it home, but there was no time to rest. Dropping the duffel bag, I went to the kitchen for three Advil and a glass of water.

There were twenty-one messages on the answering machine. I grabbed a notepad. Most of the calls were as expected. My parents, Michelle's parents, my brothers, neighbors, friends, some bullshit sales calls, and Sergeant Petrillo.

He wanted me to call him back.

Finishing my water, I got to work. The first task was using my grill to destroy the clothing. I poured on the lighter fluid, added some newspaper, and covered it up. Thick black smoke billowed out and soon there was nothing left but ashes and burnt rubber. I put one more coat of lighter fluid on it for extra measure and lit some coals to cover up the evidence. The fumes from the sneakers made me nauseous. I thought of the body that I had disposed of. Wanting to purge the sickening memory, I slammed the hood and headed inside.

The final piece of the puzzle was putting the gun back in the safe. Though I had been thorough in prepping it, the reality was I had no way of knowing that it could not be identified as the murder weapon. Either way, I wasn't overly concerned. Simply put, I had utilized every available option at my disposal and still had a couple tricks up my sleeve. I slid the .22 back into the gray cloth interior and locked the safe.

Walking downstairs, I prepared to return calls. As had been the case every day since Michelle's death, I wasn't in the mood for talking. Something as simple as conversing with friends and family left me in the pits of despair. But it needed to be done. This was something I could no longer ignore.

I called everyone back, spoke to some and left messages for others. Midway through a message on my brother's answering machine, I became paralyzed by self-loathing and guilt. I was calling the people that loved me, simply to develop an alibi. I didn't even want to talk to them. I couldn't even remember the conversations I'd just had. I was too focused on this rampage.

Michelle would be disgusted to see what I had become. I didn't have the courage to pray, but if I could, I'd pray Michelle couldn't see me.

A feeling of helplessness overcame me and I dropped to my knees, wanting desperately to escape. I didn't want to go on living but for the first time since I could remember, I was afraid of death.

I had to stop these thoughts. Opening the medicine cabinet, I crushed a Roxicodone on the counter with my license, arranging two long yellow rails. I rolled up a dollar and snorted both rails through my clogged nostrils as quickly as possible. Coughing uncontrollably, I turned on the faucet, gulped water down, and blew my nose in the sink.

The drugs hit me hard. As my vision became blurry with light trails, I laid on the kitchen floor, staring at the floodlights. I breathed heavily from my mouth, closing my eyes as the halo of the lights glowed behind the darkness of my eyelids. I was motionless. I had a feeling I might not remain conscious and rolled to my side. If I vomited, I didn't want to asphyxiate.

CHAPTER 38
CHEMICAL ROMANCE

I AWOKE TO the sound of sirens and got up in a panic. It was over. I grabbed my handgun and raced to the door.

Nothing, just a fire engine passing on the street. No one was here for me.

I put on a pot of coffee. My nose felt like it had cement in it. I sat at the table.

The fog of the opiates helped keep my mind from racing. I'd had enough of this bullshit back-and-forth. The stress that was eating away at me didn't make sense.

I put in a dip of Skoal. Fuck it. What choices are there, Jacob? Cross your fingers and hope that none of these retaliatory murders get pinned on you. Worrying every day for the rest of your life that police are going to burst down the door and put you behind bars forever? That wasn't an option, not for me.

I took three Advil and two Roxicodone tablets with a tall glass of water. I liked the feeling of the Roxy in my body. It felt different than my despair, and it was starting to feel normal. I hated myself for taking the pills but, as sad as it was, I needed them to escape. I was high, and simply in denial.

While the sickening chemicals made me feel better, I fought the urge to feel any semblance of happiness. When the cold dark waters of death take me, I will see no blue light…only darkness. The fond memories of my past would fuel the actions of my present. To punish those who harm the innocent.

I thought of a quote from *Pulp Fiction* that my platoon and I used to say in the desert. Samuel L. Jackson quotes Ezekiel 25:17. Well, he claims to quote it, but it really is just some rant with bits and pieces of the actual Bible verse.

We used to say this right before going out on missions, partly because Samuel L. Jackson says it right before shooting people with a giant hand cannon. "The path of the righteous man is beset on all sides by the inequities of the selfish and the tyranny of evil men. Blessed is he who in the name of charity and good will shepherds the weak through the valley of the darkness. For he is truly his brother's keeper and the finder of lost children. And I will strike down upon thee with great vengeance and furious anger those who attempt to poison and destroy my brothers. And you will know I am the Lord when I lay my vengeance upon you."

I laughed, thinking about the men in my unit, how we had adopted that line into our culture. I wished that I could be with them, to go back to the desert and forget the madness of Florida, the place I once couldn't wait to return to.

Slowly, my drug-induced fog started dissipating and I felt the real world pulling me back in. The brief chemical escape was winding down and once again I prepared to carry forth my mission.

There was only one person standing in my way: Sergeant Petrillo. The gatekeeper who knew everything about Michelle's killers and the facts surrounding the case. I would have no choice but to call him. Speaking to Petrillo terrified me. There was simply no way to gauge what he did or didn't know about my involvement. I must have started dialing a half-dozen times before I finally got the courage to connect the call.

As the phone began ringing, I breathed carefully to ensure a steady calmness to my voice, three seconds in, seven seconds out.

"Hello, this is Petrillo."

Standing in the kitchen, I stared out to the patio. "Sergeant Petrillo. It's Jake Bedford returning your call. How's it going?"

"Hey, Jake, I've been trying to reach you. Where you been?"

Nervously I maintained a steady focus. I needed to gather information and he was perhaps my only source of intel.

"I was away for a little while just trying to clear my head and get back into the swing of things. How's the case looking?"

There was an awkward pause as I awaited the sergeant's response.

"You been watching the local news?"

"No, haven't seen the news in what seems like ages. Why? What's up?"

"Three members of the 8th Street Kings were gunned down the other night, and another gang member is believed missing. One of the men killed was a suspect in your wife's murder who went by the name Shaggy. You haven't seen any of this?"

Now, I am not certain how Petrillo meant this. Am I a suspect yet? Does he know anything?

I paused for a moment.

"That's good, right? I mean you can take him off your list and focus on the other guys. What happened? Was it gang related?"

The urge to keep talking felt like a dam about to burst, but I held steady, remembering the old saying, "A fish wouldn't get caught if it didn't open its mouth."

"Well, to be honest, Jacob, we're not one hundred percent sure. We thought originally that it was gang violence, but there are some discrepancies that are making us look at multiple possibilities. We need to get a statement from you about your whereabouts the past couple nights. Just to corroborate some details."

Nervously I scrambled through a kitchen drawer looking for a pen and paper. I needed to keep my story straight.

"Uh, sure…no problem. But I don't understand, are you saying I'm a suspect?"

"Listen, Jake, I know this is hard, especially after all you've been though, but we have to rule out every possible scenario. Just so my guys can get back to focusing on these dirtbags that took Michelle. I hope you understand, Jake. It's just protocol with some of the findings."

I scribbled furiously the content of our discussion.

"Of course, I understand, just protocol. Well, I spent some time at a buddy's farm and then just spent a night in Lauderdale to get away. It's been hard being at the house. Everywhere I look I'm reminded of Michelle…just wanted a change of scenery. What do you think happened?"

"Me? I think these guys had it coming. They were all suspected felons with criminal histories and the one guy was a suspect in Michelle's murder. Maybe karma just got 'em. I'm sure it was gang retaliation."

I stopped writing. Something was up.

"But you said there were discrepancies? Anything that might lead to a break in Michelle's case?"

"Well, just some stuff that is out of the ordinary for a typical drive-by or gang-related shooting. Forensics and the task force are investigating the details. Michelle's case still has one hundred percent of my focus, Jake. I give you my commitment on that. We've got teams working with Broward and Dade Counties to look for Carlos Zentillo and Angel Araujo. We're pretty sure Zentillo is camped out in Miami and that Araujo may be local. Also, Shane

Tidwell is apparently cooperating with authorities. All of the information he's given has been accurate but unfortunately both Araujo and Zentillo are no longer at these addresses."

It was apparent that Petrillo was keeping information on the murder discrepancies close to the cuff and I didn't want to potentially draw any additional attention to myself.

"OK, I'll check in with you soon…. Call me if you need anything. Please help put these guys away. It is the only thing that will let me sleep at night."

"You have my word, Jake. I do need you down here ASAP to provide a statement so I can clear that off the books. When can you get down here?"

Today wasn't an option. I needed time. Think, Jacob, think!

"I can be there tomorrow. Will that work?"

"I'd prefer today, but that's fine. I know you're going through a lot right now. Make it tomorrow and let's put this behind us."

"Sounds good. Thanks, Sergeant Petrillo. Appreciate all you're doing. See you soon."

The dial tone sobered me up. I was forced to examine the true weight of my actions and the consequences they would inevitably bring. I was currently a potential suspect, and that meant I would need to act quickly, efficiently, and with deliberate intent. I had only bought myself an additional twenty-four hours and I would need all my wits about me to persevere under questioning.

I didn't know if Petrillo had bought anything I said. The thing about life is, you can second-guess everything but a lot of things just come down to chance. I guess realizing you're already dead inside helps you see how brilliantly complex and amazing life is…each moment, each decision, each day…has thousands of possibilities.

The temporary relief of the oxy had faded, and my body was

exhausted. There was a lot of work to do, I wanted to rest for a few hours, but I just knew that wasn't possible. It was time to plan for a quick strike. I needed to carefully hunt Zentillo and Araujo…and stay the fuck out of the limelight.

CHAPTER 39
SOBRIETY

I took a freezing shower to knock the cobwebs out of my head and try to gain focus. It was late in the day but I didn't know what time—the hours and days had begun to melt together.

I was starving. I needed to get some real food and figure out my next move. Driving to a local sub shop, I again considered the idea of telling my side of the story. I wanted the world to know that people like me existed on the outskirts of society. Maybe writing it all down could give my meaningless life a purpose. Maybe it could bring the closure I needed.

Of course, that was my intention, but a small part of me simply wanted to justify the things I'd done. Perhaps there was a greater need to convince myself I was still the good guy seeking justice in a world full of hypocrisy and evil. In the end, when the dust from my bones is swept away, at least my story would be left behind.

Pulling back into the driveway, I parked the truck and headed inside.

While I understood the necessity of getting moving, I needed fifteen minutes of peace.... My body was on overload and my hands were shaking. I got a cold beer and headed out to the porch to enjoy the warm glow of the sun on my face.

I could feel the summer heat radiating off the pavement into the humid Florida air. The laughter of neighborhood kids reminded me of the carefree days…when the cruel realities of the world hadn't tarnished the purity of life. It was nice to daydream peacefully about the past.

Unfortunately, they were only dreams. I couldn't look up from the grill to watch Michelle prepare salad and corn at the kitchen table. There would be no more barbecues, my buddies leaving beer cans on the table while tossing a ball outside. I tried so hard to just close my eyes and imagine, but all I saw is her face. The instant I pictured her smile, the icy grip of reality reminded me she was gone forever.

I shook my head and reached into my shorts for my pocket watch. Gently I thumbed the bezel, looking at the brick pavers, taking in the sound of cicadas chirping. I quickly finished my beer and grabbed another, hoping to take the edge off. Two would be fine, but I couldn't get drunk. There was too much on the line. I needed to find these guys.

Though limited on time, I needed to maintain the same meticulous approach used in planning my first strikes. Since anonymity would be my only protection, firearms would be my last resort. They were too loud and messy and they posed a risk to my ability to operate covertly.

I still had the unused three milligrams of etorphine in a syringe and another 4.5 milligrams in the bottle. The ability to inject my enemies with a fast-acting, lethal substance was ideal for my mission since time was of the essence. From this point forward, it would be impossible to dispose of bodies. All evidence would remain at or near the scene. I might be able to buy some time hiding a body, but true disposal was out of the question. For this reason, the method of killing would now become my most critical ally in evading authorities and remaining undercover.

Though the etorphine is extremely valuable for its instant effects, it is so rare that it raises red flags immediately when police run toxicology reports on the bodies. That fact alone could really throw a wrench in my ability to stay covert. I needed every possible angle to throw them off and maintain the illusion of innocence.

I'd mix Roxicodone and Xanax with the etorphine. It would likely provide no additional lethal benefit but would possibly give me an extra day or two while authorities ruled out overdose. Using a thick twenty-gauge needle and a spoon would allow me to boil the drugs with water and add them to the cocktail.

At my disposal was seven and a half milliliters of etorphine. I couldn't just use three like the first time, I needed to ensure I used a lethal dose. I could use a twenty-gauge, one-and-a-half-inch syringe and load up seven milliliters of etorphine with a two-milliliter cocktail of other prescription drugs. I intentionally left one milliliter empty to ensure the syringe plunger didn't dislodge.

Now that I've identified a method of taking out targets, everything came down to locating Zentillo or Araujo. Based on my conversations with Sergeant Petrillo, Zentillo was likely in Miami, and Araujo could have been local or in Broward County. Once again, my task consisted of gathering intelligence…with borrowed time. With a sigh, I walked back into the house.

There was no time to waste and I certainly couldn't drive aimlessly through three counties, hoping to stumble on my prey. There had to be a way. I'd done this before and I'd do it again. A major obstacle came in being forced to use my own vehicle to track targets while avoiding detection by the authorities.

The vehicle was a risk, but one that had to be taken. There was no alternative with my time constraints. As darkness fell upon South Florida, I prepared a plan to quickly gather intelligence and strike with minimal post-murder cleanup.

I was left to assume members of the 8th Streets were becoming increasingly weary after three had been murdered and one mysteriously disappeared. I would be at the mercy of chance… but felt confident I could make contact. These men weren't easily intimidated and it wasn't in their nature to hide.

My plan was extremely circumstantial, forcing me to lure the target to my truck. Since I didn't have time to do recon, I needed to make sure there were limited witnesses. While the truck would provide some anonymity, I'd need to be quick, efficient, and flawless.

I sat in the truck, carefully studying the features and layout of the F-150. As I reached over to gauge the distance to the passenger door handle, the headrest caught my eye. I studied it for a moment, my mind racing through options. I smirked in the rearview, talking under my breath, "This will work. It has to."

I closed the door and headed inside to get ready. I dressed in my standard recon attire with a black ball cap. From the gun safe, I retrieved the Taurus 9 mm pistol. As long as I removed my fingerprints and wore gloves, there was no way to trace it to my person. I quickly cleaned the weapon and put it under the seat of my truck, keeping my .380 pistol in my concealed holster. I brought rubber medical gloves and five hundred cash.

Heading out, I caught my reflection in the hallway mirror. My unkempt hair and scraggly beard made me look like a homeless meth addict…not a clean-cut former Special Ops soldier. I noticed that people no longer acknowledged me or smiled as I walked past them. In fact, people would walk the other direction or avoid eye contact. Barely able to look myself in the eyes, I stared at the mirror…not recognizing the reflection. I gave an uncharacteristic grin. It was just the look I needed…tonight, I wasn't myself.

CHAPTER 40
MAKING FRIENDS

IT WAS JUST after 9:00 p.m. as I entered Lake Worth seeking a glimmer of hope that might lead me to Araujo or Zentillo. The summer heat and monotonous driving agitated me. My nerves were on edge, and I was anxious to find the men. At 10:21 p.m., I cut my losses and began the journey south to Broward County. Pulling off the exit just after 11:00 p.m., I drove east to an intersection of apartments next to the train tracks. If you live in South Florida for many years, you have an idea of which places to avoid late into the evening. I headed parallel to the tracks, away from any major intersections. Slowing the vehicle, I saw a guy that looked in his mid-teens dribbling a basketball, listening to his headphones. I made a U-turn and slowly rolled down the window.

"Hey, kid." I gave a quick honk of the horn. He was startled a bit and removed his headphones. "Listen, I'm looking for a guy named Angel, goes by A-dog. You know where I can find him? I'll give you two hundred bucks."

The kid cocked his head inquisitively, tucking the basketball under his arm, and looked around before answering. "Two hundred bucks? Why, is he under arrest?"

I couldn't help but laugh. Why was it everyone around here thought I was a cop? I put the car in park and slowly leaned out the window. "I'm not a cop. I need to ask him something. You know where he is?"

I could see he was thinking as he dribbled the ball a few times and then held it under his arm again. "Not sure, probably near the ball courts up the street."

Trying to hide my frustration, I gripped the steering wheel tightly. "I'm not from around here. Where is that?"

Annoyed with my banter, he shook his head. "The basketball courts, near Eleventh. The only ones up the street," he said.

I pointed. "That way, right?" I said, confirming the location. "Yeah."

Satisfied, I reached in my pocket and counted out some cash. "Good looking-out, man, here's one-fifty. I'll give you another fifty later if I see him."

The kid approached and took the cash.

I held the cash as he tried to take it for a second. "It's a surprise, so don't tell him. You got that?"

Letting go, he put the money in his back pocket and acknowledged, "Yeah, whatever, man."

He put his headphones on and continued dribbling up the block. It was almost like it was commonplace for people to pay for info. His calm demeanor frightened me. For all I knew, he was calling Araujo now to let him know someone was looking for him.

I started my journey toward Eleventh, hoping the basketball courts might play home to my prey. I thought about the kid for a moment and felt bad. It could have been me growing up here, just a young man surrounded by thugs holding the entire community captive. As I looked in my rearview, I could see him singing and hoped he would be lucky enough to escape the streets.

I drove down the dimly lit side road, taking careful note of my surroundings and keeping an eye out for authorities. It was typical evening traffic, nothing out of the ordinary. I turned left toward the basketball courts, part of a small public park. There was a small field, with two trashcans next to a jungle gym and a few play areas for children. About fifty yards away was a basketball court. There were five guys shooting hoops. The park was otherwise empty. Turning off my lights, I quietly pulled into the back of the parking lot to survey the scene.

The guys playing were all males, I estimated between their late-teens and early twenties. One had a green shirt and black Nike shorts, another a green bandana tied like a headband. It gave me enough optimism about their 8ths affiliation to stick around.

I watched them and contemplated my approach. Strategically, the best course of action would be to gather intel and quickly eliminate the targets. If I played my cards right, I could relocate the bodies to a remote location and buy more time. As long as I was quiet and composed, I felt confident I could navigate the situation. Unfortunately, I had to *know* they were 8ths in order to proceed. The risk of killing civilians far outweighed the risk of being identified. The moment I killed a civilian, my entire mission went to shit.

I debated bringing a firearm. The likelihood of getting into a shoot-out on the ball courts was slim. Still susceptible to a beatdown, I loaded the chamber of my .380 pistol and holstered it under my shirt. At the very least, I could back them up with the .380, allowing myself time to escape. The 9 mm was not as easily concealed so I kept it tucked under my seat.

I sat there for nearly forty minutes until finally the guys took a break. The court was poorly lit by the few working lights overhead. The guys hung out for about fifteen minutes, exchanged handshakes, and three of the men started walking away. The two men that remained were the ones with the green shirt and green bandana. They lit cigarettes and continued talking. I was preparing to exit the vehicle when I saw another man walking toward the courts.

The man was obviously known by the two, though they didn't give him any type of handshake or greeting. I saw the man pull something out of his pocket. The gentlemen in the green shirt did the same and they made a brief exchange hand-to-hand. I assumed this was a minor drug deal, probably a small amount of marijuana or cocaine. The new visitor then turned his back and exited the court, walking through the park and down the street.... Another five minutes passed and he was out of sight.

There were only two other cars in the parking lot and I was left to assume they belonged to these men. One car was a Chevy Monte Carlo and the other an older-model Chevy Tahoe. I turned on my lights and drove toward the cars. Obviously this would alert them but hopefully not arouse major suspicions.

I pulled up and separated the remaining three hundred and fifty dollars I had, putting one hundred in my right pocket and the remaining two hundred and fifty in my back pocket. I adjusted the passenger headrest and took a deep breath as I exited the vehicle.

As I started walking towards the men, I muttered to myself, "Stay calm, Jake, you got this...just stay calm and focused."

They glanced over at me walking, their demeanor not signaling any alarm. I breathed slowly and deliberately.

The men casually shot a few baskets and occasionally looked down at their cell phones. With a cautious approach, I kept my hands at my sides. As I got to the court, they looked in my direction and kept shooting.

I inhaled slowly before announcing my presence. "What's going on, fellas?"

One of the men grabbed a rebound and took a shot, responding with a barely audible "All right."

I came within ten yards of the men before they stopped to stare me down. They continued shooting and made no attempt to reach for a firearm or other weapon. It was obvious they didn't consider me a threat, out of place perhaps…but nothing of concern.

I stood near the three-point line and watched one of the men steal the ball and drive the lane. I nervously gave conversation another shot. "I need an eight ball, you holding?"

The man immediately held the ball and looked at his friend. As his friend shrugged his shoulders, he laughed and threw up another shot as he spoke. "You think I'm holding?"

His friend watched curiously as he grabbed a rebound and casually dribbled my way before shooting again.

"Not sure if you are or not. I've bought here before. Just asking, need to re-up."

The men continued to play for a moment, trying to ignore my presence, but it was obvious they were focused on me and not hoops. Not a single shot had hit the rim since I'd first inquired about purchasing drugs. The man who'd spoken to me looked at me again and said, "Can't help you. Go get your fix somewhere else, faggot."

Sensing his aggression, I knew my best move would be to remove myself from the situation and reevaluate my approach. Confrontation under the lights would do nothing but blow my cover.

I turned around, feeling defeated and replied, "OK, no big deal, man."

While I had a feeling these guys were 8ths, I wasn't certain. All I knew was that they were assholes and that wasn't enough to proceed with my plan.

As I slowly walked to the truck, desperation gripped me and I clenched my jaw in anger. My time was limited, and I was tired. Tired of being bullied by these fucking thugs. They'd taken everything I had already, ripped me to shreds, and yet still managed to further humiliate me. I felt an overwhelming urge to kill like nothing I'd ever experienced. My heart was racing, I could feel myself unraveling at the seams.

"Lock it up, Jake. You've gotta keep yourself together just a little longer. Your almost there, just stay calm. Deep breaths."

About ten steps back to my truck, I heard one of them bark at me.

"Ay, one-fifty."

I stopped in my tracks. I gave a quick glance at the sky, closed my eyes, and exhaled before turning around.

Walking toward them I quietly said, "One-fifty? OK."

I met the guys on the court and handed the man with the green shirt one hundred dollars from my right pocket without saying a word.

The man looked at the folded twenty-dollar bills and contorted his face. "This is a hundred man…get the fuck out of here with this shit. I said one-fifty."

Clumsily I put my hands in my pockets and looked at the ground. As the man lit a cigarette, I looked at his face. He had a shaved head and a goatee, on his neck I clearly saw his tattoo, a black crown above the numerals VIII.

I paused, trying to hide my satisfaction.

"I know, I know…I heard you. The other fifty is in my truck. Look, I really don't like doing this in public but my dealer is out of town and couldn't deliver. I'll go get the rest of it, is that cool?"

The man took a drag off his cigarette and exhaled in my direction. I tried not to cough and felt sick inhaling the same air he was. He motioned to his friend with the bandana and pointed to the cars. "Yeah, go get it."

I turned to start walking and looked back, pointing to the outskirts of the court. "Listen, you care if we go over there out of the light? I really don't want to draw any additional heat over here in the open."

The man flicked his cigarette and looked at his friend. "I'll be right back. You staying here?"

The man with the bandana took a quick layup shot and responded. "Nah, I'm out. Let's go feast—I'm starving."

The walk to the car took about twenty seconds but it seemed like forever. I tried to mentally run through the plan but the intensity of the situation made it difficult to focus.

As the three of us approached the cars, the men walked to the Monte Carlo and I headed to my truck. I opened my driver's door and leaned in, sneaking the remaining cash out of my back pocket. As the men casually talked, the one with the green bandana walked to the Tahoe and opened the rear hatch. There didn't seem to be anything happening that raised their suspicions. Quickly, I ensured things were in order and closed the door.

I walked over and gave the guy in the green shirt the other fifty dollars, making sure he saw the other cash in my hand as I quickly put it back in my pocket. He opened the door to the Monte Carlo and got something out of the glove box. He exited, looked around, and slipped me a bag of white powder tied up very tightly. Giving a cautious glance, he put the money in his pocket and retrieved his cell phone.

I took the little baggy and knelt down behind the driver's door of my truck, taking out my key so he'd think I was going to sample it. I popped my head over the truck, needing to get his attention. "Hey, listen—I'll buy more if this shit's good. You care if I take a bump to try it?"

I couldn't tell if my voice was shaky. Every time I opened my mouth to talk, it felt like the words slurred.

Leaning against the Monte Carlo, he looked up from his phone conversation and scowled at me.

"I don't fuck around. This shit's legit. Go ahead."

The man in the bandana had closed the hatch and gotten in his Tahoe. He was messing with the radio and not paying much attention to either of us.

As the man with the green shirt chatted on his phone, I became annoyed with the situation and called to get his attention. "Hey, I'd prefer not do this in the open. You mind hopping in for a second?"

Visibly agitated, he talked into the phone, "Hold up a minute," and shook his head, muttering, "Motherfucker, all right, hurry the fuck up. I don't have all night."

Without hesitation, the man opened the door to the pickup and jumped in. As I opened the baggy, I put some powder onto my car key. "OK, thanks. I just want a quick bump. If it's good, I'll buy another." Still on his phone, he looked out the window paying me little mind. I pressed my nostril closed, blocking from view the other with my palm. I exhaled quickly pretending to inhale the cocaine.

I rubbed my nose quickly and let an audible exhale go. "Shit's good. It burns. OK…I'll buy another, you got it on you?"

Ignoring me, he spoke into the phone. "Lemme hit you back. Gotta put in work right quick. Yeah, if them bitches are there, we'll swing by. Fuck that, I'm gunna tap that ass whether she like it or not. I'll get mine. Aight, word."

Fury swept through my body at his callous disrespect for women. I thought of Michelle and how these vicious jackals ravaged her. My body began to shake uncontrollably as he put his phone down and looked directly in my eyes. "Told you I don't fuck around. That shit's pure Colombian." He leaned back into the seat, reaching into his pocket. With a quick fluid motion, I slapped the back of his headrest. He shot up in the seat, wide-eyed, gasping for air.

I had put the syringe under the headrest and lowered the rest tightly so that the needle was perpendicular with the seat. When I slapped the back of the seat, the syringe had thrust into his lower neck and trap area, and the entire chemical cocktail had immediately injected into his muscle.

His body shot forward, the syringe now dangling out of him. He looked over at me, trying to comprehend what was happening and grabbed the door handle. I had locked the door and he fumbled with the lock before blacking out.

My anger gave way to adrenaline, and the rush of killing the man had things moving in light speed. It was intoxicating.

I looked through the window: the Tahoe was still there and the other suspect was listening to the radio, waiting for his friend. I put on a pair of rubber gloves and grabbed the 9 mm Taurus from under my seat, holstering it behind my back. It was time, there was no turning back.

Exiting the truck, I walked to the Tahoe. The man with the bandana looked up at me immediately with surprise. I was fluid and confident.

"Yo, you have change for a hundred?"

He looked at me confused, as if not understanding what I'd asked. I took the 9 mm out and put it about two feet from the window, pulling the trigger. I put the hollow point through the side of his head, almost a direct shot to the temple. The gunshot sounded like thunder and he immediately slumped over in the Tahoe, dead. The bullet had penetrated his brain, spraying blood all over the interior of his car. I holstered the gun behind my back and ran back to my truck. I jumped in, gasping for breath.

I had a dead man beside me and needed to dispose of the body immediately. I had no clue where to go, and it was too late to be careful. I backed out, trying not to screech the tires and drove around the block. What the fuck was I going to do with this body? I was operating in a complete state of panic. I didn't have an alibi for this.... The entire situation was fucked as soon as I pulled that trigger. Why couldn't I just stick to the plan?

I saw some cars but there was no sign of authorities. I drove to the outskirts of the park and stopped the truck in the darkness of a side street. I removed the needle from the suspects back and took his wallet, throwing them both on the floor of the truck. I didn't know what to do and without the time to calculate a plan, I left the body on the grass next to the curb before driving away.

CHAPTER 41
BITTERSWEET REALITY

AGAINST MY BEST interest, I started driving back to the house. There would surely be repercussions for my recklessness. Every second I remained on the road put me in danger. I pulled into a bait-and-tackle store near an intercoastal canal. It was a store I used frequently for offshore fishing trips. They had about a dozen boat slips in the back.

I disposed of the syringe and 9 mm Taurus in the water. I knew the water was at least ten feet deep even on low tide so it wouldn't be visible. Even though the gun wasn't registered in my name, I didn't want it anywhere near me.

Arriving home, I pulled into the garage and sat there…my hands shaking uncontrollably. I reached to my holster for the .380 and contemplated killing myself. Carrying forth seemed impossible. How could I not get caught?

I should just end this all now. I sat there, mind racing, sweat pouring off my cramped muscles. I pictured putting the gun in my mouth and pulling the trigger…darkness. Having come this far, only to take the coward's exit. All the progress I'd made the past few weeks was washed away with angst and paralyzing fear.

Glancing around the truck, I saw the target's wallet on the floor… In what seemed like some surreal, cinematic moment, I reached for it. Opening it up, I tried for a moment to pull my mind away from the evening. I found about four hundred in cash and an ID. Closing my eyes…I glanced at the name.

ANGEL MANUEL ARAUJO
1748 SE 19th Street
Lake Worth, FL 33461
Height: 5'11"
Weight: 160
DOB: 7/19/95

I held the card tightly in my hand and started convulsing. Within seconds I was crying uncontrollably, sobbing so hard that my diaphragm started to spasm barely able to pull air into my lungs. Exhausted, I regained enough composure to exit the truck.

I put all of my clothes, the wallet, and the ID on the grill and doused them with lighter fluid. I lit a match and closed the top. I went inside and flushed the cocaine and rubber gloves down the toilet.

Outside, the charred remains of the evening hissed under a tarry smoke. I loaded the base with charcoal and lit it up, covering my tracks so it appeared that it was used recently for cooking. I had destroyed all the clothing, discarded the firearm and syringe. I needed to thoroughly clean and examine the truck to ensure there was nothing else I had missed.

Shivering, I walked outside and surveyed the scene. Everything looked in order, and I would wash the truck soon. Looking up on the garage wall, I saw our bikes and paddleboards had collected dust—symbolic of a past life. I'd forgotten who I was and what Michelle would have wanted. Weary with my own existence, I wondered if death would provide a serene escape. Like blowing out a candle, it seemed so simple.

With each murder, the killing had gotten easier. My soul was fractured beyond repair, and while their deaths brought me no peace, they were necessary. I took a deep swig from a bottle of Jack. Perhaps it was time to let go, allowing myself to drift away to the darkness.

Stumbling upstairs to the medicine cabinet, I took a couple oxys with another swig of Jack. Closing the cabinet, I pulled my electric razor out and began to shave my head.

If tonight is the night, at the very least clean up for your family.

The thick locks fell into the sink as the cool steel brushed across my skull. The familiar sight of my appearance in the mirror hurt. I turned away, focusing on the tile.

"What would Michelle think of you now? And your family? Knowing what you've become. You can't hide forever, Jacob, you cannot run anymore.... It's too late. Accept your fate and do the world a favor. Disappear."

I sat on the floor of the shower, drinking steadily, repeating the words "do the world a favor..." and buried my head between my knees. The frigid water beaded over my naked body, unable to wash away the past.

CHAPTER 42
ENLIGHTENMENT

THE SUN PEERED through the bamboo blinds along the bathroom and my eyes slowly twitched open. I was lying on the bathroom floor. Rolling onto my back, I stared at the white plaster ceiling and listened to the soft hum of the ceiling fan in the bedroom. It is a feeling I have described many times over…pain, confusion, and guilt.

I sat up, wiping the sleep from my eyes. An empty bottle of Jack lay at my feet next to my .380 pistol. My pants and the bathroom floor were covered in urine. I no longer felt impending doom around me, just the torrid feeling of a drug-and-alcohol-induced hangover. Whatever my intentions were last night, I'd passed out, here to live another day.

I drank from the faucet, gulping water into my dehydrated body. I ran my fingers over my head, feeling the bristly remains of where my hair had been. While the end of night was a blur, I remembered saying, "Do the world a favor and disappear." I glanced again at the pistol before turning on the shower, wishing I'd pulled the trigger.

I suppressed the urge to vomit, resting my forehead against

the cool tile. The frigid water took my breath away.... It was among the last true feelings I had these days, cold water piercing my skin like daggers.

Leaning against the bathroom cabinet, I stared at the bottle of oxycodone. The numbing escape it provided had once again caught up with me, clouding my cognition. I dumped the pills in the toilet, putting the night behind me.

I took four Advil and turned on the news to see details from last night's murder. Outside, two sparrows chased each other around the foxtail palm.

I pondered the plausibility of planning my final killing. I knew that yesterday's reckless actions could prevent this from happening. I had no time to focus on Zentillo at the moment—for all I knew, the 8th I shot was him, albeit highly doubtful. Either way, there were far more pressing issues that needed to be addressed.

My truck needed to be washed and I needed to prepare for my meeting with Petrillo. As I stared outside I reflected on last night's carelessness. Pulling the trigger of that 9 mm in public eliminated the ability to operate on my terms. I was no longer in control.

It was what it was. I poured a cup of coffee and raided the empty cabinets, finding only a can of tuna and some stale saltine crackers. My cell phone was on the counter and I checked the messages. Missed calls from my brothers, Michelle's parents, my parents...nothing out of the ordinary.

I had to call Petrillo and make plans to meet up. This was my wild card. My entire existence seemingly depended on where he was in the investigation. I'd either earn some time to track Zentillo, or need a drastic plan to lay low and hide. Either way, it was the only conduit I had to reality. I dialed the number and walked out to the patio.

Ringing…

The sun felt so good on my shivering body. I squinted.

The familiar voice answered, "This is Petrillo."

Breathing deeply, I readied myself. "Hey, Sergeant Petrillo, it's Jake."

"Hey, Jake. What time can you be here? It's imperative to the case that we get you cleared so we can proceed with the investigation."

My voice was raspy. "I understand. I was gonna grab some breakfast and head down there in a few hours. Is that OK?"

The always-calm-and-confident Petrillo responded immediately. "Yeah, that's fine. A lot has happened in the past twenty-four hours. I need an official statement about your whereabouts over the past week particularly last night. Plan on being here for about an hour, maybe more."

I shifted uncomfortably, leaning against a palm tree. They had to have known something. I'd been way too reckless and failed to cover my tracks.

"OK, sure. I was…" I paused. Shit. Where was I? I quickly spit out the first thing that came to mind. "I was over at a buddy's house."

Without missing a beat, the Sergeant responded, almost like playing a game. "OK, well we're going to likely need statements from both of you to corroborate that. Some events late last night are directly impacting our investigation."

I felt he was testing me, looking for me to stumble.

"Events? Really? Like what? Did you guys catch one of the suspects?"

"Well, Jake, for starters, Angel Araujo turned up dead along with a fellow gang member. We're awaiting final reports from forensics and toxicology but something just doesn't seem right."

I tried to shield my overwhelming disdain for our failed justice system.

"Doesn't seem right? I don't understand.… That's great news, right? What goes around, comes around. Hate to say it, but maybe this is karma."

An intense silence ensued. I clenched my fists, waiting for him to speak.

When he did, his tone was calm.

"Jake, I'm not saying it's bad news…but here's the thing. In the past week, two of Michelle's murder suspects, along with others, were killed. In both incidents, we believe it was a caliber round matching some of the same weapons registered to you. You know I've got your back but it is a coincidence we need to look into."

My defiance and agitation got the best of me. "So two piece-of-shit gang members are killed and now I'm a suspect in multiple homicides? Do I have that right?"

I sensed his discomfort through the phone. "Jake, calm down. Everything is going to be fine. We have protocols we have to examine and, yes, you are one of many suspects. This is standard procedure. You do have a connection with possible motive. I just wish we had caught these guys but that's not happening anymore. I personally don't think you are a vigilante killer but this is a connection we have to rule out. That's why I've been on you to get down here."

I had to play the game—he controlled the terms.… I sighed audibly. "Sergeant Petrillo, I understand, I'm just a little shocked…and confused. I mean, personally I think it's great that these guys are dead but that doesn't make me a killer. I don't think many men in my position would be expressing sorrow right now. Am I right?"

His voice softened. "I know, and I agree, but as I said, it's protocol. Get down here, bring all your unloaded firearms, and give us a statement. We should have you checked out of here in an hour or so. Every moment I don't have this done, things look more and more suspect."

Wiping sweat from my forehead, I acknowledged our mutual frustration. "OK, I understand…it's just protocol. I'll be down in a few hours. Just wanna get some breakfast and take a shower. You want me to come to the station in West Palm Beach, right?"

"Yes, the sooner the better. Keep your firearms cased and in your vehicle. We'll come get them and tag them. Then you'll be good to go and we can continue our investigation."

I walked inside, closing the sliding door. "OK, I'll be there as soon as I can. I'll call you when I'm on my way to the station. Oh, one last thing. I don't own all the guns you mentioned…sold some a while back."

"That's fine. We'll need to see the firearms transfer paperwork, so bring that with you. This will make all of our lives easier. Jake, if we have to go get a search warrant for the weapons and come take them…it's going to make a lot of folks look into this much deeper. Since I think this is likely gang-on-gang violence, I'd prefer we allocate additional police resources elsewhere. You understand what I'm saying?"

His voice was calm and direct. I felt he was truly looking out for me and it made no sense to argue. I paused before speaking. "Yes, sir, I understand. I'll bring them. See you soon."

I hung up the phone and thought about my next move.

CHAPTER 43
A LIAR'S TRUTH

You would think that my mind would be swimming with the sea of lies but I remained unusually calm. I would deal with this like anything else, carefully and methodically. I was thoroughly unprepared for his questioning but didn't need to overelaborate or come up with anything intricate…except for my whereabouts.

I needed to come up with the following:

› an alibi

› firearms transfer or bill of sale paperwork for the guns I used and destroyed

I felt that if I could come up with these, then I'd be OK. Unless of course I was walking into an ambush at the station. If that were the case, I'd be put away and locked up until trial.

Still, the fact that I hadn't heard from the police, other than Petrillo, put my mind at ease. If I truly was a key suspect, then they would have gotten a warrant and come for me. Based on my ability to *voluntarily* go to the station and give a statement, I knew they didn't have any concrete evidence that could tie me to the murders. This was very convenient in allowing me some time to cover my tracks and develop an alibi. If I could navigate these obstacles, I would have time to get back to the final chapter of my mission, pursuing Zentillo.

I figured I'd have about two hours to get my shit together, plan properly, and stop by the station. The biggest dilemma I had was my whereabouts. I knew I could buy some time with fake transfer paperwork. They'd have to check the details and spend hours seeing if it was fraudulent or legit. Even though I'd taken the time to carefully alter the .22 rifle I'd used, I didn't want to turn it in. Having the same gun used in the murders purposely drilled to remove barrel patterning was unbelievably suspicious. Honestly, I didn't even know if what I'd done would work.

With regards to whereabouts, if I didn't have a matching story, I could be held there at the station until further notice. I couldn't just call a friend and ask them to cover for me—they might end up as accessories to murder or receive obstruction of justice charges.

I'd have to say I was driving to visit a friend and they weren't home, only I could be tied to that story. The more people that were involved in this cover-up, the less likely my chances of evasion.

Drove out to Clewiston unannounced to see Dave, he wasn't there…got drunk, sobered up, and headed home. That sounded pretty untraceable. If he asked for details, I knew enough about the farm to fabricate a story.

There really was no other way. I figured it was reasonable enough. Just because I wasn't actually with someone did not automatically make me a murderer. Besides, if I was the number one suspect…as stated earlier, my door would've been beaten down so I could be booked for questioning.

The firearms transfer was another story. In Florida, firearms are not registered with the state. When you buy a gun, there is a three-day waiting period, provided you don't have a con-cealed-weapons permit, in which case, you've already been finger-printed and your background check is cleared. So when you pur-chase a gun, all information is recorded by a federal system.

A typical firearm can be sold, provided that both parties are legally able to possess a firearm. Most bill of sale documents have the details of the weapon, the parties involved with applicable signatures, and driver's license information.

I just needed to buy myself some time. I had an idea in place, and it would have to work. I went upstairs to change and caught my reflection in the bathroom mirror. I stared into my sunken eyes, rubbing my hands over the stubble on my head. This wouldn't work. I needed to look somewhat composed, or at least not like a fucking zombie. Quickly, I shaved my face and headed to my study to get things underway. Uncertainty looming, I'd need to I ensure that my house and belongings went to my family.

I typed "create a will" into Google and clicked a link for a site called "LegalZoom" that allowed me to customize and print a will for about seventy dollars. Problem solved. Within twenty minutes, I completed the paperwork and put it in a manila folder. A notarization would make it legally binding and my family would have one less worry with the impending circumstances. With no time to waste, I headed out.

CHAPTER 44
AFFAIRS IN ORDER

MY FIRST STOP was the Northlake Car Wash about ten minutes from the house. I paid eighteen bucks for the Super-Wash. As the gentlemen worked to return my vehicle to pre-felony conditions, I checked my watch. Fifteen minutes down…the clock was ticking.

My next stop was unexpected, but seemingly critical. I passed a costume store that Michelle and I had used for our annual Halloween party. Since it wasn't October, it was pretty desolate. I walked inside and was met by an older woman behind the counter leisurely doing a crossword puzzle.

She looked up at me through purple reading glasses. "Good morning."

I leaned against the counter, smiling. "Good morning. How are you?"

"I'm fine, thanks. Something I can help you find?"

"Yes, can you tell me where I can find a dark wig…nothing too crazy."

She set her crossword puzzle down and pointed behind me. "Sure, honey, the end of aisle four. Just let me know if I can help you."

Turning around, I nodded. "Thanks, will do."

I walked down the aisle, past crazy rock-star wigs, fake mullets, and mohawks. While most of the wigs were over the top, one was just a plain dark eighties costume wig. I tried it on and it looked pretty good for color match.

I paid cash and headed out.

When I got to the truck, I used the scissors on my Swiss Army knife to cut the wig and make it a bit more realistic. It took about ten minutes to fix, but it looked pretty good, especially since I'd be putting a hat over the top of it. I put the wig on under my hat and checked my reflection in the rearview. Pleased with the results, I got back on the road.

Almost an hour had passed and I still had two more stops to make. I pulled up to the bank at the end of Northlake Boulevard and looked in the mirror, laughing slightly at my reflection. The wig color was a spot-on match, although it was slightly curlier than my natural hair.

As I walked in, I removed my sunglasses and carried my manila folder with my will and testament to the front desk. The customer service agent was on the phone, finishing a call. I surveyed the lobby. There was a security camera at the entry point and above each of the teller windows. To the right were three offices where the bankers and loan officers kept their quarters.

I was greeted by a service agent. "Good morning, sir. How may I assist you today?"

Smiling sheepishly under my wig, I spoke slowly, hiding my tension. "Good afternoon. I need to get some paperwork notarized and need assistance with a retirement account and equity line withdrawal."

The young lady pointed to a clipboard at a nearby table. "OK, sir, no problem. If you could please sign in and have a seat, one of our financial specialists will be right with you."

I signed a form with some scrawled letters and had a seat adjacent to the banking offices. I fumbled carelessly with my phone and waited.

A middle-aged banker came from his office and checked the clipboard.

"James?"

I had my hand in my pocket clutching my pocket watch for comfort. "Yes, that's me. It's actually, Jacob, sorry...bad handwriting."

The man shook my hand and introduced himself as Ronnie George before leading me to his office.

There were two chairs facing the desk and our backs were covered by opaque privacy glass that encased the office. Ronnie had a picture of himself, his wife, and a daughter with a black lab.

As we exchanged pleasantries, I explained that I needed assistance with a notary and some withdrawals from my IRA and equity line.

Ronnie used my driver's license to look up my account information, glancing over the top of his computer to explain I'd incur stiff tax penalties for the early IRA withdrawal. After politely declining his suggestion to apply for a bank loan, I acknowledged a full understanding of the tax implications and gave him my requests.

I withdrew four thousand dollars from my IRA and nine thousand from the equity line Michelle and I had opened as an emergency fund. All in, I was withdrawing thirteen thousand in cash from the bank. Nervously, I glanced at a clock on his desk.

He prepared the paperwork as I rolled my pocket watch through my fingers. Looking out the window, I lost myself staring at the family picture on his desk.

I envied the happy life he was living. A wife and family...something I wanted more than anything, something I could never have.

Ronnie broke my trance. "How would you like your cash?"

Looking at my manila folder, I responded, "Mixed bills are fine. Ronnie, could you also assist with notarizing something?"

Ronnie stood up. "Sure, what documents do you have?"

I pulled out the two pages that needed signatures and handed them over.

Ronnie took a look at the forms, surveying the lines.

"I'm doing some preliminary ground work before I meet with my finance guy and our insurance agent.... They printed them out for me."

Ronnie removed a brown binder from his drawer. He opened it up and I saw a list of names, signatures, and thumbprints of other notarizations he'd done.

I signed the paperwork as he started recording my driver's license information in the notary book.

Ronnie stamped the notary seal on both pages, put his signature and date on the forms, and I was good to go.

I put the pages back in my folder and thanked him.

He nodded. "No problem, sir. I'll be back in a moment with your money. I'll also need you to sign a few forms for me before you leave."

Ronnie left to go to the tellers and get the cash. The brown notary book was on still on the desk.

I leaned around peering over the security glass to see what was going on. I estimated I had about three minutes before he returned. The lobby had some traffic and the customer-service agent looked as disinterested as a giant tortoise staring into space.

My heart was racing as I quickly grabbed the notary book and opened it up. I quickly scrambled through the pages of notary stamps done earlier in the week. I needed two Florida driver's licenses to make my plan work.

David Durbin Fairley DL# W857-847-39-167-0
Michael Howard Maier DL# S453-580-18-934-1

I scribbled furiously, consumed with panic. Quickly glancing around the opaque glass through the doorway, I saw that Ronnie was behind the teller desk reviewing my paperwork with a bank employee.

I slid the notary book back to the desk, wiping the sweat from my forehead and waited. Ronnie came back in and returned to his seat. "OK, Mr. Bedford, you're all set."

I nodded, trying my best to act calm despite the profuse sweat pouring through my shirt. Ronnie counted the money on the desk before putting it into two envelopes. I signed my IRA distribution paperwork and equity line withdrawal forms.

It was done.

My body trembled as I shook Ronnie's hand one last time, put the envelopes in my pocket, and headed outside.

When I got into the truck, I took the envelopes out of my pocket and looked at the money. It was a strange feeling to hold thirteen thousand dollars in my hand. I'd never seen this much money at once, but right now it was nothing but meaningless paper. The one thing I needed was time.

CHAPTER 45
THE LAST STOP

THERE WAS ONE more stop to make before heading to the police station. With the deadline looming, I was anxious to get going. If things fell into place, these stops would be nothing more than a brief inconvenience allowing me enough time to finish what I'd started. I raced back home to finalize the details for my meeting, readying myself to meet with Sergeant Petrillo.

As I drove, Luke Bryan's "Kiss Tomorrow Goodbye" played in the background. The title alone was a final reminder of Michelle's death, and of the loneliness that now defined me. Pulling into the garage, I headed to my office to prepare documents.

Bill of Sale: Transfer of personal firearms
Seller: Jacob Bedford
FL DL #S938-483-48-485-0

Buyer: David Durbin Fairley
FL DL #W857-847-39-167-0

Firearms:

> › 1 (one) Sig Sauer .380 ACP, serial number: JS384759

> › 1 (one) Colt AR-15 A3 tactical carbine semiautomatic rifle, serial number: 49534939u5

> › 1 (one) Glock 21 .45 ACP semiautomatic pistol, serial number: VSD405830204

Bill of Sale: Transfer of personal firearms
Seller: Jacob Bedford
FL DL #S938-483-48-485-0

Buyer: Michael Howard Maier
FL DL #S453-580-18-934-1

Firearms:

> › 1 (one) Smith & Wesson MP15-22LR rifle, serial number: 64304345

> › 1 (one) Benelli M4 Tactical 12 gauge shotgun, serial number: BD1608TX478

I completed two separate papers, each with unique dates, prices, and signatures. I folded the paperwork and rubbed them on the floor to give them a used look and feel.

I packed my camo rucksack. Along with my clothing and dopp kit, I packed my weaponry as requested by Petrillo. I cased my Rock River AR, Springfield XD-9, Beretta 9 mm, and my hunting rifle, a 30/06 Springfield. I put the gun cases in the bed of the truck, closed the hatch, and locked the contents.

I had another large camo hunting bag that housed my Colt AR, Glock 21, Benelli tactical shotgun, and plenty of ammo. I figured I'd also bring a dozen MREs, and some duct tape. I put all of this together and left it sitting inside the front door of the house.

All of the guns I left at the house were listed as "sold" on the paperwork, so I had an alibi for not bringing them to the station. I tied up a few loose ends with the house and started toward the police station. As promised, I called Petrillo to let him know I was heading down.

I dialed and waited.

"This is Petrillo."

"Hey, Sergeant Petrillo. It's Jake. I'll be there in about ten to fifteen minutes. Will that work for you?"

Petrillo responded with his usual pleasant tone. "Hey, Jake. That's fine. We'll be waiting."

As I drove to the station, I wondered again if I was walking into an ambush. It was the perfect setup. Maybe the forensics team had pinpointed a fingerprint that matched mine. I assumed that my file from the military, along with my concealed weapons permit, had shown a match of my prints from one of the bodies during my killing spree.

I'd walk in casually, then be surrounded and placed under arrest. "Kiss Tomorrow Goodbye"—that might be a fitting song for me right now. I couldn't bring a firearm into the station and I wasn't going to kill innocent officers for doing their job. To my knowledge, I'd never killed anyone who didn't have it coming and I wasn't going to start now. I could only manage a semblance of hope that the swift nature of my deeds hadn't allowed the CSI team to pinpoint me to the crime scene, but unfortunately, it was a gamble I *had* to take… It was the only way I could clear myself temporarily.

The fact that I was allowed to voluntarily surrender my weapons and appear for questioning alleviated many of my concerns but then again…who knew.

CHAPTER 46
THE LION'S DEN

I PULLED INTO the police station and parked outside. I waited in the car for a couple minutes, both of my hands on the wheel. I had this feeling of fear unlike anything I'd felt in recent weeks. I was walking into a place I could not escape from or defend myself in, and I was doing it voluntarily.

I looked in the mirror, contemplating removing my wig. Figuring the best-case scenario would be to buy myself a little time, I left it on. After all, if Petrillo put out an APB on me, it might at least buy me some time by varying my appearance. I put the envelope of money under the floor mat of the passenger seat and looked around to see if anyone was scoping me out. I didn't see anyone, just oak trees lazily hanging over the parking lot.

I had my wallet, keys, the firearm transfers, and my phone. Not knowing the situation, I quickly erased my calls and browsing history. As I raced through the data, I looked at my voicemails. I still had one from Michelle.

It was dated about a week before her murder. "Hey, baby. It's me. I'll be home in a little bit. If you can take the taco meat out of the fridge, I'll get things going when I get there. Love you."

I rested my head in my hands, tearing up. Since Michelle's death, I'd listened to her messages over and over, even calling her voicemail just to hear her voice one last time. I wiped my eyes, got out of the truck, and headed inside.

I walked to the front desk, checked in, and went through a metal detector, emptying my pockets into a small white bowl. I waited in a chair for Petrillo to come get me.

As confident as I was that the police didn't yet have evidence to pin me to the murders, I was panicked. So much had happened in the past week and I didn't want everything to end here in this dirty police station. My throat was so dry I could barely swallow. I wanted to be with Michelle so badly, to hold her in my arms. There was nowhere on earth I'd rather not be than this station. I needed her strength. I took my phone and called her voicemail. "Hi. This is Michelle. Sorry I can't take your call. Please leave a message and I'll call you back. Have a great day."

I called over and over, my eyes welling up. "Hi. This is Michelle. Sorry I can't—"

"Jake?"

I looked up to see Petrillo. He was wearing a shirt and tie, with his badge on his waist and a Glock holstered at his side. He was alone and walking toward me with his hand outstretched. My eyes were red and I tried to quickly wipe away my tears, though it was obvious that I had been crying. I hoped he wouldn't say anything.

I stood up and extended my hand to Petrillo. "Hey, Sergeant Petrillo. How's it goin'?"

Petrillo forced a smile and greeted me. "Another day in paradise. You doing OK?"

Shrugging, I looked at the ground. "I'm holding up as best I can. Good days and bad days, ya know."

He stared at me, and I could see pain in his eyes. There was an awkward pause.

"Come with me. You want some coffee, soda, water?" he said before putting his hand on my shoulder and pointing down a hallway.

"Nah, I'm OK. Thanks."

I followed Petrillo down the hallway to his office. There were a series of cubicles and dry-erase boards where they were working on various cases.

We sat down at a desk. Behind him were various plaques and medals he'd been awarded. There was a picture on the wall of him with the police softball league holding a trophy. Another picture on his desk of him, his wife, and two young sons. I gazed intently at the picture, lost in thought. He took notice and turned the picture so we could both look at it.

"These are my boys. Love 'em to death but they've given me a lot of gray hair."

I forced a chuckle.

Petrillo stared at the picture in a momentary trance, saying, "They grow up so quick. I worry about bringing them up in such a wicked world. It's one of the things that keeps me so motivated in this line of work."

I nodded. "I'm sure it does. How old are they?"

Petrillo pointed to the youngest of the boys. "Tyler is four and William is…" He paused. "Ya know what, Jake, I believe he's gonna be seven soon." He shifted uncomfortably in his chair and stared at the picture for a moment before letting out a sigh. His voice lowered, just above a whisper. "To be honest, I've been so wrapped up in work lately I don't even remember at the moment."

He rubbed his eyes with his thumb and index finger. "That probably sounds crazy but I've been at the station more than home lately. Really having trouble keeping everything…" Petrillo stopped midsentence and turned to face me. "Shit, I'm sorry Jake. I got off topic, my apologies."

Seeing that Petrillo was flustered and embarrassed, I responded, "No worries."

Petrillo turned his chair facing me. His tone returned to one of confidence and authority. "I want you to know we have made some significant progress in the case. We've had Tidwell in isolation for a while and he's started talking. Based on his intel, we have gotten some major leads within the past week, particularly on Angel Araujo and Mario, though, as you know, they were murdered before we could get to them. The murders do seem sudden, bearing the circumstances of your wife's murder. Do you understand why I had to get you in here?"

I shifted in my seat and pondered my response for a moment before speaking. "Yeah, I do, sir, I understand completely. As you said, it's protocol. I'm here to help in any way I can. I just want to get some closure for myself and our families. The past few weeks have been harder than anything I could ever have imagined."

Looking down, he fumbled with a pen. "I can't even fathom what you've been going through, Jake…I truly can't. I want you to know we think we have a strong lead on Zentillo and I think we are gonna nail this guy any day now. Once we have him…he's never going to see the light of day again.

"But before we can proceed with certain leads and facts, we now have more homicides to account for, and their relation to Michelle's case is throwing a shitstorm into my investigation.

"We have to rule out all possibilities. You are a tactically trained soldier with firearms that match those used in the homicides, and obviously you have a tremendous motive to go after these pieces of shit."

I sat in silence as Petrillo stared at me, waiting to see how I would react. I had been listening carefully the whole time and focused on the plaques on the wall, breathing methodically. Everything he said made perfect sense. I started feeling a bit better about the situation. If they had concrete evidence, they would have arrested me by now. I shifted my eyes and looked directly into his stare.

"Sergeant Petrillo, if I had killed these men…you would never have found the bodies. I was trained by one of the most elite tactical units on the planet…. We are meticulous in nature.

"I understand why I'm here, and rest assured…I'll do everything in my power to assist in your investigation. At the end of the day, no one…and I mean no one will sleep better at night knowing these men are behind bars. Just tell me what you need from me."

I was calm, calculated, and direct. I kept my voice composed without a hint of anger or aggression. Petrillo kept his gaze for a few seconds and looked down at some paperwork. He sighed and grabbed a pen. He questioned me for about fifteen minutes regarding the dates of the murders. I stated that one night I had driven out to Okeechobee to visit a friend but got to his farm and he wasn't there. The other night, I was at home drinking.

The thing was, even without another person to corroborate my whereabouts, they needed evidence. In order to build a solid case against me, the police would need to dial in matching DNA evidence and ballistics details from the firearms.

Petrillo seemed to have a genuine concern for my well-being and was passionate when he spoke about solving Michelle's murder. I knew he was doing his job in interrogating me, and I was happy to assist in *hopefully* clearing my name. Still, I could tell he wasn't really sold on my whereabouts the nights the murders occurred.

I folded my hands on the edge of the desk and brought my eyes to meet Petrillo's.

"Sergeant Petrillo, I know it would be convenient if I was playing cards with the guys or out at a bar the night these murders happened…but I wasn't. I haven't really done much of anything lately. I haven't even seen much of my family. I've been alone, drinking…sleeping…crying. I don't know one day from the other. I haven't paid my bills…gotten groceries…half the time I don't even shower. I wake up midday, hungover, waiting for a call from you telling me these guys are in custody. That's the truth, no matter how inconvenient it is for the case. I just don't have much fight in me anymore."

Petrillo's eyes softened. We sat in the comfort of silence, taking in the gravity of the situation.

He tried to speak a couple times but stopped before finally breaking the lull. "OK. OK, Jacob. I really appreciate you coming down here. I know this is hard for you."

I nodded. "And I appreciate all you are doing, sir. Is there anything else I can help with?"

Petrillo shook his head, putting his pen down. "Nope, I think we got enough from you. Did you bring your firearms with you?"

"Yes, sir. Out in my truck. Wanna go get 'em?"

He moved his chair back and got up. "Yes, let's go."

We passed through the hall and out the entry door. I squinted in the sunlight and we walked side by side in silence.

My visit to the station was winding down. I needed to play the game a little longer and I was free. The gut-wrenching anxiety and anguish were gone. I wasn't out of the woods yet but they didn't have anything on me.

I unlocked the bed cover and slid the cased weapons onto the truck bed. I opened the cases and showed them to Petrillo. I could tell he was a gun enthusiast by the look on his face but he didn't say anything.

Petrillo closed the cases and said, "I'm gonna need one of my guys to help carry them in. Give me a second."

He made a call into the station. A younger officer came out the door.

I put my hands on both cases and told Petrillo, "These are all the guns in my possession, here is the paperwork for the firearms transfers."

I reached into my pocket and pulled out two envelopes. Petrillo took the envelopes and started looking over the paperwork. He looked up briefly as the other officer came to us. I looked at the other officer, and nodded to him. He looked to be about twenty-three years old and his nametag read "Yates."

Petrillo turned to Yates, saying, "Take these inside to my office. I'll get 'em logged when I get in."

He handed the officer the two rifle cases.

Petrillo stacked the remaining cases and went back to inspecting the paperwork. I saw disbelief as he read over the firearms that had been transferred. I cannot say the good Lord's name for fear I'll be struck down by lightning for the atrocities I've committed…but if I'd ever sworn before…I swore then he knew.

I saw it on his face…Petrillo knew that one of the transferred firearms was the same caliber as those used in the murders. He stared silently at the two transfers, studying the names and the details repeatedly. I could read his expression…as if to say, I can't believe it…it was you. It was you this entire time.

He looked up and caught my stare. His eyes widened with a look of bewilderment and concern before quickly looking away into the distance. He fumbled for what to say.

Petrillo spoke softly, "Well, this is all I needed. You happen to have any contact information for these individuals?" His tone had changed completely. There was no confidence, almost as if he couldn't quite process what was going on.

Adjusting my hat, I shook my head. "No, sir. I sold these items at a gun show. They were both Florida residents though. Should be able to look them up pretty easily, right?"

Looking back at the paperwork Petrillo replied, "Sure. We'll just run them through the system. Jake, typically I'd have you stay here while we confirm the transfer documents and run some tests on the weapons, but I don't want to do that to you. You should probably go spend some time with your family. I'm sure they love you very much. Is there anything else you want to tell me?"

His response caught me off guard. I hesitated before responding, "No, sir, nothing I can think of…just that I appreciate all the work you and your team are doing. It's good to know there are still some good guys out there."

Petrillo raised his brow in silence. I could tell he wanted to ask me something, but couldn't. He scanned the pavement at a loss for words.

He looked up at me with a bewildered stare. "Jake, thanks for your help. I'll be in touch soon."

Nodding, I said, "Yes, sir. Again, appreciate all your help."

Petrillo extended his hand and we shook. He held my grip unusually tight and stared at me with fierce intensity. He nodded, looked down on the ground, and headed into the station.

And just like that…I was free to go.

CHAPTER 47
ON THE CLOCK

As I HEADED back to the house, I found myself compulsively monitoring the rearview. I mean, if Petrillo *really* had suspected anything, I'd be waiting at the station until the transfer paperwork checked out, right? Either way, I began thinking about evasion tactics or the possibility of being caught in a standoff. These were serious and highly likely outcomes. I figured that I'd need to get the heck out of dodge as soon as possible. It likely wouldn't take long to figure out my paperwork was bogus.

As I scanned the rearview yet again, I tried to shake the image of Petrillo's intense stare as he shook my hand.... It almost gave me the chills. I'm telling you, right as rain, I felt something in his expression, an understanding. Like he had known all along, but he let me walk anyway.

Impatience had me heavy on the gas pedal. Each passing second was of consequence to my survival. I pulled in the driveway. I knew this would probably be the last time I ever saw our little home again. I studied all of the pictures of Michelle and me hanging on the wall. It was hard to pull my concentration away from her beautiful face looking back at me from those frames. I felt bad that our dream home was in such disarray. It hadn't been cleaned since she had passed and my fury had laid waste throughout the home. Through the broken glass, spilled alcohol, and pills scattered across the counter…my only peace was knowing the memories that we had created here in our home would stay with me forever.

Reminiscing, I stared at a photo in a small white frame of Michelle and me kayaking in MacArthur Park. It had been a hot summer day as we'd paddled through the mangrove trails surrounded by small uninhabited islands. Sweat beaded off my face onto the yellow kayak as I paddled over the shallow water, watching mullet jump in the distance.

"I can't believe you've never been kayaking, growing up in Florida," I said to Michelle.

She smiled as she slowly drew her paddle through the water. She wore aviators, and her long black hair was pulled through her baseball cap.

"I know, crazy, right? We really should do this more often. It's beautiful out here. Doesn't even feel like Florida…it's so tranquil."

Looking ahead, I saw a small island in the distance. The low tide had exposed enough sand for a landing point.

Turning around, I said, "You wanna go over to the island and hang out for a while?"

Michelle was focused on a heron in the distance catching lunch. "Sure, babe."

I paddled hard toward the island, sweating profusely, awaiting the cool refuge under the tall mangroves. The kayak shifted back and forth, ripples splashing off of the paddle.

With each stroke, we gained only the slightest bit of distance and I was getting frustrated with our lack of progress. I grunted, displacing as much water as possible with each thrust. Exasperated, I turned around to see Michelle.

She sat, legs crossed, with the paddle resting on her lap. Her olive skin radiated in the summer sun as she watched the sunburst cascade on the rippling water. Realizing I'd been the only one laboring didn't agitate me but instead satisfied me for some strange reason. As we drifted for a moment, I enjoyed the comfort of her presence.

Michelle looked at me and smiled. It was a moment without words, yet it said so much. We were both entirely content and in love. It was just us, surrounded by nature, and it was perfect.

Smiling, I told her I loved her. Then I focused on the island, paddling harder than before, invigorated with the feeling of being the engine that was carrying us forward.

When we reached the island, I pulled the kayak onto the beach and opened a bottle of water. We sat under some trees, watching the tide pull seashells from the sand.

Michelle held my hand and leaned against my shoulder. As we talked for an hour, the blue skies gave way to a brief thundershower and we sat in the rain, enjoying the reprieve from the afternoon heat. We watched the mist rise from the water and the birds shaking water from their wings.

Michelle turned to me. "Do you think they instinctively learn to hunt fish or is that something they are taught?"

Pondering her question, I cocked my head. "I'm not sure… never really thought about it. Why?"

Michelle watched them inquisitively. "Just curious. It will be fun someday to come here with kids. I wish I'd done more of this stuff growing up."

I held her hand and smiled. I had never felt more complete. I had never felt more at ease with life as the two of us stood there alone on that little beach.

I touched the frame of the picture and breathed deeply, hoping to exhale the pain that immediately filled my soul from knowing she was gone.

Perhaps our love was the only pure thing in my life. A calmness fell over me—she could suffer no more.… She was safe in heaven. Someday soon I would fade away to eternal darkness, free from the gut-wrenching emptiness consuming me.

Clearing the broken glass on the counter, I grabbed my phone. While the final chapter of my life seemed inevitable, I had to do my best to prepare those I loved. It was hard to fully grasp never seeing my family and friends again. They had shared my misery following Michelle's death and though they never felt the depths of pain I had, they had been affected.

I knew that the decision I was prepared to make would profoundly impact their lives and bring about more pain. Unfortunately, I didn't see another choice. The cold hard truth is seldom easy to take, but, as it stood now, I would never talk to my family and friends again. There weren't enough hours in the day for me to call all the people I loved, that had made me the man I used to be. The familiar pain pierced my gut again as this sunk in. This was it. A lifetime of memories and only a moment to reminisce.

The first call I made was to my parents. While I, as their son, loved them with all my heart, I just didn't understand how everyone was coping with Michelle's death. I resented their ability to heal.

As the phone rang, I felt the impending darkness that loomed in my future.

My mom answered.

My voice was hoarse. "Hey, Ma. How's it going?"

Mom's voice softened to that of a mother consoling a child. "Hey, sweetie. How are you doing? We've missed hearing your voice."

I felt a teardrop falling as my voice quivered. "I'm OK, Mom. Just wanted to call you guys and check in. Wanted to hear your voices."

"Oh Jake, we're holding up…just been thinking about you every moment. We've been trying to call you and leaving messages. Your father and I have been praying a lot and missing your face."

As the tears streamed down my face, I did my best to hold it together. I didn't want her to hear the pain in my voice. "I miss you guys more than you know. I am going to take off for a week and do some surfing or something. Wanted to see if you could stop by in a day or so to bring the mail in."

"Of course, sweetie. No problem. Can we do anything else? You need your dad and me to pick up some groceries or help with anything? We'll tidy up the house a bit…maybe have a family dinner when you're back."

I felt guilty lying to my mom. The last conversation I'd have with her felt cheated. I paused in silence, before saying, "I'm good on groceries, thanks. Is Dad around? Wanted to say hi real quick."

"Sure, hun. He's outside fixing the weedwacker. Let me go get him."

I tried to sound as upbeat as I could. "Thanks, Mom. I love you so much. Thank you for everything you guys have done…I really mean it. You are the best."

I could hear my mom tearing up as her voice began to tremble. "You are our son. Of course, we'd do anything for you. Love you so much. I'll get your father."

"Thanks, Mom."

As I waited, I checked the clock, wiping a tear from my eye. I still had time left.

"Jakie!" my dad said.

"Hey, Pop. How you doing?"

"Oh, we're holding up OK, just working on the weed-wacker...damn thing needed some WD-40 to get going. How are you doing, Son? I can't tell you how much you are in our thoughts. We love and miss you so much."

The call pained me and I actually looked forward to the silence of the car.

"Thanks, Dad. Love you guys too. I'm heading out of town to surf for a week, and Mom said you guys would bring in the mail."

"Sure thing, bud. Where ya going?"

I didn't have time for formalities, this was exhausting.

"Not sure yet. Just gonna clear my head. I love ya, Pop. Just wanted to hear your voice."

My dad was silent, and when he finally spoke, it was in a concerned and calming tone. "Son, take care of yourself. We love you. Call us when you're back so we can catch up."

"Will do, Dad. Love you, bye."

As I hung up the phone, I dried my eyes. I had more calls to make and I didn't want to wear myself out.

I started dialing but hung up, staring at the pile of unopened mail on the kitchen table. I never realized how hard it would be to say goodbye.... The gravity of my situation set in like cement.

I leaned down, drinking from the faucet, then slumped back into a chair, wiping my face. I picked up the phone and dialed. I called Michelle's parents and my brothers.

I called my closest friends.

Everyone was still very concerned about me, particularly since I had been virtually out of touch since the funeral. As always, I blamed my disappearance on the need to heal by myself.

I had hoped that speaking to everyone would make me feel better, like I'd have some closure to this sick journey. It didn't. I felt worse. The calls felt forced and no matter how supportive friends and family were, I felt defensive about why I had been out of touch. Perhaps I felt bad for the pain and attention they would suffer at my expense. I truly loved all of them with all my heart.

Before the initial phone call regarding Michelle's death, I had never realized how emotionally fragile I was. Once my world was shattered, there was simply no way for me to pick up the pieces and move forward.

After everything that had transpired in the past couple weeks, there was just one final chapter in my legacy. I needed to leave my story for the world.

Moving aside bottles, I cleared the kitchen table and sat down with my yellow notepad, wondering where to start. The road I'd traveled had taken me this far, but I still had more ground to cover. I began pouring my thoughts on the light-blue lines, filling up page after page.

CHAPTER 48
MY BROKEN SOUL

I AM JACOB Bedford. I am not a writer; I do not wish to be remembered as a hero…I just want to end the pain that has consumed me. Time cannot heal the wounds left by Michelle's murder. As the days pass, the rage grows, coursing through my veins like venom.

This is not a tribute, but a warning to those who harm the innocent…so that the innocent may know a lifetime of love and happiness.

As I continued to write, the words flowed freely, my intensity focused on the abridged version of my story. Filling up one notebook, I began another…

I have no feelings of remorse for what I've done. I was consumed by an obsession to destroy those responsible for Michelle's murder, nothing could stop me. My actions will inspire a small percentage of people to defend the lives of loved ones with lethal force, not relying on the resolve of an inept legal system.

I rapidly scribbled details of the past weeks stopping abruptly.

I was at a crossroads where my past met this very moment. Rubbing the cramps out of my right hand, I pondered how to finish a story that hadn't ended.

I looked up at the clock, sighing. I'd written nonstop for nearly three and a half hours only to arrive at an impasse. I had not yet finished my journey, though I knew how it would end. Burying my head in my hands, I exhaled deeply, wiping a tear from my eyes. I lifted my head, picked up a pen, and finished the sickening finale of what had…and would become of my life.

Setting the pen down, I organized the notebooks on the kitchen table. I knew that the final chapter of my life would bring a great deal of pain and suffering to our families. It was only right that I took the steps to alleviate difficulties in dealing with that suffering. I carefully placed my will and testament on the center of the table, next to my journal and some other documents I left for our parents. The time to reflect had passed.… It was time to move forward.

I grabbed my bug-out bag and stood in the doorway, peering one last time into our empty home. The Florida heat stung my back, and the cool air conditioning tried to seduce me back inside. I breathed the cool air in, then locked the door and headed to the truck. It's all in the past now. Focus on the future.

CHAPTER 49
SUICIDE MISSION

I PULLED ONTO the highway and began my journey south. I'd have an hour of drive time to concentrate on every detail of my mission. My plan was to locate and kill Zentillo before the police could capture him alive. As I was no longer working off the grid, this would be my most high-profile risk yet. Once the police discovered the forged firearm transfer documents, it wouldn't be long before I became the prime suspect in their homicide investigation.

The strategic military decision would require recon sniper tactics, patiently awaiting a perfect opportunity to strike. Unfortunately, patience required time, which I certainly didn't have.

I exited off Linton Avenue in Delray Beach for some necessary prep work. I pulled into a Lowe's parking lot and located a truck similar to mine. It wasn't hard—you can't drive more than ten minutes anywhere without seeing half a dozen Ford F-150s. My electric screwdriver allowed me to switch plates with a similar color truck in less than a minute.

Theoretically, if authorities pulled behind me and ran plates, they'd match the make and model of a similar truck.

Unfortunately, I thought there would be an APB out on me within the hour, so I didn't have the luxury of researching other people's criminal histories. I hoped the guy didn't have any outstanding tickets or worse.

After a quick glance of my surroundings, I continued south toward Miami.

Entering Dade County, I pulled off toward Overtown. Overtown was notorious for leading the Miami area in violent crime. I figured it was the most likely place to locate members of the 8ths. Approaching a stoplight, I had a moment to reflect. All the anguish and suffering of the past few weeks was about to end. This was in every sense of the word, the final chapter of my twisted horror story. I had perhaps only hours before potentially becoming one of America's most wanted.

I rolled down the windows and I threw the wig I'd been wearing into the backseat. The air brought a tingle to my shaved head as sweat trickled down my temples. As I neared the "Historic Overtown" underpass, my phone started ringing. It was Petrillo.

Petrillo!

I scanned the rearview but it was clear. A sickening tingle of nausea hit my stomach as the fourth ring finished sending him to voicemail. I waited.

Nothing. The phone rang again. He was calling back. Again I ignored the call.

Still no voicemail.

I started panicking, not knowing what to do. It didn't seem possible that they could have tracked the individuals from the gun transfers that quickly. Not knowing if they could trace my location with my phone's GPS, I pulled over, throwing my phone down a storm drain. I glanced at the AR and shotgun on the floor of the backseat. My Glock was at my side, ready for action. I kept driving.

This was Miami's gang central. In fact, sometimes police had even been known to "miss" patrols because they were concerned about violence against law enforcement. I knew this was likely the right area to search, but didn't know what gangs hung out where.

Just as in every major city in America, you get a feeling when you're out of place. I knew I'd raise a few eyebrows in an area heavily protected by gangs. Even as dangerous as Overtown was, there was very little chance someone would just open fire on me. Gangsters don't hustle on the street for years without developing a high level of street smarts. I might get some hard stares, but guys typically don't shoot lost civilians. Gangs survive by bringing in money, and it's bad for business to create an unnecessary homicide investigation in your workplace.

As I drove around, activity was minimal. Most of the streets had dead ends, nothing was connected, so I had to go to the end of each street, carefully scanning for spray-painted gang signs or symbols nearby. As I turned down the third street, I saw a small, run-down park with an old basketball court. This was a shitty place for a kid to grow up. The rims were bent and had no nets. There were beer cans strewn across the yellow grass and large weeds grew from cracks running the length of the court. There were double pitchforks spray-painted with some letters over a park bench about thirty feet from the court. I knew they were gang signs, but they certainly weren't 8ths' symbols.

I headed west for ten minutes surveying every detail. Miami always puzzled me. You could be surrounded by million-dollar condos on Miami Beach, then drive fifteen minutes to the most dilapidated parts of the city. I knew there were a lot of good families that lived around here and I felt badly that these thugs made the streets so dangerous. It helped me justify assassinating these dirtbags.

I turned right under a small overpass by some drainage pipes.

There was a broken fence that had been ripped down and the sidewalk was covered with garbage. The daylight disappeared into darkness, and through the shadows the entire underside was covered in graffiti. There were a couple pitchfork symbols covered by sprayed Xs...and the number eight was painted everywhere in green and black paint. The gangs seemed to have their own code, not that it mattered. All I needed to know is that they were here.

It was dark enough under the overpass that I was able to park for a moment and survey the surroundings. I adjusted my side and rearview mirrors to maximize visibility behind me. All of the recon for my missions had started on the same canvas, young kids and teenagers hanging around, seemingly with no place to go. It could have been any neighborhood in America, but the difference was that, here, entire neighborhoods were held hostage by the fear and violence of gangs.

In shadows of the overpass I felt like a predator stalking my prey. I was becoming more proficient in identifying traits unique to members of the 8ths. I studied two guys hanging around an old water fountain and bike rack. They were sitting on bikes, one wore a green bandana underneath a Miami Heat hat, the other had a green belt and jeans sagging over green Reeboks. They looked young, couldn't have been older than sixteen.

I suppressed my hatred, knowing my composure was the only chance I had to succeed. I needed certainty, not emotion, right now. I came for Zentillo...and I needed to start hunting.

Time and patience were something I could not afford to abuse.

I grabbed a thousand bucks from my envelope under the floor mat and put another five hundred in my pocket. My Glock was at my side covered by a T-shirt as I slowly drove toward the men.

I hoped they'd play it cool. If either of these guys reached into their pocket or behind their back, they would get shot.

As I pulled up, the two looked at me, resting on their handlebars with look of curiosity.

Putting the truck in park, I rolled down the window. "What's up, fellas?"

The kid with the bandana was extremely confident in his demeanor and answered with a vocal air of authority. "What's up, bro? You *must* be lost."

While I was taken back a bit, his confidence was refreshing. I sensed he knew the area and everyone who prowled these streets.

"Nah, just looking for someone that lives around here."

The guy with the green belt leaned further into his handlebars and said, "We don't know anyone round here, and we don't talk to cops. See ya."

The familiarity of the conversation was comforting. "Well, you're in luck, 'cause I'm not a cop. And I'd have to tell you… otherwise it would be entrapment."

Saw that in a movie once—don't even know what it means. They looked at each other in silence before the one with the bandana chimed in. "Like my man said, we don't know anyone."

I pursed my lips and peered over my steering wheel into the distance. Shaking my head, I stuck with the routine that had served me well in the past.

Leaning out the window, I quietly addressed them. "Well, I assume that you're both young entrepreneurs and you *do* want to make some money. So, you help me find this person and I'll give you a thousand bucks.

"If you're not interested, then fuck it…I'll find some other kid that wants to make some quick money. Looks like you two have shit all figured out. Big ballers, huh?"

I put the car in drive and slowly crept up a couple inches. They took the bait.

As they looked at each other, the lure of easy money got the best of them and the guy with the green belt yelled back to me, "Yo, you got the money on you? A thousand bucks? Who you looking for worth a G?"

Putting the car back in park, I immediately responded, "Zentillo. Carlos Zentillo. You know him or not, I've got shit to do.... Don't waste my fucking time."

I held up ten fresh hundred-dollar bills. They looked nervous. I could tell that it was likely they knew Zentillo...probably knew where he was, but were terrified to give me the information.

Gang members are typically financially motivated, and will put this over any loyalty or so-called oath. That being said, rats get killed.

Glancing at the clock, I counted to ten while they pondered their move. Growing impatient, I took a shot. "Look, fellas, I know you aren't making greenbacks like this for nothing. Give me some info and I'm on my way. No one will find out."

They shifted nervously on their bikes.

I adjusted my rearview, looking behind me, and addressed the pair. "I'll tell you what. I'll give you fifteen hundred bucks now if you tell me exactly where he's been staying. I know he was staying at his girlfriend's a while back but can't find him now. That's fifteen hundred cash...right now, and all you gotta do is say the words. You know where he's at or not?"

I glanced around to see if anyone was watching us. Nothing unusual, everything looked clear.

With only a moment's hesitation, the guy with the bandana spoke softly, barely audible with the sound of overpass traffic in the background "I know where he's at. I'm not sure if he there now, but I know where he stay."

Backing up his friend, the other chimed in. "Yeah, he probably there. Been posting up there for weeks."

My patience was on the verge of exploding. I shook my head and looked at the sky before speaking. "I'm sorry, does 'there' have a fucking address? 'Cause I'm not familiar with 'there.'"

Without hesitation the kid with the green belt said, "Give me the money and I'll tell you."

I held the bills up for a moment. "OK. Here's the deal, kid. I'm gonna give you this money right now. If I find out you're lying or you told someone about this…you're gonna wish you were never born."

I pulled the Glock from under the T-shirt, setting it clearly on the center console and keeping my hand on it.

"There's a reason I'm driving through with stacks of cash, not worrying about a fucking thing. I can be your best friend or your worst fucking enemy. Don't make me kill you both. You feel me?"

The kids were buying into this—I could tell from their intense expressions they realized I meant business. They looked around quickly before the one with the green belt reached toward me and took the money.

Sliding the cash into his back pocket, he looked around again and eased into his handlebars. "He's not at his girl's. Place was full of heat. He's about ten minutes away, staying at his boy's gramma's house. She got a couch and shit in the garage. Been letting him crash there for a minute."

I was at the edge of success but knew, based on their immediate discomfort, that it would require some probing. "All right… so where is this house?"

The two looked up again. I could see them squirm.

Skittishly the green-belted kid spoke. "It's just past Tenth Street, near the corner of Caldwell and Piatt. House got a blue

LeBaron in the driveway, just sits there…he stay in a little garage off the back."

Backing him up, his buddy added, "That's the truth, man. Word is bond."

I hoped they weren't giving me some bullshit. I needed to test them real quick. "So I turn out of here, go past Tenth and it's on the corner of Caldwell and Parks?"

I purposely said the wrong thing to see if they'd correct me.

Without a second of hesitation, the kid with the bandana said, "No, man. It's near Caldwell and *Piatt*, a few houses in, blue LeBaron in the driveway."

I nodded and pulled the remaining money out. "Good, here's the other five hundred I promised. Fellas, if you want to make more easy money, keep your mouths shut about this. You got me? Your lives don't mean much to me."

I gave the guys a quick once-over and nodded, putting the car in drive before one of them said, "You didn't hear shit from us, word?"

I nodded again. "We never even talked. Word."

I slowly rolled up my window and floored it up the block… hopefully never to be seen again. I saw them in the rearview, staring wide-eyed at my taillights.

CHAPTER 50
RELIEF

I passed Sixth Street, slowing down to monitor my surroundings. It didn't matter that Petrillo was looking for me—I was too close to the end to care. I knew success would hinge on my ability to remain clandestine in my approach. I breathed slowly, picturing how this would go down. I wanted to see the panic in Zentillo's face before I killed him, to watch as my smile reflected from his lifeless, glassed pupils.

I tried using Michelle's memory to fuel my intensity, but couldn't. The only pure thoughts I had were of Michelle and her innocence. They could not be tarnished by the savagery of my existence.

I turned onto Tenth Street, which ran parallel to Caldwell. Something was up, there were two black, unmarked Chevrolet police cars parked on the street ahead. They were empty, no police or anyone in sight.

Had they possibly beat me here to Zentillo's? It didn't make sense. Tactically, police bring multiple units and block all escape routes, swarming a criminal to ensure there is no loss of life.

I slowly drove past the empty police cars, then turned left

onto Piatt, looking through the backyards. I didn't see anything until I looked six houses down and saw some officers were talking to a neighbor on the opposite side of the street.

For all I knew, they were responding to let some kid's parents know he got caught with a dime bag at school. Without a police scanner all I could do was speculate.

Ahead, I could see the blue LeBaron in the driveway but didn't want to park anywhere near the cops. I drove past Caldwell down the opposite street to improvise.

There was a parking spot along the street beyond the back-yard of my target house. The entire neighborhood was comprised of small one-floor houses probably built in the late '50s.

I slowly pulled the truck in and surveyed my surroundings. It was midday, so there was minimal activity. Clouds of doubt hovered over my thoughts and I became pessimistic of Zentillo's whereabouts. If he'd heard about the cops in the area, chances were he was already gone. Either way, I'd come too far to start second-guessing now. This might be my only chance.

The police couldn't see my entry from this side of the street. I only needed five minutes and it looked clear to proceed. My heart was racing and I licked my parched lips. Closing my eyes, I took a deep breath, exhaling slowly. The sunlight danced off the concrete, radiating the Florida heat. The time had come.

I cocked the shotgun and wrapped a long-sleeve T-shirt around it for concealment. Glancing in all directions, I quietly closed the door to the truck. Quickly crossing the street, I leaned against a house, crouching below the windows, scanning my surroundings.

I cleared a short chain-link fence and approached the back of the house. Exhaling deeply, I leaned against the garage, peering toward its only window, a bed sheet covering the opening. If Zentillo was there, he'd be looking out the window frequently, particularly if he heard about any police presence in the area. I army-crawled just past the window, using shadows and sight angles to stay hidden.

Side-crouching in a combat position, I looked at the door lock. The deadbolt was not fastened and I slowly gave the door handle a quarter turn…. It was locked. It was a shitty twenty-dollar lock, easy to breach.

A bead of sweat dripped from my nose onto the concrete and I looked up at the sky, feeling the sunshine on my face. Dropping the T-shirt off the shotgun, I readied myself.

Inhaling a long, slow deep breath…three, two, one…

BOOM!

I kicked the door and it exploded inward.

Inside, a shirtless man looked up wide-eyed, darting toward a semiautomatic handgun on a small desk.

My index finger reacted immediately and thunder roared from the short-barrel tactical Benelli, two shots slamming into his chest and one into his stomach. He fell limp against a small cot where his bags were. He was dead within seconds, blood pooling under his body. I caught a glance of the VIII tattooed across his chest.

I threw the shotgun down. There was no time to hide or destroy it. My hands, face, and shirt were covered in blood spatter.

It had been only eight to ten seconds since the shots had been fired. I grabbed my T-shirt, sprinted across the backyard, and hopped the fence toward the truck.

Dogs were barking like mad and people were looking around outside. Luckily sound gets muffled in an open, populated area. It would have been extremely difficult to immediately pinpoint the source of gunfire. I crouched low and got in my truck, holstering the Glock at my side. It was my intent to slowly exit and get out of here.

It was done. I felt relieved, but feared the unknown.

What now? Where could I go?

I started the car and slowly pulled out. The police would be calling for reinforcements, but it was clear for now. There were people outside talking. They looked at me but didn't seem too interested.

I drove past Piatt as two marked police units sped, sirens blaring, toward my intersection. One unit slowed and turned left toward the crime scene…the other slowed, preparing to follow the first car. The officer hesitated. I saw him look directly at me through his dark sunglasses. He quickly turned in the intersection to get behind me.

He yelled through the vehicle speaker, "PULL YOUR VEHICLE TO THE SIDE OF THE ROAD NOW!"

Slowing down, he pulled behind me, preparing to stop. I could say I lost my license…maybe he'd run the tag and I'd be fine. I stopped briefly. He parked, preparing to exit the vehicle.

I saw the blood splatter covering my hands and forearms, glanced at the Glock at my waist.

Fuck it!

I floored it toward the end of the street, gaining distance before he could catch up. I needed to get to open road. Navigating the neighborhood would be impossible at high speeds. I pushed the engine beyond redline, sirens blaring in the distance.

CHAPTER 51
PANIC ENSUES

THE SPEEDOMETER CLIMBED to seventy miles an hour as I flew down the side street. Control was slipping away and it took all my strength just to keep the truck steady.

The sirens grew louder and with each passing second I was reminded of the cruel, harsh reality I was facing…that in all likelihood I was only moments away from death or, worse…incarceration.

With my right hand, I buckled my seatbelt to keep from moving around so much. I glanced at the speedometer, seventy-five miles per hour and climbing. In the rush of speed, the world seemed to peel away around me.

I pictured Michelle, hoping her memory could allow me a moment of clarity. She was somewhere we'd never been before and was wearing a blue hospital gown. She slowly lifted her head and smiled as my eyes met hers. In the sea of confusion, I smiled and tears streamed down my face as the truck rumbled over the poorly paved road.

I slammed the breaks hard and the truck fishtailed down a

side street. The smell of rubber hit the cabin as a cascade of red and blue lights flashed behind me.

Speaking aloud, I tried to make peace with life. "It's OK, Jake. You're finally finished. It's time to head home."

All I had to do was let go. But I couldn't.… Inside me was a drive to keep going. I wanted just a few more moments to remember Michelle.

Sweat beaded off my forehead, blurring my vision. The world slowed, my ability to control the car starting to slip away.

Thud!

A police cruiser slammed into my bumper, thrusting the truck forward.

The highway exit is ahead.… It's not that far.… Hold on as long as you can.

They can't take you alive…it can't end this way!

"Michelle!

"Why…why did this happen! I miss you so much!" I screamed, trying to wipe the tears against my sleeve.

I could see the ramp to 95 just blocks ahead…perhaps my only salvation. I just wanted some time, time to think.

The vision of Michelle came to me again, I still had no clue where we were. "It's a girl!" said the man in green scrubs, wrapping the baby in a blanket. Michelle was exhausted, but her face lit up as she held the little girl in her arms. I felt warmth come over my body. She nodded. "Come here, hold her…she's yours." Smiling, I tried reaching out—she was so beautiful, I'd never felt anything like…

Fuck! The police had set up blockades at all exit points and I could see traffic building up behind the blocked streets. The slight shimmering hope of reflection was fading.

The sight of her holding a little girl, our little girl, swept an icy emptiness through my body as I realized it had never happened.

"Just a few more fucking minutes…please, PLEASE!"

Adrenaline pumped through my body and I slammed the emergency break and used all my strength to turn the wheel hard left.

The truck shrieked across the pavement and spun around, slamming into the side of a police cruiser. I accelerated in the opposite direction.

Zoom, zoom, zoom, zoom, zoom.

I glanced ahead and saw a police chopper in the distance.

Gritting my teeth, I tried again to envision Michelle in the hospital. Real or not, I just wanted some time with her. Her dark hair swept back from the hospital gown, Michelle leaned in to hand me my daughter. I looked down at the swaddled bundle…

Her eyelids slowly crept open but all I could see were the glassy eyes of Michelle's killers…

"AHHHH, you motherfuckers!" I went into a rage as I picked up speed.

The police had laid out spike strips ahead. The street between was desolate, just me and row of concrete telephone poles.

I breathed deeply, removing my seatbelt, gripping the wheel with all my strength. I clinched my jaw, grinding my teeth as the tears flew back across my temples.

I glanced at the speedometer.

Fifty miles per hour and climbing.

I stared at the gray concrete pillar ahead, intently focused on the center, lightly shadowed as it was by the cloud cover.

Eyes closed.

CRASH!

CHAPTER 52
AFTER LIFE

SMOKE BILLOWED FROM the engine compartment, I heard the hiss of engine fluids leaking onto hot metal. My vision blurred, I blinked rapidly, trying to regain my bearings.

Was I dead?

I could see the telephone pole about twenty yards in the distance. Turning my head, I saw the mangled unmarked police cruiser at the intersection. He'd sideswiped me into the curb before I could make it.

I drifted in and out of consciousness. I struggled to focus through the sunlight glaring through the broken windshield. I heard that sound…that familiar ringing.

I'd heard that ringing once before after a grenade had hit our platoon. The sickening echo hung in the air now, piercing my eardrums as it had done in the desert.

The airbag was covered in blood. My nose was broken and blood was pouring from my nasal cavity. My mouth was swollen and quickly I realized I was missing teeth.

Sharp pain resonated through my left shoulder as I slumped against the door. My arm was badly broken.

I coughed, clearing the blood pooling in my throat, struggling for air.

Through the clouds of smoke, the police surrounded me, peering through the wreckage of blood and twisted steel.

Reaching down between my legs, I looked for the Glock. I didn't have it.… It must have been in the car somewhere.… Where was it? Everything was scattered from the collision.

Unarmed, I could not end this myself. They would have to take me…

The yelling got closer.… I started deciphering the dialect.

Police (blaring over a speaker): "You are surrounded. Exit your vehicle now or we will fire!"

The smoke dissipated and I saw a dozen or so police officers had their guns drawn directly on me from a short distance away.

An officer yelled through the PA, "Exit the vehicle now! We can see you moving. Exit the vehicle now!"

I could barely move. My nose was broken so badly my eyes were starting to swell shut. The world blurred into a kaleidoscope of red and blue lights.

Civilians had gathered in the distance, examining the sick reality sideshow I'd become.

The officer shouted again, "Get the fuck out of the car now or we will shoot you! Exit the vehicle immediately!"

I tried to move but couldn't. I stared through the window at the men, squinting through the sunlight. I coughed blood onto the floor and noticed my pocket watch lay beneath the pedals. A piercing pain radiated through my left arm as I grabbed the watch with my right hand, clutching the cool casing in my palm. I slumped against the door and put the watch into my back pocket, wheezing for breath. Slowly reaching for the door handle, I see the police starting to close in.

I slowly opened the door, bracing my body against the inside of the car… not sure if I could stand.

An officer crouched behind his car yelled, "Exit the vehicle slowly with both hands above your head."

Other officers yelled in a show of force, "Get out of the vehicle NOW!"

"This is your last warning—we will fire! Exit your vehicle NOW with your hands above your head!"

Lowering my legs out the door onto the concrete, my whole body nearly buckled under my weight. My shirt was covered in blood. I leaned my back against the car, trying to stand.

The officers slowly started moving in as they shouted, "Hands above your head! Hands above your head!"

I put my right hand above my head—my left arm could barely move.

They stepped closer. "Step away from the vehicle now!"

Drifting away, I thought of Michelle. I could see her face, smiling in her hospital scrubs.

A sensation of warmth passed over me. My eyes welled up and I felt my lungs fighting to pull air through my clogged windpipe.

I would have given an entire lifetime just to hold my wife for a few seconds. I took a slight step forward. I was so disoriented and my eyes struggled to focus.

I thought of the vision of Michelle holding the daughter we would never have. There would be no weekends at baseball games or ballet recitals. Just pain and emptiness.

Two officers stepped forward with their guns drawn. "Step forward! Keep your hands above your head!"

I took a step forward…

The officers closed in, ready to take me in cuffs. "Walk forward now!"

As tears filled my eyes, I felt shame for the spectacle I had become. I reached for my pocket watch. Feeling the smooth brass case, I rubbed my fingers along the engraving, pulling it from underneath my blood-soaked T-shirt.

BOOM BOOM BOOM BOOM!!!

The sound of air whistled through my lungs.

I fell to my back, feeling the heat from the concrete. I tried to focus on the blue sky as four officers kicked at my arms, ensuring I had no weapons.

"Suspect down! Suspect down!"

The one officer shouted into his radio, "It's not a weapon! It's not a weapon! Clear! Clear!"

I stared directly into the sun, blinded by its overwhelming brilliance.

I couldn't breathe. It was like trying to gasp for full breaths through a coffee straw.

The sounds of an approaching ambulance dissipated as my lungs filled with blood. The world began fading away in the echoes of sirens. "Please forgive me, Michelle, I love you, please forgi…"

CHAPTER 53
LOOKING BACK

"Hɪ, ʏᴏᴜ'ᴠᴇ ʀᴇᴀᴄʜᴇᴅ Jake. Leave a message." I shook my head, carefully setting the phone down on my desk. Leaning back in my chair, I scanned the research report from Jake's firearms transfers, muttering under my breath, "Always trust your gut…"

Within hours of Jake's departure from the police station, our research team concluded that the firearm-transfer paperwork was forged. I immediately put an APB out on Jake and was granted a search warrant for his home. I'd like to say I was in shock but I wasn't. For the first time in my career, my emotions had blinded my instincts. I'd looked into Jake's eyes and seen only confidence and calculation, not the glassy vacant stare of the psychopaths I'd come face-to-face with in my years on the force.

All the signs should have brought me to Jake, but I simply refused to believe he was a serial killer. His tragic loss shook the very fabric of my existence as a father and as a husband. I'd wanted to believe in him, I'd wanted to help heal his pain at all costs.

I felt no closure. There were so many unanswered questions. While he was certainly our prime suspect, the bogus firearms transfers still didn't provide any concrete evidence that could link Jake to the murders. It was too early for a nationwide manhunt and too late for second chances. I needed to find Jake and talk to him.

I tried calling one last time but as expected, it went straight to voicemail. Frustrated, I needed to clear my head. I grabbed my keys and started walking down the hall.

"Excuse me, Sergeant Petrillo," a younger officer named Chaves called from his desk.

"What's up, Chaves? I'm kinda busy right now."

Chaves looked anxious. "Sir, we have units keeping an eye out for Jacob Bedford's truck and they wanted to know when we should execute the search warrant."

I glanced at my watch, then looked at Chaves. "I'm going to follow up on some leads. Get in touch with Corporal Smith and tell him to touch base with me in an hour. OK?"

Chaves hastily replied, "Yes, sir."

I knew in my heart that Jake had taken matters into his own hands but I needed hard evidence. I fired up the black Dodge Charger and peeled out of the station.

As I headed to the house, I pondered Jake's whereabouts. As is often the case, we usually track suspects to the homes of friends and family. I dialed Jake's parents' house and waited. If you've worked interrogation for years, you can sometimes tell from the inflection or tone of people's voice if they are hiding something. Obviously it wasn't foolproof, but at this point I'd settle for any break in the case.

"Hello."

"Yes, Mrs. Bedford? This is Sergeant Petrillo of the Palm Beach County Sheriff's Office. Do you have a moment?"

"Yes of course, Sergeant Petrillo. How are you? Do you have any information in Michelle's case?"

"Yes, ma'am, we have had some unsettling discoveries today

and I need to make you aware of where we are at with the case. I know that however unlikely it may seem, Jake is one of our key suspects in the murder of six people, all members of the 8th Street Kings gang. As you know, this is the gang directly responsible for Michelle's murder."

There was a temporary silence on the line.

"Sergeant Petrillo? What? I don't understand…. That's, that's just not possible. How can you say that?"

"Mrs. Bedford, I can't even imagine how hard these past few weeks have been on Jake and your families but there is mounting evidence that Jake was seeking revenge for Michelle's murder. Unfortunately, as this is an ongoing investigation, I cannot go into all the details but…"

Her tone shifted to sheer anger and frustration. "All the details! Sir, you are telling me my son is a possible murder suspect and can't go into all the details…. I just don't…"

"Mrs. Bedford, I'm sorry to tell you this…. I know this is a lot to take in. I promise you, as soon as I can, I'll be in touch but right now I need…"

"That's just not possible. Jake is not a murderer…. This is a mistake. It has to be!"

"No one hopes so more than myself, ma'am. Your son is an incredible young man who went through a horrific tragedy. I know this is painful but we have to follow up on any and all credible leads we get. I assure you I'll update you as soon as I can but right now I need to know if you or Michelle's family might have any clue of Jake's current or possible whereabouts. When was the last time you talked to him?"

I could hear Janet Bedford crying as she paused to blow her nose. "We spoke to Jake today. He said he was going to get out of town for a while…but I have no clue where he went."

I slowly pulled into Jake's neighborhood and continued talking.

"OK, I'll be in touch soon. Please notify me immediately should you learn of his current or possible whereabouts."

Silence.

"Mrs. Bedford? Are you there?"

"Yes, OK. Please let us know what's going on as soon as possible."

"Mrs. Bedford, you have my word. I have to say this, as hard as it may be, but you need to be aware that harboring a potential fugitive is a felony.... I need you to be honest with me as we proceed through the investigation."

I felt her pain reverberate through the phone, her audible crying and tone was that of a strong woman pushed to the brink.

Clearing her throat, she did her best to gather strength. "OK, Sergeant Petrillo, please call us as soon as you have any details."

CHAPTER 54
WAIVER OF PROTOCOL

I PULLED INTO Jake's driveway and sat in the car for a moment. This entire investigation could make national headlines at a moment's notice, certainly something I didn't want to deal with. I knew my instincts were right but I had to be certain that evidence existed proving that Jake was indeed the man behind the murders.

Having spent so much time with Jake in recent weeks, I realized my emotional attachment to the case had pulled me in too deep. I'd worked in the sheriff's special gang task force for nearly seven years and I'd never seen anything like this. I had a vested interest in protecting him and understood the compelling desire to take vigilante justice.

As much as I understood it, I had taken an oath to uphold the law...not to determine how it should be enforced. Admittedly I was torn between my oath as an officer and my obligation as a husband and father who would do anything to protect my family.

The Florida sun blazed overhead as I emerged from the cruiser and walked to the front door to check the locks. It wasn't dead-bolted but I'd still need a breaching tool to break the key lock. I went back to the cruiser and retrieved the heavy, black steel battering ram stored there.

As I approached, my emotions got the best of me. Pausing before the porch, I thought of how I would react if my family were murdered in cold blood.

"C'mon, can't think this way." I squinted and shook my head, hoping to purge the thoughts. I held the door ram steadily and looked beyond the police cruiser. The neighborhood was quiet and no one was outside.

Breathing deeply, I counted, "One, two, three…"

I couldn't do it. This was entirely a waiver of protocol to enter the premises alone. I knew I couldn't execute the warrant without a support team. This *could* be career suicide.

"Make the call, man," I muttered.

Paralyzed by my emotional investment, I couldn't call for backup yet. Selfishly I was compelled to know the truth. I simply needed to know what had happened. At worst, I could fudge my reason for entering alone and get a smack on the hand by my superiors…. As for my subordinates, hell…they'd think it was bravery.

"Jacob…what have you done? Give me some answers." The overwhelming uncertainty was maddening and I felt possessed.

I looked around one more time—the coast was clear.

"Fuck it." I fixed my arms tightly on the door ram and prepared for impact. My heart raced as sweat beaded onto the concrete stoop.

BOOM!

The door swung open, shattering the small lock, and cool air rushed out through the doorway.

Dropping the ram, I unholstered my 9 mm Glock and prepared for a tactical sweep of the premises.

"JAKE! Jake, are you in here?"

I gave a quick five count and double-checked behind me to

ensure that no one had seen me. Pulling the broken door closed, I crouched behind the stairwell, peering upstairs.

"Jake! If you are here, come out. It's Sergeant Petrillo. I am alone! We need to talk. Please come out. Make this easy on both of us."

Silence.

I used a tactical crouch to clear the bottom floor of the house. It was empty as I proceeded upstairs to check the bedrooms.

Clear.

Closets.

Clear.

I felt the sickness of Jake's depression, seeing the once-beautiful home in complete and utter disarray.

"Where are you, Jake? Give me something, man…"

Heading downstairs, I passed a picture in the foyer of Jake and Michelle. Jake was lifting Michelle up in his arms—it was a wedding picture. Michelle had blue shoes on, and their smiles radiated the elation and joy of young love. Their eyes sparkled… so much life ahead of them.

I thought of my wife and I thought of our boys.

A tidal wave of sadness hit my very core. I holstered my Glock and sat on the stairs. My eyes welled up with tears and I buried my face in my hands, sobbing like a child.

"You can't do this. You don't have the time. Lock it up for the sake of everything you know…" I tried my best to get my shit together and brushed away my tears.

I had never felt so disconnected from work. Over the recent weeks, I'd felt a connection with Jake and a remorse for the unthinkable tragedy he endured. Perhaps I saw Jake as a younger version of myself. I was about his age when I started my own family. We were forged from a common core. Was I a fool to think I could bring this man true justice?

Wiping my face on my shirt, I scanned the residence, absorbing the pain of its condition. There was trash sitting in bags near the garbage can, and empty liquor bottles were everywhere. On the kitchen counter, an empty bottle of oxycodone lay open with pill remnants scattered along the granite. One corner of the room was covered in broken glass, the remains of half a bottle of Jack Daniels lay upon the tile.

Every fiber in my body just wanted to know where Jake was and to talk with him, if only for a minute. More than anything I wanted to know he was OK.

I felt claustrophobic in the cluttered kitchen. I needed a breath of fresh air and headed to the back door. As I unlocked the slider to head out, I noticed a neatly organized stack of paperwork on the kitchen table.

It struck me immediately among the chaotic wreckage of the house.

"What the hell?"

Approaching the table, I stared in silence. Amid the shattered contents of the home, the table had been completely cleared except for the following:

› multiple notebooks and binders meticulously organized and clipped together;

› a last will and testament;

› a handwritten note providing the combination to his gun safe.

I brushed the notebooks aside and took the gun-safe combination. Heading upstairs, I swept the rooms and found the safe in a bedroom closet. I opened the door and peered into the gray cloth interior that seemingly might hold critical answers to the case.

I fell into silence, fighting back the tears of inevitable truth and evidence. Amongst the contents were some of the exact fire-arms from the phony transfer paperwork…and the same caliber of those in the homicides.

I loathed the killer that Jake had become, knowing he had to face justice, but I felt the internal struggle between right and wrong.

"What if it were me? What would I have done?"

The lines of reality blurred and I couldn't resist feeling an acceptance for Jake's vigilante justice.

How could you not feel for a man avenging his family against remorseless killers?

My head was spinning and I felt nauseous. I closed the safe and headed down to the kitchen.

I moved an empty bottle of Jack Daniel's and Crown Royal from the sink and splashed water on my face.

I dried my face on my shirt and sat at the table. It had been nearly an hour since my arrival and I knew I had to wrap things up soon. I sat at the table, neatly placing the safe combination back on the piles of paperwork.

I moved aside Jake's will and testament, revealing a stack of yellow notebooks.

I held the pad in my hand and read the top.

"My broken soul? What the…"

CHAPTER 55
THE MANUSCRIPT

WITHIN SECONDS OF reading, hanging on every word, I began to see the shocking truth of Jake's transformation.

With every page I turned, I felt more deeply enveloped in a world of darkness.

My eyes raced across the pages, absorbing the surreal reality of Jake's final weeks.

Ring.

My cellphone pulled me from a cathartic trance. I yearned to dive back into Jake's thoughts, and the interruption of reality was unbelievably annoying.

Agitated, I answered, "Yeah, this is Petrillo."

"Sergeant Petrillo, it's Corporal Smith. Where ya at, sir?"

Immediately I realized the reality of the impending search warrant closing in.

"Ugh, I'm finalizing some details on the 8th Street Murders. What's up?"

"Nothing. I was told to call you. What's the plan for executing the warrant for Jacob Bedford's residence?"

"We are going to move soon. Go prep the team and remain on standby for orders. I'll call you soon and we'll get mobile."

Smith responded, "Yes, sir. I'll have a unit ready on your command."

"Thanks, Smith. I'll be in touch. Remember, standby until further notice."

As soon as I hung up, I returned to the notepads, pouring over the methodical brilliance that had kept my investigation at bay.

As I finished the final notebook, I was lost beyond words.

"What the..."

I looked at the patio in complete confusion, racking my mind for answers.

"What the hell is going on here?" I shook my head and peered out the window. "It just doesn't make any sense." The final journal entries just didn't add up.... I didn't know what was real and what was fabricated. It seemed like the lines of reality blurred between fact and fiction. I wanted to analyze Jake's words for hours but there was no time to waste.

It had been forty minutes since Corporal Smith had called and I needed to make a move.

For the first time in my career, I had ignored sound judgment and acted on emotion.

I took the entire stack of paperwork from the table and hid it in the trunk of my police cruiser.

I glanced around nervously. My hands trembled as I dialed.

Corporal Smith answered. "Sir, I've got a breach team ready and on standby. Say the word."

"It's time. What's your ETA?"

"We can be there in fifteen minutes, sir."

"Sounds good, Smith. Get the team mobile and head over. I

just got here and am going to do a perimeter search. If it's clear, I'll breach the entry point and I'll need backup."

"Yes, sir. We're on our way."

Placing the phone in my pocket, I locked the back door and headed out front. Carefully, I placed the breaching ram outside and checked my tracks. As I waited, I thought of Jake's eyes earlier that morning…those brown eyes so often filled with pain and confusion had been different. There was an air of confidence and clarity.

Now I knew that somewhere locked beneath that tortured soul was a depth of anger and calculation I'd never expected. He had gotten the best of me—he had utterly abused my trust and yet I felt no anger from the betrayal. I felt no vindication from catching him. I felt guilt among a confusing sea of questions. It was the guilt that I could not bring peace to Jake…that he felt compelled to take this route.

As four marked units came down the street, I adjusted my sunglasses and focused on centering my emotions.

"I can't believe it was you the whole time, Jake…. Now where the hell are you?" I said to myself.

The officers exited the vehicles in full tactical gear and assembled on the porch under the awning, awaiting orders.

The sun was starting to fade and the increased police presence had more than a few neighbors cautiously watching from behind their curtains..

Removing my sunglasses, I wiped the sweat from my forehead and spoke. "Take a knee, gentlemen."

The eight officers knelt down, weapons on their sides, adjusting their bulletproof vests as they anxiously prepared to move.

"Men, I've breached the premises and done a quick perimeter and interior sweep. Our subject, Jacob Bedford, is not present currently. In the event he does return, he is considered armed and extremely dangerous. Approach with caution. Lethal force may be used if necessary. Are we understood?"

In unison the eight officers responded, "Yes, sir."

"Good. The subject is a key suspect in a murder investigation. Our objective is to clear the premises and identify any evidence that might potentially be used in linking the suspect to the murders. While we will have a forensic-evidence team working with us, we need to conduct a quick sweep and ensure all areas are clear. Understood?"

"Yes, sir."

I put my sunglasses back on and drew my Glock.

"Again, I've already swept the premises, but stay alert. Need two men out back, two on each side, and two with me." I pointed and the men took positions. "Let's go!"

As the men and I combed the house, I stayed focused on the task at hand, suppressing the emotional drain of earlier.

For each of the officers working, the tactical sweep was simply all in a day's work.... The broken glass, the pill bottles, the pictures on the wall had no bearing on their emotions. Seeing that reiterated how much I'd overstepped the boundaries of this case.

I watched the search unfold as the men scoured the rooms and closets.

"Sir, there is a safe upstairs. Want me to call the PD and have a technician arrive?"

I pretended to ponder the question. "Yes, call it in. Thanks."

As the search came to a close, we logged all the firearms and some clothing into evidence and secured the area for a forensic team to search.

Night had fallen and I was mentally exhausted. I just wanted to go kiss my kids goodnight, take a shower, and crawl in bed, but I couldn't. After all the units had left, I sat in my car and let the air conditioner blow full blast, drying the sweat to my face. I had so much going on in my head.

I made a quick call home to my wife but got the answering machine. She was probably finishing dinner with the boys or giving them a bath.

"Hey, hun, it's me. I'll be heading home soon. Long day. Tell the boys I love them and I'll give them a kiss when I get back. Love you, bye."

My day was almost over but I still had one more stop. As I backed out of Jake's driveway, I called his parent's house.

Ringing.

Mrs. Bedford answered, "Hello."

"Hello, Mrs. Bedford? This is Sergeant Petrillo."

Her voice filled with excitement. "Yes, Sergeant Petrillo? What's happening? Please tell us something…anything."

"Are you and Mr. Bedford at your house right now?"

Her excitement turned to panic. "Are we at the house? Yes, why? Is everything OK? Is Jacob OK?"

"Listen, I need to stop by and can be there in ten minutes. I'll explain everything. Would that be OK with you?"

Silence.

"Mrs. Bedford? Are you there? Is it OK if I stop by?"

Her tone changed—the excitement had faded and she sounded terrified. "Yes, yes, Sergeant Petrillo. That's fine. See you soon."

CHAPTER 56
TRUST

I SAT FOR a moment in the Bedfords' driveway, trying to think about what to say. To be honest, I couldn't even think. The day had drained me to the point of sheer exhaustion; simply holding a thought was arduous.

There was so much I wanted to talk to the Bedfords about but I couldn't. I was taking a tremendous risk already, no need to add fuel to the fire.

Opening the trunk, I retrieved the stack of paperwork that Jake had left on the table and proceeded to the door.

I rang the doorbell and was greeted by Jake's father, Art Bedford.

"Good evening, Mr. Bedford. May I come in?"

I shook Mr. Bedford's hand and entered the house. Jake's mother, Janet, came in to meet us.

"Good evening, Sergeant Petrillo. We've been waiting to hear from you all day. What else can you tell us?"

The possibility that they could be hiding Jake hadn't even entered my mind. I tried to be the good officer and scan my surroundings for clues, but it was useless. I simply didn't believe he was here.… He was way too calculated for that.

"Listen, Mr. and Mrs. Bedford, I don't have time to explain but you need to listen to me…and listen to me very carefully." I gazed at them, intently absorbing their concern and fear. They remained silent but I could tell from the intensity in their body language they had so many questions. "You told me you spoke to Jacob today, right? What did he say to you?"

Janet looked at the ground and wiped a tear from her eye. "He said he was going away for a little while and asked if we could stop by the house to get the mail. That was it. I'm so confused.… Listen, all we want to kno—"

I calmly interrupted. "I'm sorry to cut you off, Mrs. Bedford, but I don't have much time. Please allow me a moment."

They gazed at me, awaiting my words.

"We executed a search warrant today at Jake's house. We are still awaiting a forensic sweep, so you won't have access to the house. We believe we may have found some guns matching the description of those used in the murders I described earlier. Again, I cannot go into details on the investigation but there is something you need to have."

Their faces contorted in disbelief and confusion. I handed over the notebooks to Janet Bedford.

She took them and looked up at me. "What is this? I don't understand. What are these and why on earth do you believe Jake may be responsible for murder?"

I took her hand and looked directly at her and Art. Fixing my eyes on theirs.

"Jake left these for you. You both need to read these tonight. I cannot spend a moment more talking with you now, but trust me, you'll understand why soon enough. You did not get these from me. I have no knowledge of these existing and we never had this conversation. I need you to acknowledge me now."

I waited, without blinking, as they stared at me in stunned silence.

"Mr. and Mrs. Bedford. Do you understand what I just said? I need you to acknowledge that."

The confusion in their eyes was piercing as they stood there in silence. They looked briefly at the paperwork before sheepishly responding, "Yes, yes...we understand. But, what abo—"

"Listen, all I can say is that I do believe deep down your son Jacob was a very good person, but every man has his breaking point. I need you to read these and understand I'll be in touch very soon. Do you understand what I've just told you?"

They nodded clearly. I shook their hands and thanked them for their time.

As I prepared to leave, I looked one last time to Mr. Bedford. "Once you read them, you'll have more clarity. I will be in touch tomorrow."

He thanked me but looked utterly deflated and frustrated that I refused to answer any questions.

I closed the door to the car and headed home. I could barely hold a thought and needed a shower.

CHAPTER 57
WORK-LIFE BALANCE

PULLING THE CRUISER in the driveway, I sat for a moment, breathing deeply, releasing my death grip on the steering wheel. Closing my eyes, I focused on decompressing, allowing each exhalation to carry away the weight of the day. This was my ritual.

During the day, work was my top priority, but at night I wanted to be the best husband and father I could. I vowed never to let my dedication to protect and serve jeopardize my ability to provide a loving home for my family. This case had tested the very mettle of my existence. Perhaps it was the true innocence of Michelle Bedford and the fact that her murder had been so brutal, or maybe it was that I could see a younger version of myself in Jake.… Whatever the circumstances, I couldn't stop thinking about this case. I'd worked homicides for years but had never seen anything like this in my precinct. Most of the cases I worked were criminal- or gang-related homicides, one low-life against another.

It struck me to the bone because my wife and family meant more to me than anything. I would give my very life for them in an instant, and I felt the shame in Jake's eyes because he couldn't protect his wife. He was entirely lost without her. For the first time in my life I understood the rage of a man who sought vengeance. After all, if it were me, could I leave closure in other men's hands? He was a goddamn combat marine.... This guy's entire MO was to hunt and kill bad guys!

I took a few breaths but it was futile. I opened the door and walked into the house.

My wife, Dana, was wiping off the kitchen table and held up her finger, telling me to be quiet. I whispered, "Hey, hun. How was your day?"

She smiled. "Crazy. Just put the boys in bed. How 'bout you?"

I tried to shield my frustration with work. "Still looking for bad guys.... As soon as we get one, three more pop up. Wish sometimes I'd been a park ranger."

Dana tossed a paper towel in the trash. "Well, that's why you do what you do…not everyone else can or is willing to, right?"

"I guess."

I opened up the fridge, prepping a plate with leftover chicken and mac 'n' cheese.

As I punched the microwave keys, Dana came up behind me and leaned against my back.

"Honey…"

"Yeah," I muttered, with a smile, thinking I might just get lucky tonight.

"You really stink! Go take a shower…" She laughed as she took a seat behind the counter.

Laughing under my breath, I pulled the plate out of the microwave. "You try running all around in the Florida heat all day…see if you still smell like rose petals."

Dana handed me some silverware. "Don't even start with me. Those boys are like wild animals and you've been working so much I'm pretty much raising them on my own. Tyler is having trouble reading and William got in a fight at school. As a matter of fact, I had to pick him up early today."

"A fight? What happened? Is he OK?"

Dana sighed deeply. "Yeah, he's fine…just playground stuff. Some kid has been bullying him and pushed him to the ground on the basketball courts."

"And what happened?"

"Apparently, he got up and threw a basketball at the kid. Then they got in a tussle before the teacher's aide broke things up. He's fine, just really upset, that's all. You really should talk with him in the morning. He needs to hear from his daddy that everything is going to be OK. I can't do this alone, John, they need you. *We* need you."

A surge of anger ran through me, pissed that my son was being bullied. This was matched by a sense of pride that William had stood up to the kid, knowing that I'd told the boys to stick up for themselves if someone was picking on them.

"I know, Dana. I've been working way too much and I'm sorry. You guys mean the world to me, I'm doing the best I can. I will definitely sit down with him at breakfast. So, what's gonna happen? I mean how can we make sure this doesn't keep happening?"

Dana finished the last sip of her wine. "It's really exasperating. There doesn't seem to be much the school will do. They can send them to detention and hope that works and they want to send them to the counselor to explain that violence doesn't solve problems."

I was pissed. "That's a load of crap! What's the counselor gonna do to help this? It's gonna be the same issue over and over. I'm glad he stood up for himself. He's not going to put up with this all year, enough is—"

Dana cut me off. "I know, and I agree to an extent. But remember, we want to raise these boys right. I'm not going to let others dictate the way we raise our children. They will be well-mannered, respectful, hard-working boys.… I want to make sure they don't get in trouble."

Eating in silence, I contemplated Dana's comments.

"OK, I'll talk to him. But understand, these boys will know they don't start fights…but they can finish them if someone strikes first."

Dana rolled her eyes. "OK, but remember if he gets tossed out of school for fighting, you're going to be right alongside me for the parent-teacher conferences. Are you ready to commit to that?"

I paused, knowing full well that it was my wife who really had to deal with this.

"All right, I will."

I washed my dishes and headed to the bathroom. "Hun, I'm gonna go take that shower now."

Down the hallway I heard Dana say, "All right."

After showering, I snuck in the boys' rooms to give them a kiss goodnight. They were both sound asleep and I kissed their foreheads. Tyler was tucked up in a ball under the covers and William was clinging to his toy giraffe. He had previously "outgrown" the giraffe and was focusing on being a big boy. We noticed he only had it around when he was stressed. I knew his tussle on the playground had upset him and I felt helpless that I wasn't there for him earlier. It was my fault he still carried that burden to bed. I was absent when he needed me most.

As a parent, I understood all kids had obstacles to deal with as a part of growing up. Nevertheless, it frustrated the hell out of me that he was going to have to potentially face more bullying tomorrow. I knew something had to be done on my end, as detention and guidance counselors didn't seem like the optimal bully deterrent.

Dana and I finally settled into bed and talked for a while. She drifted away but I couldn't sleep.

Perhaps I was overanalytical because of my years in uniform, but I couldn't help but think of the irony of life. I knew my son William would have to stand up to this bully on his own, even if it meant a physical altercation. There was no way the school authority could solve this with their inept counseling and half-assed attempts at discipline.

As I thought of this, I realized what a hypocrite I was. That was fine for *my* family, but what about Jake? His innocent wife had been savagely murdered and society expected him to sit on the sidelines while justice took its course.... That's the way it had to be. He couldn't stand up to the brutality and answer with violence.... That's not how the civilized world behaves.

Perhaps I was as guilty as anyone. How naïve I was to think we, as police officers, could get true justice for Jake and his family. It's easy to give advice on something you've never experienced. I can't imagine letting this bullying thing slide, let alone if my entire family was murdered.

My mind had only just given me the reprieve of sleep when I was awoken by the buzzing of my work phone on the nightstand.

Half-asleep, I wiped my eyes and looked at the screen. It was 4:27 a.m.

"This is Petrillo."

It was Sergeant Chris Rodriguez, my friend and counterpart in Miami. We'd come up together in the ranks and he was one of Dade County's finest.

I leaned over the bed and whispered quietly, trying not to wake Dana, who pulled the covers over her head. "Chris, what's up?"

"Hey, Petro. Look, man, sorry to wake you but you gotta hear this. We have Carlos Zentillo in custody."

I sat up and raised my voice. "What? When?"

Quickly I closed the door to the bedroom and went to the kitchen, doing my best to not wake anyone.

Rodriguez chimed back in. "We just got the fucker an hour ago. He was hiding out at some fellow banger's house in Hialeah. One of our street-level informants gave us a tip and we set up a covert predawn entry. As soon as we went in, he opened fire and took off running."

I couldn't resist my excitement. "Sonova…sorry, man. Go on."

"He shot one of my guys in the chest, no injuries, as we were tacked up. We had a brief shootout in a neighborhood and hit him twice. He's in critical condition at Hialeah General with twenty-four seven supervision. You'd better believe when this shitbag comes outta the coma or whatever the fuck he's in…we'll make him talk."

Chris took a moment to breathe then continued. "I knew we were working on this together so I wanted you to be the first to know. I'll update you with any and all details as soon as I have 'em. Hit me up if you need anything. I'll be working on this all day."

"Chris, can't thank you enough, brother. Keep me updated…. I'll be in touch."

"You got it, man. Get some sleep," Chris said before hanging up.

I knew there was no chance of going back to sleep, so I put on a pot of coffee and prepared for the day ahead.

CHAPTER 58
A NEW DAY

I SAT AT the kitchen table, sipping coffee, contemplating my day. I wanted to go immediately to the station and start drawing up case details on the big board but couldn't. I had to wait for William to wake up so we could talk about this bullying situation at school. He needed me, and work would just have to wait. Until then, I could at least brainstorm.

My plan was to head to the station and brief our team on the Zentillo details and ensure that Miami Homicide could handle the particulars relating to the arrest. I wanted to be included on interrogation but most likely Zentillo would be in the ICU for a while, if the bastard even lived, and to be honest…I didn't give a shit either way.

I liked my day cut and dry, indecisiveness drove me crazy… and never had anything in my life weighed on my mind as much as Jake Bedford's case. There were simply too many complexities to get organized.

My first order of business would be continuing a streamlined investigation to the 8th Street Kings murders without looking inept. This is much easier said than done when not withholding a literal admission of guilt meticulously written and orchestrated by the killer.

Then I had to figure out what the hell was going on with Jake's manuscript. The entire journal was a literal time stamp of his role in the murders with one exception...the ending. I had no clue where to connect the blurred lines of fiction and reality.

The only concrete solution I could come up with was delivering some new intel to the investigation unit and saying I needed to talk with Jake's parents to get information on his potential whereabouts. I needed answers and they were the only possible link I had to the case.

As I pondered my every move, a light went on in the hallway.

Slam!

The bathroom door shut and I heard Tyler pounding on the door.

Crying.

Tyler came into the kitchen, dragging his blanket and wailing, "Daaaaddddy, William won't let me get my toothbrush."

And so my day began.

I scooped Tyler up and held him tightly. "OK, buddy, it's gonna be fine. We'll get your toothbrush in a couple minutes. You want some eggs?"

Tyler nodded and I set him up at the table with some toys as I prepared breakfast.

I put a plate in front of Tyler. Dana came out in a robe and I handed her a cup of coffee.

"Morning, sweetie."

"Good morning," she stated, quietly taking in the chaos of our kitchen.

William soon entered and sat at the table without saying a

word. I knew immediately something was wrong. He usually would run up to me if he hadn't seen me since the day before.

I put some eggs on a plate for him and sat down at the table.

Leaning in, I put my hand on his hair. "Hey, bud, I missed ya last night. How ya doing?"

He wouldn't look at me and stared at his plate, fumbling with his fork.

William mumbled at me. "I don't wanna go to school today, Dad. I'm sick."

I glanced at Dana and raised my brows. "Sick, huh?"

I put my hand on his head. "You feel fine to me. Bud. Let's talk about what happened at the playground. Everything is gonna be OK, I promise. Tell me what happened."

William's eyes softened up and he started to cry.

As his teardrops fell, he spoke quietly in a hoarse voice. "Andy was being mean to us. He always takes the basketball from us and then hits us if we try to get it back."

I brought him close, hugging him, and whispered, "Shhh, it's gonna be OK. What happened when he hit you?"

William sniffled his congested nose and took a breath. "I threw the ball at him and told him to stop hitting me!"

"OK, then what happened?"

"He hit me again and I hit him back. Then Ms. Riley came and yelled at us…and told us we were in trouble…and mom was gonna yell at me…"

The tears flowed again.

Dana looked at me with the I-told-you-so expression, though I'm not sure what for.

"It's all right, bud. You're not in trouble."

The tears let up, and William looked at me with his big blue eyes. "I'm not? But they said I can't go to recess today and… and…"

I put my hands on his shoulders. "William, listen to me. I love you and your brother so much. And what did I tell you about hitting others? Do you remember?"

William looked up, drying his tears. "Yeah."

"What?"

"Don't hit others unless they hit you first. And to stand up for myself and to let Ms. Clark or my teacher know if someone is bullying me or Tyler."

"Exactly. Good boy."

"Now listen, Mommy and I aren't upset with you at all. When you go to school today, focus on school. If Andy hits you or bothers you, tell him to stop or you'll hit him back. Let your teacher know he's hitting you and you are tired of it. If it continues…"

I saw the look in Dana's eye but ignored it.

"If it continues, you have my permission to punch him right in the nose! You know where that is right?"

He stopped crying and looked at me. "Yes, Daddy."

"Good. Remember, if he hits you, and you've alerted your teacher, and he hits you again…you take this fist," I made his hand into a fist, "and you hit him right here as hard as you can." I pushed his tiny fist into my nose. "*But* only if…tell me, William, only if…"

William finally smiled a bit and started looking like the boy we knew and loved. "Only if he hits me first, I tell him to stop, and I tell a teacher that he's hitting me."

"That's my boy!"

I kissed him on the head. "OK, now go get ready for school."

Dana looked at me. "Just know if I get a call today, you'll be right next to me putting out this fire, hotshot!" she called back as she took off down the hall to help the boys.

Quickly, I put the dishes into the washer and went to get my uniform on. I kissed Dana and the boys goodbye and headed to the station.

I arrived before most everyone else and made an outline for our case briefing. At this point, we had contributors from multiple counties and law enforcement agencies and the report for this case was becoming more complex by the day.

CHAPTER 59
WITHHOLDING EVIDENCE

AT 8:45 A.M., I gathered the team for a meeting to update the officers on the case, providing tasks in conjunction with forensics findings and informing them of Zentillo's arrest. While everyone had their marching orders, I was going to personally visit Jake's parents to seek any additional details on his potential whereabouts.

At 9:15, I headed to my cruiser and called the Bedfords.

Mr. Bedford answered on the third ring. "Hello?"

"Mr. Bedford, Sergeant Petrillo. Good morning?"

Art Bedford's voice was calm but concerned. "Yes, good morning, Sergeant Petrillo."

He was silent. I took this as him awaiting my instruction following last night's conversation.

"Are you and Mrs. Bedford at your house? If so, I need to stop by and discuss the case with you. Would that be OK?"

"Yes, we are both here. What time can you be here?"

I scanned the clock in the car. "I can be there in fifteen minutes."

He hung up and I headed over. While I didn't have a

definitive plan in place, what I did have was an objective I needed to accomplish.

I needed to find out more about Jake, I needed to get inside his mind to find out where he might be and get answers about the mysterious manuscript ending.

As I pulled into the Bedford's driveway, I put my phone on vibrate and headed to the door.

Art Bedford opened it before I could even knock. We shook hands and he led me inside.

We walked into the living room and I had a seat on the tan leather sofa.

Art looked at me. "Can I offer you something to drink? Water, tea, coffee?"

I smiled, adjusting my belt. "Yes, a water would be great. Thank you."

He headed to the kitchen and I scanned the room. There was a wooden chest that served as a coffee table—it was beautifully stained and showed the well-worn marks of years of use. The room was quiet with the exception of the careful ticking of a grandfather clock in the corner.

On the walls were pictures of the family. Jake, his brothers, and, of course, plenty of their grandkids. With few exceptions, the pictures showed the family on the water, at the beach, or outside. One picture showed the boys with skis on. I got up to examine the picture.

"Seven Springs," a voice said from behind me.

Startled, I turned around to see Janet. "Good morning, Mrs. Bedford."

"Good morning. We took the boys to Seven Springs, Pennsylvania, many moons ago so they could see some snow. They all took to it, especially Jake…he was a natural on skis."

I turned and took a seat on the couch as she sat opposite of me in a loveseat.

"That's cool. I've wanted to take my boys somewhere so they could see a change of the seasons."

Art Bedford walked in and handed me a large glass of ice water and sat down next to Janet.

"Thank you, sir."

As I took a sip of water, Art and Janet were gazing at me intently from the edge of the loveseat. The intensity was unnerving. I realized they had read the manuscript and must have been filled with questions.

"So, before we get started, I do have an update that I want to make you aware of. We have Carlos Zentillo in custody. As you know, he was one of the key suspects in Michelle's murder. We received Intel that he was hiding at a friend's in Hialeah. He fired at pursuing officers, they exchanged fire, and he was shot twice. He is currently in critical condition under police supervision at a nearby hospital. You are among the first civilians to have knowledge of this. I sent one of our officers to inform Michelle's parents first thing this morning."

Art and Janet looked at each other, wide-eyed. It was obvious they wanted to speak but there were no words. Art gently took Janet's hand and nodded at her. She covered her mouth and began to cry.

As Art consoled Janet, he looked at the ground, and then me. "Sergeant Petrillo, I know what you told me and I respect that, but please...allow me a moment, father to father, as a parent that loves his kids more than anything. Please." He paused looking for acknowledgment.

I nodded and he continued.

"From the moment Jake received your call, our entire world collapsed. Since then every detail of Michelle's murder and your investigation has been ingrained in our memories. What we read last night in that manuscript was a spot-on documentary detailing every single murder…"

I shifted uncomfortably in my seat, quietly allowing Art an opportunity to vent.

He continued, "*But*…it cannot be true! It doesn't make any sense!"

I remained silent.

"How could he have written about killing Carlos Zentillo? How could he write about his own death? None of that's true! The entire story must just be his way of venting, right? Jake isn't capable of these actions, right?"

I felt sweat trickle down my face as they awaited my response. The silence was palpable and they looked at me with a penetrating stare. I sighed, wanting so much to speak openly but couldn't. I knew all of the murders had happened exactly as laid out in Jake's manuscript.

Jake had killed these men, but completed his manuscript the way he *wanted* to finish things, but couldn't. His manuscript was intended to leave a message, a task that consumed his existence. In projecting his own demise, he demonstrated the true calculation and precision of recent weeks. There was no way he'd be caught. He knew the repercussions of carelessly pursuing Zentillo, and wisely opted for the safer alternative…disappearing.

I started to speak but held back. I breathed deeply and looked at the portraits of the Bedford family.

"Mr. and Mrs. Bedford." I paused. "I have no clue what on earth you are referring to when you say 'Jake's manuscript.' Just know I'm sincere in my commitment to this case and getting justice for your families. I am doing everything in my power to find your son and get some answers."

I paused again, meticulously choosing my next words. "I

know how hard this must be for your families. Rest assured, it may take time, but I'm doing as thorough an investigation as possible. Leaving no stone unturned to ensure we punish those responsible for Michelle's senseless murder."

Art and Janet stared at me with vacant, pained expressions. I believed they understood the reasoning behind what I did but were frustrated nonetheless.

I took the opportunity to get back to the purpose of my visit.

"Mr. and Mrs. Bedford, as of this morning all of the suspects responsible for Michelle's murder are either dead or in custody. Carlos Zentillo may or may not live to see trial and the only other survivor is a gang member going by 'Shay T.' He will likely be facing life in prison without the possibility of parole, upon an assumed conviction."

I paused briefly.

"While we will soon be able to close Michelle's case, another has opened. I have told you that Jacob is a key suspect in the murder of these gang members. The reason we, being the authorities, believe this is bec—"

Mrs. Bedford chimed in, "I just can't believe he'd do this…I mea—"

"Mrs. Bedford," I interrupted. "Please let me finish…. It's important that you both hear me out."

Continuing, I spoke directly, feeling as if each word had significance. "We believe Jake is a suspect because he forged firearms-sale documents for weapons matching those in the homicides. Along with that, there is a definitive motive for going after these men. *But*…as of right now, while he is a key suspect, we have no definitive evidence that can tie Jake to these murders with absolute certainty. Most of the firearms we've found matching those from the homicides have been destroyed to the point they may or may not serve as admissible forensic evidence. At the very least, it could take weeks to sort that out."

I finished, sitting in silence, allowing the gravity of these words to set in before proceeding. "Now, I hope you understand why I am here. I wanted you to know why we have to pursue Jake as a suspect and that I'm going to make every attempt possible to locate him. I need you to tell me about the Jacob Bedford that I don't know. Where he could be and who could help me locate him?"

I took a sip of water, and the Bedfords looked at one another. Art got up and went to the kitchen for a moment.

Mrs. Bedford held a Kleenex to her nose and looked at me. "All the faith and prayer in a million lifetimes couldn't have prepared me for this. We all knew, our family and Michelle's, that her murder would have a profound and irreparable impact on Jake…but we didn't see this coming."

Art came back with a glass of water for him and Janet. She nodded and continued. "After Michelle's murder, Jake changed drastically. It wasn't a state of mourning that time could heal. Jake became completely withdrawn and sought isolation instead of the comfort of friends and family."

Her eyes welled. I could feel the anxiety as Art held her hand, saying, "It's OK. Take your time."

"I need a moment," she said and headed to the back porch.

Art stayed and continued for her. "Jake went through a transformation. I truly feel he was pushed beyond his breaking point. Nothing could have prepared him for Michelle's murder—it was well beyond anything he saw in combat. Once he changed…we kind of felt there might be no turning back. He didn't respond to calls, stating he needed time to cope. Even when we stopped by to check on him, he was desolate and agitated. He said he wanted time to heal on his own. We tried to respect his wishes, but obviously we were…"

Their home phone began ringing.

Art looked at me as he stood up. "Excuse me for a moment, please." Looking at the caller ID, he said, "It's Michelle's father, Victor. I'll only be a moment."

I nodded and looked at my watch. I knew I needed to get *some* information for our police report, as much of our discussion couldn't be mentioned.

Art hung up the phone and briefly checked on Janet, who came back inside. As they both sat down, we stared at each other in awkward silence.

"Everything OK with Michelle's father?" I asked.

"Yes, he spoke earlier with one of your officers, who informed him of Zentillo's capture. He was relieved to know that all of these men are off the streets. You'll have to excuse me, Sergeant Petrillo, where were we?"

"Well, I really need to get some information for my police report. I need you to tell me some places Jake might have gone or whom he might have seen."

Janet's eyes were red but there was a confidence to her. "Well, Jake could be anywhere. You know much of his military background, but he was also an avid fisherman, surfer, and hunter."

"Go on," I said.

"He hunted in Okeechobee and Clewiston quite a bit. He fished locally and would surf in Central America sometimes. I think he'd been to Panama and Costa Rica sometime in the past, right?" she said, turning to Art.

Art nodded.

"Honestly, he hadn't traveled that much lately between deployments and marriage. I believe him and Michelle would just take weekend trips locally in Florida."

I scribbled the details in a small notebook. Looking up, I said, "Thank you, this is helpful. Other than his best friends and brothers, is there anyone he might have seen?"

Art and Janet looked at each other. Art responded, "I'm really not sure. Other than the guys in his wedding, Jake was pretty tight-knit…didn't see too many other people. He was a home-body, loved spending time with his wife. They really wanted to have kids, you know."

I didn't know how to respond, so I just stayed quiet. For a moment we all sat in comfortable silence, perhaps lamenting on the beauty of Michelle and Jake's life together.

I stood up, putting the notebook in my pocket.

I shook Mr. Bedford's hand. "I thank you both again for your time and information. I promise I'll keep you updated on this case and if I hear anything of Jake's whereabouts. You both have my cell phone number. Please call me if you hear anything that could help us out."

Mrs. Bedford began crying and gave me a hug. She grabbed both of my hands and looked at me through the tears. "Thank you. This has been so hard on all of us. Thank you for catching those men and giving us some hope for justice. Thank you for giving us some closure."

I looked at her and held back tears of my own. "You're welcome, ma'am." I nodded to Mr. Bedford, "Sir," and headed out front.

I turned on the car and sat in the driveway. Intuitively, I understood the true dynamics of the situation. Jake's parents knew that we were kindred spirits but that I was bound to the law.

I'd come too far to turn back; I'd made my decision.

Heading to the station, I called Dana to check in and see if William was OK getting to school.

Dana answered, "Hey."

"Hey, hun. How did it go getting William to school?"

"Honestly, much better than expected. I talked with the teachers this morning and we are optimistic that all this may be behind us."

My eyes scanned the road. "That's awesome! What makes you so confident it won't happen again?"

"Well, it appears Andy's parents weren't very pleased with him and are cracking the whip, so to speak. So, maybe after some detention and understanding from both sides, things will fall in line."

"First bit of good news I've had in a while. I'm heading into the station. Will give you a shout later. Love you."

"Love you too. Have a good day."

I pulled into the station, grabbed my case files, and headed inside to the briefing room.

The briefing room had a large dry-erase board we called the "big board" and two rows of tables and chairs. I grabbed a black marker and got to work, talking myself through things.

"OK, Bedford Case 058497."

I wanted all the updates ready to go so I could conduct a quick briefing and we could update the case file.

"Key suspect/person of interest is Jake Bedford."

After writing the details of the forged firearms documents, weapons identified from the residence, motive, and summary of his military training, I continued with follow-up items.

"Awaiting forensic and ballistic analysis on firearms. Awaiting bank and travel records."

The case was at a virtual standstill without these items. After all, we found Michelle's passport in the safe but Jake's was nowhere to be found.

As I finished writing, I stood back, analyzing everything I'd noted, ensuring nothing had been overlooked. While I'd noted all the evidence at our disposal, the fact remained that without the notebooks, there was no concrete evidence that Jake was indeed the killer. There was a great deal of work to do and it was time. I went to gather the team for a briefing.

CHAPTER 60
ONE STEP CLOSER

OVER THE COMING days, we worked tirelessly with the forensics team to gather and process evidence. Knowing the duress the Bedfords were dealing with, I allowed Art and Janet to visit Jake's house accompanied by an officer to pick up Jake's mail and see the condition of the premises. They had been very patient, but both families were on the verge of a breakdown.

Three days after our briefing, we had a major break in the case that provided some clarity on the twisted reality that had become Jake's life. While searching bank and travel records, authorities found that five days prior to his disappearance Jake had booked a flight from Fort Lauderdale to Panama City, Panama. They had documentation that he had indeed checked into the flight, landed in Panama, and cleared customs. From there they were searching for his potential whereabouts, but the case went cold. We immediately began working with Panamanian authorities in an attempt to locate and extradite him.

Once Jake arrived to Panama, there was no record of him checking into a hotel, buying meals, or paying for anything. In fact, nothing had been charged on any credit cards and there was no usage of any ATMs whatsoever. This wasn't much of a surprise, as the seized bank records showed an IRA withdrawal that had been made at his bank earlier in the week. It was assumed he had enough money to get by for weeks. We knew that Jake would certainly need to replenish resources soon but his ability to remain entirely undetected was concerning to police, federal agents, and the Panamanian authorities.

While working with a joint task force that included federal and international authorities, I was enjoying every moment of the mystery. It was truly unlike anything me or the other agents had ever seen. It was as if Jake had bought a ticket to Panama and been erased from existence. We anxiously awaited any details that could lead us to Jake. More often than not, every lead we chased was a dead end, with one major exception that occurred over the next forty-eight hours. This brought the investigation to a boil.

Someone assumed to be Jake had recently attempted to use his American Express to book one-way flights departing from Panama City. The purchase was placed on a computer in the hotel lobby of a small Panamanian hotel called the San Roque. It was an older hotel, so apparently there was no surveillance footage that could be used to identify the person making the transaction. The card he had was disabled, being monitored by authorities, and the purchase was denied. The credit card activity showed an attempt to book a flight to Liberia, Costa Rica, which was immediately reported to cooperating authorities.

The authorities assumed Jake was stuck in Panama City and they prepared an international manhunt to bring him to justice. It was a slight blow to the police that there was no surveillance footage from the San Roque as there typically would be with a Marriott, Hilton, or other large hotel chain. Either way, it was a landmark clue for the case, or so they thought, but with each hour…things seemed to get more and more bizarre.

With the federal agents now assisting with the international case component, I was able to conduct field research and assist their workload. The agents were extremely confident that they were getting close to finding Jake but I wasn't so sure. I knew how calculating he was. It just didn't make sense that he'd so meticulously hide his whereabouts only to risk everything using a credit card. Either way, no one asked for my opinion and I kept my mouth shut as I kept busy running errands for the feds. In all honesty, I was enjoying each and every moment wondering where on earth Jake was and if he could really pull this off.

The Panamanian authorities immediately began monitoring hours of airport surveillance videos. After a couple days, they finally found what they were looking for. A suspect believed to be Jake was spotted at the Panama City airport purchasing one-way tickets for flights. As soon as this information became available, the federal contacts sent me a Webex teleconference invite hosted by Panamanian intelligence officer Eduardo Pinedas. My team and I sat in the briefing room and gathered around a laptop, prepared to take notes. Officer Pinedas introduced himself and immediately began his intel briefing.

"We believe Jacob Bedford was at Tocumen International Airport within the past forty-eight hours, purchasing tickets with cash at a ticket counter. We are hoping to follow up on this because we're not one hundred percent certain it's him. We are collaborating with US authorities, using facial recognition technology, and hoping for some fingerprint match at the counter or nearby. He was wearing a baseball cap and had longer dirty-blond hair and sunglasses. He was wearing a long-sleeve shirt and traveling with only a small duffel bag. He bought two one-way tickets, both of which were under separate names. One name was David Stirling and the other Marcus Joseph. The tickets were purchased and the flight boarded with proper identification. It is important to note that as vigilant as we try to be, the fact remains that sometimes Central America is not as diligent as the United States in verifying appropriate authenticity measures of individual identification. One flight departed Panama City and landed in Majuro, an airport in the Marshall Islands. The other landed in Antananarivo, Madagascar. We are monitoring both leads extensively and will continue our investigation with the help of our counterparts in the United States."

As the teleconference ended, we stared at each other in disbelief. One of the officers looked at me. "You believe this guy? Un-fucking-believable…he's like a Liam Neeson movie."

Placing my hand to my chin, I leaned back in the chair, taking a moment to think about everything I'd heard and process my thoughts.

Glancing at my watch, I saw it was 11:38 a.m. and we'd been steady all morning.

"OK, take some time to process this information. I'll reach out to our federal contacts and see where they want us to take this and how we can assist. Meet back here at thirteen hundred ready to work."

The men nodded and took off. I stopped by my office, grabbed my wallet, and headed to the police cruiser.

I turned the AC on full blast and watched the station through my shades. Thinking.

My intuition may have been right. It was likely that Jake had intentionally attempted to book with his Amex to check if his card was active. If it was declined, he knew the investigation was full bore and he had limited time to make his moves. It was fitting that he'd been calculated enough to do this in a place without any video surveillance…knowing full well he could use this information to his advantage.

I struggled with Jake's precision. Everything simply seemed

too well thought out. How could a man under such duress, a man that endured so much, be capable of orchestrating such strategic deception? Was it possible that he was playing me the entire time?

I didn't know…but wanted answers. I called the Bedfords to check in. It had been days and I'd promised to touch base with them.

Janet Bedford answered the phone and politely asked me to give her a moment as they were unloading groceries.

She returned to the phone a moment later. "Hello, Sergeant Petrillo. Good to hear from you. Any updates?"

"Well, nothing much that I can share at the moment. I just wanted to check in and see how things were going. You mind if I stop by the house shortly to get your feedback on some things?"

"That would be fine. We'll see you soon."

I had spent a fair amount of time with the Bedfords over the past weeks and we had developed a bond as parents. It was an unspoken understanding that respected the boundaries of our unique situations.

When I arrived at the Bedford's house, they invited me in and we sat at the kitchen table.

"I know you visited Jake and Michelle's house with one of our officers, it wasn't in pleasant condition. How are you both holding up?"

Janet Bedford looked misty-eyed but kept her composure. "It was extremely difficult to see the house so shattered. It was, for us," she held Art's hand, "a culmination of the pain, suffering, and struggle Jake was enduring. We felt helpless. It was everything we feared, and we feel as though we failed as parents."

We sat in silence. I wanted to speak but couldn't. What could I say after that?

Janet wiped her eyes. "I just hope that Jake is safe. I hope that someday he finds peace after so much suffering and tragedy."

Art put his arm around her and we all took in the moment.

"Mr. and Mrs. Bedford, I'm sorry you had to see the state of the residence but I felt you deserved the opportunity. Was there anything, other than the disarray, that you noticed that might have been a clue to Jake's plan? Personally, we all just want to know that he's safe…and right now, I don't where he is."

Art and Janet looked at each other and stared away deep in thought.

I glanced at my watch, trying to give action to the awkward silence.

Art saw me and quickly put his hand to his chin with a look of surprise. "Ya know, I don't have the slightest idea where he is… but I'll tell you this." He grabbed Janet's hand and looked at her. "He's safe, I just know it. His watch was missing, and he takes that with him everywhere."

Janet put her hand on his and smiled, as if they had some secret understanding.

I hesitated, looking at both of them inquisitively. "His watch? I don't understand."

Janet spoke up. "When Michelle and Jacob honeymooned in the Marshall Islands, she bought him a watch from the local market. It never even worked, I believe, but he had that thing in his pocket every single day without fail."

Pausing for a moment, she looked beyond me, daydreaming.

"Every night, he put it on his nightstand, and every morning it went in his pocket. And when we went to the house, the watch wasn't there. In the weeks following Michelle's death, he was rather possessive over it, would sometimes just rub the casing. It was a comforting reminder of their time together."

I tried to hide my shock; I remembered the briefing from

Panamanian intelligence stating that one of the ticket purchases was for Majuro, an airport in the Marshall Islands. I hadn't even heard of the Marshall Islands before that call and my mind began to race.

When I spoke, my voice cracked. "Int…that's very interesting. I know in the past you both mentioned Jake surfed in Costa Rica. Do you think that's a place he'd potentially go?"

Art shook his head. "Nah, I don't think Jakie would go there. The last time he went, he said it was becoming very Americanized and the beauty of the country was being overtaken by commercial business. His last trip there they had paved the main road and put in a Pizza Hut, so that may have been it for Costa. Why? Is that where you think he's at?"

Trying to focus my thoughts, I stared out the window and responded, "Well, there was some thought that it was possible, but I agree, wouldn't make much sense. After all, if he's hiding, why would you choose a location with increased development or a large American presence?"

Art looked at me. "Exactly, if he's not wanting to be found… he's probably not going to be. No offense to law enforcement, but Jake is very unique in his ability to immerse himself in his surroundings to avoid detection."

I smiled at the Bedfords. "No offense taken. I have no doubt that Jake is more than capable of operating under the radar."

I looked at my watch and realized I'd need to get back to the station soon.

"Mr. and Mrs. Bedford, I've got to get back to the office. Thanks as always for being so helpful with our investigation."

I began to stand and Janet Bedford took my hands and looked up at me. "Sergeant Petrillo, as a parent, you know there is nothing more powerful than the love we share for our children. While I cannot forgive or condone everything he's ever done, they are his decisions and he must live with them. I cannot judge Jacob. It is in God's hands to judge...not mine. What I can do is respect our son's wishes and share his story with the world. Someday this must be done. I want you to know that we'll always look at you with the highest regard and can't thank you enough for the closure you've given us. That's all I'll ever say on that matter."

As she loosened her grip on my hands, she gave me a hug. I hugged her in silence and shook Art's hand. Emotions were getting the best of me and I did my best to fight back tears.

"Mr. and Mrs. Bedford, when the time comes, I know you'll do the right thing. Just bear in mind, with modern technology, anonymity is tough to come by. Be careful, that's all I'll say."

Janet nodded.

"Thanks for all your patience as we work through the case. It's unfortunate that we met under such circumstances, but it has been a pleasure meeting you. I'll be in touch soon."

CHAPTER 61
GEOGRAPHY LESSON

I ARRIVED AT the station shortly before 1:00 p.m., ready to conduct a meeting with our team. After some discussions and assignment prep, we headed out to work the case.

Having not had lunch, I got some coffee and a granola bar from the vending machine and sat at my desk. I hadn't brought up the Marshall Islands honeymoon yet and knew it could be a key fact in the case. I wanted to do some research and delay its inclusion to the investigation.

I typed *Majuro* in Google and began some research. Majuro was the capital of the Marshall Islands. It was definitely off the beaten path, and travel time from the United States ranged from sixteen to twenty hours, probably slightly less if traveling from Panama. I also spent some time studying Antananarivo, Madagascar, where the other flight had landed, just so I could provide stateside briefing on both locations and their relation to Jacob.

Both islands seemed like the perfect place for an individual with Jacob's background to flourish and adapt undetected. I studied the languages, religions, economics, climates, and government structures. Both countries had a significant number of people who spoke English as a first or second language and used the US dollar as currency.

What perplexed me most was that either country could be an ideal fit for Jacob and the two islands were over 8,500 miles apart. The international manpower and collaboration required to search both places would be nearly impossible. Hell, searching one of these places was a monumental task!

The intriguing thing was Jake himself. Would he return to the spot of his honeymoon or was he factoring on this information coming to fruition to lead us astray? Who the hell knew? He surely would know that the government agencies could track his past travels and know he'd been there.

Over the coming days, I finalized our police reports and intelligence briefings, adding the information about Jake's honeymoon and how he could assimilate on either island with ease.

Steadily, the entire collaborative justice effort kept on the case. The forensics team felt they had a potential match in ballistics analysis but were forced to utilize verbiage that was not one-hundred percent reliable due to the condition of the weapons…essentially meaning any attorney worth his salt could have a field day with the results.

We kept working and waiting, and yet there was absolutely no sign of Jake. All we knew is that it was likely he was on one of two islands with nearly nine thousand miles between them.

CHAPTER 62
RUNNING ERRANDS

As the weeks continued to pass, the authorities followed every potential lead but became increasingly frustrated with their lack of success. I believe our sheriff's unit was the only department not the least bit surprised that the case was at a standstill. After being commended for our investigation, the Feds politely asked us to step aside and become errand boys. Over the coming weeks, our unit was assigned various tasks to contribute to the investigation, little of which utilized the extensive casework we'd gathered since Michelle's murder. While we did as commanded, the whole team was pissed off that our efforts were given only marginal consideration in the case.

Between the FBI, Panamanian authorities, and various state agencies working Jake's case, it became a glorified pissing contest among the commanding officers in each department. The head honchos were so busy trying to make a name for themselves they seemed to lose touch with the foundation of the case. That was never my forte. I just wanted justice for Michelle's murder and needed to know where the hell Jake was.

Nearly a month had passed since our team had watched the

intel briefing with Eduardo Pinedas, and no one seemed any closer to locating Jake. I leaned back in my office chair, staring at a stack of reports on my desk, becoming increasingly frustrated at the situation. I missed real police work and couldn't focus. The only thing I thought about was Jake's whereabouts and how he'd pulled this off.

My phone began ringing.

"Ah shit, it's Captain Anderson. It's not even 9:00 a.m. and somethings up," I said to myself.

I took a deep breath and answered. "This is Sergeant Petrillo."

"Good afternoon, Sergeant," Captain Anderson bellowed into the receiver.

"Good afternoon, sir. What can I do for you?"

"Well, I know you guys are knee-deep picking up coffee and doughnuts for these assholes on the taxpayers' dime but I got a call from Sheriff Bradley himself with a task."

I paused, answering reluctantly, "Yes, sir, what can I do for you and Sheriff Bradley?"

"Well, apparently he got a call from the Department of Homeland Security and they want you to meet with an agent named Timothy Patrick in Miami. The objective is to do some research on whether or not this Bedford guy was able to procure forged US passports somewhere stateside. I have a feeling you'll be runnin' around like a one-legged squirrel burying acorns on a frozen pond…but this is coming from top level and I need you to reach out to the guy."

"Yes, sir, I'll get in touch with agent Patrick today."

"Thanks, John. I'll send his contact information over shortly. Ya know, we've worked together for a long time, and if I haven't said so lately, you're a damn good sheriff. I appreciate you dealing with this bullshit. It's out of our hands until the Feds finish their investigation. You did an unbelievable job on the case, and it showed in the intel briefings. Keep up the good work."

I forced a smile. "Thank you, sir, that means a lot. I'll get on this today. Be well. My best to the family."

"Thanks. You too, John. Give my best to Dana and the kids."

I hung up the phone and gave a long sigh. The last thing I wanted to do now was drive to Miami to do busywork for the DHS. At the very least, maybe I could salvage the day and connect with Sergeant Rodriguez. I hadn't talked to him since the morning he'd updated me on Zentillo being shot and captured. It would be good to catch up, reminisce about the days we had time to actually hunt bad guys.

I headed outside the station, stopping for a moment under the shade of a tree to check my phone. The morning humidity hung thick in the air and my sunglasses fogged up. As promised, Captain Anderson had emailed me the contact information for Agent Timothy Patrick. It was 9:18 a.m. and I had Dade County traffic to navigate.

I dialed the number, feeling a drop of sweat glide down my temple.

"You've reached Agent Timothy Patrick with the Department of Homeland Secur—"

Annoyed, I pressed the pound key to bypass the voice-mail system.

I left a message with my contact information, letting him know I'd be stopping by to touch base on the potential passport forgery per our superior's instructions. It was my hope he'd call me back to confirm his availability…but to be honest, I really didn't give a shit. These guys rarely returned calls, opting instead to leave instructions via paperwork for their mind-numbing admin tasks.

The DHS headquarters in Miami was off Twentieth Street, so

I'd at least have an hour or so to catch up on phone calls. I fired up the Charger and headed south.

Pulling onto 95, I called Chris Rodriguez.

"Petro!" he answered. "What's up brother? How you been?"

I smiled. "What's up, Chris? All good, man. Just running errands for the Feds. How 'bout you?"

"Me too, bro, me too. I just finished a meeting about how to properly send email attachments that meet the FBI server requirements…. What a fuckin' joke. Anyways, when are we catching up? I have some updates on that shitbag Zentillo to fill you in on."

"Funny you ask. I'm heading down to DHS headquarters now. Wanted to see if you could swing by that Cuban joint for lunch, the one near Twenty-Ninth Street."

"Hell yeah, anything to get me out of the office for a bit. What time you thinking?"

I looked at the clock on the dashboard, it was 9:45 a.m.

"I can be there around eleven or so. That work for you?"

"Done. See you there."

CHAPTER 63
CAFE CUBANO

I PULLED INTO Cafe La Havana Vieja shortly before 11:00 and finished my call with Corporal Smith. Not only were we coordinating efforts to the federal investigation of Jake Bedford, but we still had our normal case load. My top priority was ensuring that Shane Tidwell and Carlos Zentillo never saw the light of day for their role in Michelle's murder, so I was doing my best to ensure the case was iron clad.

I turned off the car and a black Chevy Tahoe came flying into the gravel parking lot, blasting reggaeton music. Chris got out of the truck and walked towards me with his arms open. His tight black sheriff T-shirt clung to his large tattooed biceps. He had black tactical pants, his badge fixed to his belt, and his gun holstered at his side.

"C-Rod, I see you still can't drive worth a shit."

Chris laughed as we briefly embraced.

"Whatever, Petro. You Palm Beach boys could learn a thing or two about our tactical driving skills. You guys staying busy tracking down silver alerts in late-model town cars?"

We laughed and headed inside.

La Havana Vieja was a tiny bustling restaurant that exemplified the true Cuban flare unique to Miami. There was a coffee and pastry bar along one side of the room surrounded by small wooden tables. Classic Spanish music filled the air and in the corner some older Cuban men played dominos and laughed with one another.

Outside was a little covered courtyard with four additional tables. Only one of the tables was occupied, as the summer heat kept most of the traffic inside.

"Let's head outside," Chris said.

We sat down at the small wooden table and I looked around. Though it was hot, the canopy over the courtyard made it tolerable. There were potted palm trees lining a small bamboo fence that marked the border of the cafe's courtyard.

The waitress came and Chris flirted with her briefly before ordering us a couple cafe Cubanos and some pollo a la plancha.

Chris took a sip of water, and said, "So what's going on, man? You still absorbed in that Bedford case?"

"Well, yeah...I am. So much more than I should be. I just can't help it. This guy, Jake Bedford, I mean he potentially took out six 8ths and then disappeared without a trace. How could I let that go?"

Chris looked at me behind the dark lenses of his sunglasses.

"I dunno, man, it's crazy. I know you said you spent a fair amount of time dealing with him. He must've been a badass motherfucker, right? Dude like that, with his training...losing his entire world. I'd probably do the same thing if I were him."

We both paused, thinking of Jake's situation. Chris perhaps contemplating how he'd cope with such a catastrophic loss. I was transfixed thinking of the journal. I was one of three people on earth that knew exactly what had happened up until Jake left the police station and headed to the airport. After that, it was simply a brilliant fabrication of reality. A testament that he knew what would happen if his emotions got the best of him one more time.

"Petro…hey, man. You OK?"

"Huh?" I said, breaking my trance. "Yeah, I'm fine…just thinking about where that guy could be, that's all."

Our food and coffee arrived. Taking a sip of his coffee, Chris looked at me and asked, "So, what was that Jake guy like? To pull off something like he did, man, you have to be a little crazy, right?"

I took a sip of the coffee first and shook my head. "Ya know, Chris, that's what makes this so perplexing. He never seemed so out of sorts that this would be possible. I wouldn't have guessed in a million years what he may have been up to. He was quiet, confident, and had this overwhelming sadness about him. I really can't describe it. It was like an emptiness that you could feel just in talking to him. I've never in my career had a case, or an individual for that matter, affect me quite like Jake did. Honestly, I can't stop thinking about it."

Chris took his sunglasses off, putting some salt on his chicken before responding, "I know, man. I can tell this case got to you. You just seem kinda like your mind's somewhere else. I hope you can let it go soon, because things are gonna get even crazier…"

I looked at Chris puzzled. "Why's that?"

Chris talked quickly while wolfing down some beans and rice. "Well, here's what I know. Of the four suspects in his wife's murder, two are dead…one is in custody looking at life in prison. And that leaves Zentillo."

I sat back in the chair, "Yeah, what about him?"

Chris washed down some food with a glass of water, "Well, he's fucked."

Puzzled, I put down my fork, "What do you mean…fucked?"

Chris smiled. "Fucked. He's pretty much a vegetable and the doctors don't seem optimistic that he'll have any brain function again, even *if* he comes outta that coma. Fucked, my man. Wish we'd have just killed him when he started shooting at us because this complicates things."

"Jesus," I exclaimed. At that moment, I wasn't sure how I felt…. It was a whirlwind of emotion.

"Wasn't expecting that news at all," I said.

"Yeah, me neither. It's a real pain in the ass dealing with the red tape on this because you can't just pull the plug…. There are all types of legal protocols, lawyers, case investigations, and of course the department is trying to keep it all under wraps. It's all bullshit, Petro…and we're gonna be dealing with it for a while."

I weighed Chris's words and took a sip of coffee.

"Sorry, bro. I'm sure I'll be right alongside you, dealing with the madness."

Chris wiped his face. "Yeah, you will, to an extent. But it's gonna bog down my guys for a while. Guess it's just a part of the job."

"Chris, is this something I can share with Jake and Michelle's families?"

Chris held his hand up to his chin, pausing to think about it.

"Well, it's not been made public yet—hell, I just found out myself. But if you think it will help the families get some closure and they can keep it quiet, that's fine by me."

"Cool, man. Thanks."

I looked at my watch. It was just after noon.

"I gotta get going, man. Hoping to finish at the DHS and beat rush-hour traffic."

I finished my coffee, stood up, and put forty dollars on the table. "Lunch on me. You can get it next time you're in the palm beaches."

Chris stood up, shook my hand, and gave me a hug. "Thanks,

bro. I'll keep you posted on any updates, you do the same on your end. Tell Dana and the kids I said hello."

I nodded. "Will do. Be good, man."

Putting the AC on full blast, I backed out of the gravel parking lot and headed to the DHS office. The news on Carlos Zentillo's condition was unexpected, and strangely enough it didn't really impact me emotionally one way or another. Whether he rotted in prison for eternity or died on life support, I would feel that somehow justice would be served.

I pulled into the DHS parking lot and showed my credentials to the gate agent. After clearing me, he nodded and the white motorized gate slid aside, allowing me entry. It was 12:25 p.m. when I parked. As I sat in the car, I thought about how the Zentillo news would impact Jake's and Michelle's parents. I hoped it would bring them some peace of mind but, then again, he was still alive and we were all waiting in limbo for some closure.

Removing my sunglasses, I rubbed my eyes and turned the volume down on the radio. I called Michelle's parents, Victor and Linda, but they weren't home. After leaving a brief message, I hung up the phone, slightly frustrated. I started to call Janet and Art Bedford but opted to wait for the ride home. I wasn't sure how long this DHS visit would take, and I hoped to beat Miami traffic.

CHAPTER 64
A QUICK VISIT

I EXITED THE cool confines of the Charger and started walking. The Department of Homeland Security's Miami location was a tan three-story building that didn't look much different than a commercial office unit, with the exception of the security gates all around.

The front door was large paned security glass with a giant DHS logo overhead. I walked in the entrance, cleared security, and headed to a reception area. A middle-aged woman was on the phone, but she smiled at me, holding a finger to let me know she'd only be a moment.

She hung up the phone and greeted me. "Good afternoon. Can I help you?"

I glanced at her nametag. "Hello, Pam, I'm here to meet with Agent Timothy Patrick. My name is Sergeant John Petrillo of the Palm Beach County Sheriff's Department."

Pam nodded. "One second, Sergeant. Let me see if I can track him down for you."

Pam picked up the phone and dialed as I scanned the bustling office. I couldn't help but think of the sheer volume of manpower being utilized on this case, and the fact that none of us seemed close to locating Jake. I drifted for a second, trying to picture what he might be doing, before I was interrupted.

"Agent Patrick's line was busy. Would you like to have a seat and I'll try back in a moment?"

"Sure. Thanks, Pam."

I sat down in a small waiting area and looked at my watch. It was almost 1:00 p.m. and I sincerely hoped Agent Patrick wouldn't keep me waiting all day. I could see Pam on the phone and figured I might as well check in with the station to update the team on when I'd be returning. Just as I started dialing, I heard Pam call for me.

"Sergeant Petrillo?"

I hung up the phone and headed to the reception desk.

"Yes, did you get in touch with Agent Patrick?"

Pam nodded. "Yes, sir, I did. He's in a meeting but left a folder for you here at the office. He said he'll be in touch soon and thank you for stopping by."

I tried my best not to seem annoyed. "Okay...thank you, Pam."

She smiled. "Anytime. I'll go get that folder. Be right back."

Typical interdepartmental bullshit—instead of just mailing the damn folder, I'd wasted an entire half day driving to Miami to pick it up. It was amazing that we ever accomplished anything at a federal level.

Pam returned with a large brown folder and handed it to me with a big smile. "Here ya go, Sergeant Petrillo. Have a great day."

As salty as I was, her enthusiasm took the sting out of a wasted day heading to Miami.

"Thank you, Pam. Have a wonderful day as well."

I headed to the car, squinting at the intensity of the midday sun. I cranked the AC full blast and opened the folder, removing a stack of pictures and documents about two-inches thick. Each one was stamped with the DHS logo and had confidential printed alongside in red. On the very top was a handwritten note on DHS letterhead saying, "Sergeant Petrillo, we've identified six potential leads that could have provided fake documents to Jacob Bedford. Our database doesn't show any affiliation to the suspect but our COs wanted to run these possible leads at a ground level. Please circle back after you check with your team. Look forward to talking. Thanks for your help. Agent Timothy Patrick."

I tossed the folder on the passenger seat and made my way out of the security gate. I couldn't help but laugh. He'd probably had this dropped in his lap by his CO just like I had. Still, the asshole could've mailed the folder and saved me the trip to Miami. For that fact alone, I'd make damn sure it sat on my desk a couple days before we looked at it.

As I headed north, I called the station, informing them we'd be doing a briefing upon my return. As Michelle's parents hadn't yet called me back, I figured it would be a good time to check in with the Bedfords.

I passed the ramp for 195 and started dialing. After a few rings, Janet Bedford picked up.

"Sergeant Petrillo, good afternoon. How are you?"

"I'm good, Mrs. Bedford. Thanks for asking. I have some updates that I wanted to share with you both."

"Okay, please do. I have been meaning to call you as well about something."

I paused for a moment, wondering what she wanted to tell me.

Breaking the brief silence I began, "Well, when we spoke last about Carlos Zentillo, he was in critical condition at Hialeah General Hospital. It appears that he's in a completely vegetative state and the doctors aren't sure if he'll ever have any brain function again, if he survives. As he's on life support, I'm not exactly sure how or when this ends. The only thing I'm certain of now is that unless he either recovers, which seems unlikely, or they pull the plug…we're kinda in limbo with his prosecution."

I waited for her to digest the content of the words.

"I see," she said at last. "I appreciate the update. Have Michelle's parents been informed yet?"

"No, ma'am. I left them a message earlier today but haven't heard back. I'll try them again in a little bit."

"OK, they just left yesterday for a few days so if we talk to them before you do, I'll certainly inform them of this."

"I appreciate it. I wanted to inform you and them first, as I just found out earlier today. It hasn't been made public yet, so please bear that in mind. I'm just sorry that this keeps dragging on. I know tha—"

Janet saved me from a rambling response. "Sergeant Petrillo, we are a family of faith. We appreciate the updates and understand that much of this is entirely out of all of our hands. These men, whether dead or alive, will all have to face their maker to answer for their sins. Knowing that is what has allowed us to carry forth. I love Jacob with all my heart, but someday, even he will have to face his demons in the eyes of the Lord."

We both paused for a moment before Janet began speaking again. "Sergeant Petrillo, are you alone, where I can talk freely for a moment?"

I cleared my throat, and responded nervously, "Uh…yeah, why?"

"There is something I need to tell you, and please don't feel compelled to respond. I mailed the manuscript yesterday. I remember quite clearly what you told me about anonymity, and while my identity may someday be exposed, it was something that had to be done. As far as anyone in the world will ever know, I'm the only one who has ever seen the journal."

I took a moment to think. Her confession didn't surprise me in the least. It was inevitable that she would follow Jake's request to mail the manuscript. I was filled with concern, not for myself, but for her. I knew that if her identity was exposed, the comforts of privacy that she takes for granted would disappear. Her entire life would be under the microscope, and there would be a lengthy process with the legal ramifications.

I cleared my throat again. My voice was hoarse.

"Mrs. Bedford, I have no doubt that you thought carefully about your decision. Just know that my commitment to support your families is unwavering. I wish you the best of luck."

"Thank you for all you've done and for who you are. God bless you, Sergeant Petrillo."

"Thanks. I, uh…I really have to get going. I'll keep you both posted if I have any updates."

I hung up the phone and drove in silence. If the authorities identified her, this whole case was about to explode. I thought of Mrs. Bedford and the ramifications of her actions.

I pulled into the express lane and shrugged my shoulders. "It is what it is. Nothing you can do about it. Besides, the Feds are gonna run with it anyway. It's outta your hands."

As I sped back to the station, my mind once again was consumed with the whereabouts of Jake. I wondered where the hell he was, and how he'd react to his story finally being told.

CHAPTER 65
A STORY IS TOLD

TRUE TO HER word Janet Bedford sent anonymous typed copies of the manuscript to three major newspapers around the United States and included the *Palm Beach Post* and *Miami Tribune*. She included a typed note stating:

"I certainly don't condone violence or vigilante justice, but these were Jacob's final thoughts. While I know not if this is fact or fiction, it is a story that will run deep in the hearts of those who have had loved ones taken from them. In his own words, this is not a tribute but a warning to all who harm the innocent…so that the innocent may know a lifetime of love and happiness."

Within twenty-four hours of the press running stories on Jake's manuscript, the case developed into sheer insanity. This was unlike anything we'd ever seen—complete mayhem from an investigative authority perspective.

In the first day alone, the FBI, Department of Homeland Security, and the sheriff's offices received over five hundred calls with leads on possible sightings of Jake and his potential where-abouts. The public perception was wildly supportive of Jake and it was believed that most of the calls were actually done to throw our case further into chaos…and boy did it work.

No matter how ridiculous a potential lead was, it had to be examined to determine if there was any potential validity. We were so inundated at every level with sifting through bullshit that the actual investigative work came to a grinding halt. I sat in a briefing room with my team and we prepared to tackle the additional workload.

"OK, guys, so we've now had potential sightings of our suspect Jacob Bedford in Madagascar, Costa Rica, the Marshall Islands, San Diego, Key West, the Dominican Republic, and Colombia. So, this means that—"

Corporal Smith chimed in, "Don't forget Panama, sir. Another lead came in this morning about some airport incident, and, of course, as you can imagine, the guy looked *just* like our suspect."

The guys chuckled. I tried not to join them but did smirk briefly.

"OK, thank you, Corporal…. And Panama. So, I'm going to delegate these out so we can hopefully sift through them and get back into the nuts 'n' bolts of our investigation. I think it is critical for everyone to review the manuscript details that were sent to the press one more time. We do firmly believe that this document contains elements of truth that will provide clarity in our investigation. Again, I'll reiterate that we still believe it is highly likely that our original intel is accurate and Jacob Bedford is residing in either the Marshall Islands or Madagascar based on previous research."

I stopped briefly as our office secretary waved at me from the door. I held up my hand to inform her I'd only be a moment.

"So, gentlemen, review the manuscript details and stop by my office within the hour so I can assign your leads. It is imperative that we knock these out as soon as possible and continue with our caseload."

Pausing, the men stared at me intensely. Over the past few weeks, I'd pushed the team well beyond our normal workload, and they'd answered the call flawlessly.

"Men, I know that the past few weeks has been tough on all of us. You've tackled the additional assignments without fault… and for that, I cannot thank you enough. I wish I could stand here and say things are gonna get easier, but, as you can see…they aren't. You are here in this unit because you are exceptional, and part of that is handling the unexpected. Keep up the great work. If you need anything, anything at all, my door is open."

I paused again, letting the words sink in.

"OK, take fifteen. I'll see everyone within the hour to assign leads. Let's get to work. Dismissed."

The sound of chairs moving and the guys getting up filled the room and I motioned for the secretary, Janie, to come in.

"Hey, Janie, how are you doing?"

"Good, thanks. Dana called and said it was important, wanted you to call her as soon as you had a moment. Just passing along the message."

"OK, thank you. Was everything OK?"

"I believe so, she sounded fine…just said it was important."

"Got it, thanks again. I'll give her a call right now."

Janie smiled and walked out the door. I quickly gathered my folders and headed to my office, closing the door behind me.

I turned my chair away from the door, quickly glancing at the picture of our sheriff's team hoisting the championship trophy for the police softball league. I sighed, remembering a time when I wasn't entirely consumed in police work.

I dialed Dana and waited.

She answered, "Hey."

"Hey, hun, what's up? I'm buried right now."

"Nothing. Wanted to make sure you remembered you're taking William to karate tonight at five thirty. I've gotta take Tyler to soccer and can't do both."

A piercing anxiety hit me in the gut.

"Oh shit, honey, I'm sorry. I completely forgot."

"John! We just talked about it this morning. You forgot last time and he missed class. Don't you remember how upset he was?"

I let out a long sigh and rubbed my eyebrows with my thumb and index finger.

"You're right, Dana. I'm sorry. I'll make it work. It's just frickin' crazy here right now. Can you have his stuff ready and I'll be home in time to pick him up?"

"Yes, I can." I could hear the frustration in her voice.

There was an awkward silence, and I heard a knock on my office door.

"Look, honey, I'm sorry. I'll be home to take him, but I've gotta go, have someone at my door."

"John, we need to talk tonight. I know you have a lot on your plate with work, but you have two sons that need a father. You've been so wrapped up in this case the past month or so that I feel like I'm raising them alone. You've never been like this. I'm not sure what it is or why it's happening, but we need you here at home when you finish work. That's all I'm gonna say. I'll see you later."

"I understand, I love y—"

I heard the dial tone before I could even finish.

Burying my head in my hands, I breathed deeply and exhaled, hoping somehow to alleviate some anxiety.

Knock. Knock.

"Gimme just a minute," I answered.

I looked at the photo on my desk of Dana, William, Tyler,

and me at the beach. It was only a year ago but the boys looked so much younger. We were all embracing one another, big smiles on our faces as we sat in the glistening blue waters of the Jupiter Inlet park. I felt an overwhelming guilt, knowing that this case had absorbed so much of me and that I'd been neglecting my own family.

Knock. Knock.

"God dammit!" I said under my breath. "Come in!"

Deputy Yates poked his head in the door.

"Sir, you asked us to come in for our lead assignments."

"Yes, I did. Come in."

Glancing at two stacks of paperwork on the desk, I grabbed four folders and handed them to the deputy. "Here you go, Deputy. You have any questions about the assignment?"

"No sir, I'm clear."

"Good. Anyone else outside my door?"

"Yes sir. Some of the guys are waiting."

"OK, send them in. Thanks, Deputy."

Deputy Yates nodded and headed out the door.

By the time I had finished distributing leads to the men and answering their questions, I was mentally exhausted. My day seemed far from over as the emails kept piling up and leads kept rolling in on Jake's *potential* whereabouts. I began typing a case briefing but stopped thinking about my conversation with Dana. I was agitated at myself for allowing the case to become so detrimental to my personal life. I'd sworn to never let work interfere with my ability to be a good husband and father, yet here I was, so consumed with Jake's case I could barely keep up with my own family.

I shut the door to my office and closed my eyes for a moment, trying to clear my head. The brief reprieve from reality was interrupted by the ringing of my office phone. I looked down to see

Department of Homeland Security on the caller ID. Rolling my eyes, I let it go to voicemail. I was in no mood to talk to anyone.

I needed to finish this briefing and sort through some additional leads. I began typing again and glanced at my watch.

It was 5:07 p.m.

"Shit, I'm gonna be late." I quickly gathered some folders from the desk and raced out to the car.

CHAPTER 66
CROSSROADS

PEELING OUT OF the parking lot, I dialed Dana and got her voicemail.

"Hey, hun, I'm on the way. Tell William to be ready…." I paused, the phone still recording. "I love you.'

It was 5:22 p.m. when I pulled up to the house. Dana was in the driveway with the boys in her car, waiting for my arrival. William raced out and jumped in the Charger.

Dana started backing out and rolled down her window. I could see the displeasure on her face. Tyler was waiving to me from his car seat.

"I'm sorry, hun. We're just gonna be a few minutes late. I'll get him there," I pleaded.

Dana shook her head. "You're unbelievable, John. I'll see ya at home."

William buckled his seatbelt. I leaned over to give him a kiss on the head and ruffled his hair.

"You ready, bud?"

"Yeah, let's go, Dad. We're gonna be late! Can you use the siren?"

I backed up hastily and sped off.

"No, we can't use the siren…"

William looked over at me, his big blue eyes filled with concern. "Dad, are you and mom fighting?"

"What? No, why?"

He shrugged. "Just wondering, I don't want you guys to fight."

We drove in silence for a minute as I sped between cars, trying to make up time. I felt emptiness and guilt fill me as I paused, thinking of how to answer.

"We just need to talk. Your mom and I are just fine. OK?"

He smiled and stared out the window.

It was 5:37 p.m. when I pulled up to the plaza and dropped William off at the karate studio. He raced out of the car.

"I'll be right here when you're finished."

"OK, Dad!" he said, not looking back as he went through the door.

I pulled into a parking spot and stared out the window, trying to shake the looming anxiety of the day. The sun had started its descent but the afternoon heat and humidity still hung thick in the air. I rubbed perspiration from my forehead, loosening the top collar button on my uniform.

I breathed deeply, watching a sandhill crane hunting in a bush near the shopping plaza. My personal life was starting to unravel and I was nowhere close to locating Jake. I knew, no matter how hard I tried, letting go simply wasn't an option. The more bizarre the case became, the more invested I became in its resolution.

The release of the manuscript showed Jake's true brilliance. It turned a chaotic investigation into a complete and utter clusterfuck, overwhelming everyone involved. The Feds were livid, and dead set on making an example of not only Jake but of whoever was responsible for withholding the critical manuscript evidence from the case. As much as I secretly enjoyed the organized chaos following these new developments, I was desperate to locate Jake. It drove me crazy not knowing the details of where he was and how he had pulled this off.

Exhaling, I glanced at the clock, it was 6:22 p.m. and class was almost over. I thought for a moment about my situation and the choices at my disposal. I got out of the car and went inside to watch William finish class.

When we arrived home, Dana's car was already in the driveway. William raced in the house and I slowly carried his karate bag, pondering what to say to her.

There was pizza on the table and she was putting paper plates and napkins.

"Hey, sweetie," I said, leaning in for a kiss.

Dana forced a smile and turned away from me, addressing the boys.

"You two, come wash your hands before dinner."

I washed up with the boys and sat down to dinner. The boys talked about their day, but Dana all but ignored my existence.

After dinner, I cleaned up while Dana got the boys ready for bed. Finally, when they were in bed, she came into the kitchen.

I sat at the table, sipping a glass of bourbon. I wanted to feel sorry for myself but couldn't—it was my own damn fault we were at this crossroads.

Looking up, I caught her eyes.

"Dana, listen. I'm sorry that I've been so wrapped up in this case. You might not believe me, or even wanna hear this, but I feel terrible about it."

Her eyes softened a bit but she remained silent.

"This Jake guy, I spent so much time with him after his wife was murdered. He was a good guy, reminded me a lot of myself in my younger da—"

"John, he was a serial killer! I understand that he had a

catastrophic loss but come on! You can't just take matters into your own hands and murder people. That is what happened, isn't it?"

I sat in silence, feeling a hint of anger at her disregard for what he went through.

"Well, yeah it is but…these guys he killed, they weren't g—"

"Look, John, I know how good you are at your job, and how you seem to find the best in people. But at the end of the day, *we* are your family. You need to make a choice. I'm not asking you to throw in the towel, but I am asking you to be the man I married and the father that William and Tyler deserve…and lately, I don't know who you are."

An awkward silence ensued as she waited for the words to sink in. I took a sip of bourbon, pondering our situation.

"I'm going to go take a shower and do some reading before bed. I hope you'll think about what I said. We need you back, John."

Dana walked towards the bedroom and I took another sip of bourbon. I stared at the family pictures on the wall and thought of the ones at the Bedfords' house.

I thought of the moment I called Jake and reflected on all that happened since that day. I knew I needed to let go, to let justice run its course. I just didn't know if I was capable of doing so. I finished my glass, set it in the sink, and walked to the bedroom, desperately hoping a good night's sleep would help me clear my head.

CHAPTER 67
REPERCUSSIONS

As THE SUNRISE broke through the clouds, I pulled up to the station and was met by a young television reporter from a local news station.

"Sergeant Petrillo, any comment on the belief it was Jake Bedford's mother that leaked the manuscript to the press?"

I brushed past the young lady.

"We cannot comment on an ongoing investigation. You'll have to wait for a press briefing. Sorry."

Within just days of mailing the journal, Janet Bedford had received a call from federal authorities saying that she was going to be charged for the intentional withholding of evidence to a murder investigation. Unbeknownst to her, the authorities were able to trace the mailings and her anonymity quickly faded. The Feds wouldn't share their intel, even with the sheriff's office, but the belief was that they had obtained security footage from a strip mall showing Mrs. Bedford placing the manuscript in a FedEx drop box.

The story had already received nationwide attention as the manuscript resonated with both the nation and international community. People were fascinated with this unknown vigilante who had taken revenge for Michelle's murder and eluded authorities in a worldwide manhunt. Once Janet became involved, things heated up even more and the press became obsessed with unwrapping the lives of the Bedfords and all those close to them.

While Mrs. Bedford did not address the media and remained silent, her potential indictment garnered attention from some of the most experienced criminal defense attorneys in the nation, who offered their services pro bono to defend her.

I sat at my desk, overwhelmed by the investigation and the leads that continued to pile up on a daily basis. I wanted to resent Jake for making this entire situation a complete circus but couldn't. As I made a list of the day's priorities, my cell rang. It was Captain Anderson.

"Good morning, sir."

"Good morning, Sergeant. I'm calling to check in on you, and the case. How are things going?"

I could barely hide my frustration. "Well, sir, we are doing the best we can with the tools at our disposal. We are severely understaffed for the additional workload, even with the guys pulling OT and I'm just doing my best to keep it all tog—"

"John, take a deep breath. We've known each other for a while. I know you are doing everything humanly possible within your unit. I want to know how *you* are doing."

I paused, not really knowing what to say.

"Sir, permission to speak freely?"

"Please do," said the captain.

"I'm on the verge of a breakdown. I'm fine, but it's a lot to take in."

Captain Anderson was silent for a moment but spoke slowly.

"John, that's exactly what I was worried about. You have one speed, and that's full-throttle. It's my understanding you've pretty much been living in the office or the field the past month and I'm worried it's catching up with you."

I didn't respond. I was caught off guard and slightly offended.

"How are things at home?"

"Well, they've been better. I'm just trying to keep everything together until we solve this case or at the very least…make some significant headway."

"I figured. Look, John, I'm allocating an additional homicide unit to assist you guys starting tomorrow. I want you to take a week of paid leave to recharge the batteries. Take Dana and the kids on a trip, get away and get your mind off this case for a bit."

"Sir?"

"Look, we can handle things for a week until you return but you need to clear your head and make sure things are fine on the home front. I'm not asking you, John, I'm tellin' ya! You are too valuable to this department to have a breakdown and that's where you're headed."

The first thing that popped in my head was that this was the perfect opportunity to find Jake, to get out of town on unofficial police business. I leaned back in my chair and glanced at our family photo, feeling the anxiety of my predicament.

"John, you there?"

"Yes, sir. If you think that's the best thing for the department, I'm fine with that."

"Good. I'm assigning Sergeant Timmon's homicide unit to assist you. I'd ask that you brief him as to your current status and take the rest of the week with the family. OK?"

"Yes, sir. Thank you, sir."

"My pleasure. I'll have Gary call you shortly so you can start the briefing. Look forward to catching up when you return."

"Yes, sir, will do."

I hung up the phone. Maybe this was exactly what I needed, some time to clear my head.

CHAPTER 68
OUT OF TOWN

DANA LOADED THE kids up in the car. I gave them a kiss and went to the driver's side window.

"Honey, did you pack William's medicine?"

"Yeah, it's in his bag. I'll be back soon, you need anything while I'm out?"

"No, I'm good. Call me after you've dropped the boys off at your parents and you're heading home."

"OK."

I kissed Dana and watched the car slowly pull out of the driveway. Heading inside, I set our suitcases on the bed, preparing to pack. My mind was racing, Jake's whereabouts still filling my thoughts. Details of the investigation still filled national headlines and every department felt increasing pressure to bring Jake to justice.

I'd had no contact with the Bedfords and desperately wanted to talk to them. It would be far too risky to touch base. I knew they were likely being monitored with the federal investigation. True to her word, neither Janet nor Art made any mention of how they came across the journal and only stated they found it in their mailbox.

I smiled as I began packing, thinking of Jake with a full beard blending into the surroundings of a foreign land. Every day I hoped for the slightest clue, so I'd know he was OK. That day might come but as of this morning, not a single person on earth knew where the hell Jake Bedford was.

During our research, we noted that no signed extradition treaties existed between the United States of America and either Madagascar or the Marshall Islands. He was always a step ahead, out-thinking his adversaries as he'd been taught in the Marine Corps.

I opened the safe and retrieved our passports before heading back into the bedroom. Putting the last of my clothes in the suitcase, I zipped it up and caught myself staring at a wedding picture that hung above our bed. Our first kiss as husband and wife recorded by the photographer at our wedding ceremony. I thought of the picture at Jake's house. Him lifting Michelle in his arms, her blue shoes and their radiating smiles. A chill ran through my spine.

"Get it together, John," I muttered.

How the hell was I going to disconnect for a week?

"You've gotta let it go…you've gotta le—"

My phone rang in the other room, snapping me from my thoughts.

"Hey Dana."

"Hey, I'm on my way home. I'm gonna pick up some subs for us at Publix and I'll be back in about an hour."

"Sounds good. Look, there's something I want to talk to you about when you get home. Slight change of plans."

"Change of Plans? Is everything all right?"

"Yeah, everything's fine. I'll tell you about it when you get back. Everything's good, trust me. I love you."

"Uh…OK. Love you too, John. I'll see you soon."

ABOUT THE AUTHOR

Kevin Wallace was born in Silver Spring, Maryland. One of four siblings, he was drawn to writing at an early age after winning a statewide creative story contest. He continued his passion for writing while majoring in business at Elon University in North Carolina.

Unsatisfied with books about muscle-bound superheroes, Kevin set out to create a high-intensity revenge thriller with a dark, troubled character we can all relate to.

Gathering insight from military family and friends he began working on BROKEN SOUL as a bucket list project. Working full-time as a healthcare sales manager, his writing was limited to nights and weekends. After a three year labor of love, he finally completed the novel.

Kevin is currently working on the second installment of Broken Soul. When not writing, he is an avid marksman, fisherman and hunter. He enjoys all things surrounding the ocean or the outdoors.

He currently resides in South Florida with his wife and daughter.

Made in United States
Cleveland, OH
12 June 2025

17701639R00201